TWO BRONZE PENNIES

TWO BRONZE PENNIES

An Inspector Tom Harper Novel

Chris Nickson

This first world edition published 2015
in Great Britain and the USA by
SEVERN HOUSE PUBLISHERS LTD of
19 Cedar Road, Sutton, Surrey, England, SM2 5DA.
Trade paperback edition first published
in Great Britain and the USA 2015 by
SEVERN HOUSE PUBLISHERS LTD.

British Library Cataloguing in Publication Data

Nickson, Chris author.
  Two bronze pennies.
  1. Murder–Investigation–Fiction. 2. Jews–England–
  Leeds–Fiction. 3. Great Britain–History–Victoria,
  1837-1901–Fiction. 4. Detective and mystery stories.
  I. Title
  823.9'2-dc23

ISBN-13: 978-0-7278-8491-6 (cased)
ISBN-13: 978-1-84751-608-4 (trade paper)
ISBN-13: 978-1-78010-659-5 (e-book)

All Severn House titles are printed on acid-free paper.

Severn House Publishers support the Forest Stewardship Council™ [FSC™],
the leading international forest certification organisation. All our titles that
are printed on FSC certified paper carry the FSC logo.

Typeset by Palimpsest Book Production Ltd.,
Falkirk, Stirlingshire, Scotland.
Printed and bound in Great Britain by
TJ International, Padstow, Cornwall.

For all those who came to Leeds seeking life and safety

The rabbi walked down to the river, gathered up clay and shaped it into the form of a man to defend the Jews of Prague. He wrote the name of God on a piece of paper, placed it in the figure's mouth and the creature came alive.

'I can give instances of how the regular working staff becomes reduced on the streets from 41 by day to very much less . . . so that it may well be asked, "Where are the Police?"'

—Leeds Chief Constable Webb, 1892, in a memorandum to the Watch Committee requesting money to appoint more men.

ONE

'Have you heard a word I said, Tom Harper?'

'Of course I have.' He stirred and stretched in the chair beside the fireplace. 'You were talking about visiting your sister.'

Annabelle's face softened. 'It'll only be for an hour. We can go in the afternoon, after we've eaten.'

'That's fine,' he told her with a smile. He was happy, finally at home and warm for the first time since morning.

He'd spent the day chasing around Leeds on the trail of a burglar, no closer to catching him than he'd been a month before. He'd gone from Burley to Hunslet, and never a sniff of the man. But it was better than being in uniform; half the constables had been on patrol in the outdoor market, cut by the December wind as they tried to nab the pickpockets and sneak thieves. It was still blowing out there, howling and rattling the window frames. As a police inspector, at least he could take hackney cabs and omnibuses and dodge the weather for a while.

Tomorrow he was off duty. Christmas Day. For the last five years he'd worked it. Not this time, though. Christmas 1890, the first together with his wife. He turned his head to look at her and the wedding ring that glinted in the light. Five months married. Annabelle Harper. The words still made him smile.

'What?' she asked.

He shook his head. 'Nothing.'

He often glanced at her when she was busy, working in the kitchen or at her desk, going through the figures for her businesses. Sometimes he could scarcely believe she'd married him. Annabelle had grown up in the slums of the Bank, another daughter in a poor Irish family. She'd started work here in the Victoria public house and eventually married the landlord. Six years later, after he died, everyone advised her to sell. But she'd held on and kept the place, trusting her instincts, and she'd built it into a healthy business. Then she'd seen an opportunity and opened bakeries in Sheepscar and Meanwood that were doing well. Annabelle Harper was a rich woman. Not that anyone round here called her Mrs Harper. To them she'd always be Mrs Atkinson, the name she'd carried for so long.

Whatever they called her, she was his.

'You look all in,' she told him.

Harper gave a contented sigh. Where they lived, in the rooms over the pub, felt perfectly comfortable, curtains drawn against the winter night, the fire in the hearth and the soft hiss of the gas lights. He didn't want to move.

'I'm cosy,' he said. 'Come and give me a cuddle.'

'A cuddle? You're lucky I put your supper on the table.'

She stuck out her tongue, her gown swishing as she came and settled in his arms. He could hear the voices in the bar downstairs. Laughter and a snatch of song from the music halls.

'Don't worry,' she told him. 'I'll send them on their way early tonight. They all have homes to go to. Then we can have some peace and quiet.'

But only for a few hours. Annabelle would be up before dawn, the way she always was, working next to the servants, stuffing the goose that was waiting in the kitchen, baking the bread and preparing the Christmas dinner. Dan the barman, the girls who worked for her, and God knew who else would join them at the table. They'd light candles on the tree, sing, laugh, exchange gifts and drink their way through the barrel of beer she'd set aside.

Then, after their bellies were full, the two of them would walk over to visit her sister, taking presents for Annabelle's nieces and nephews. For one day, at least, he could forget all the crime in Leeds. Billy Reed, his sergeant, would cover the holiday. Then Harper would return on Boxing Day, back to track down the damned burglar.

Annabelle stirred.

'Did you hear that?' she asked.

'What?'

He gazed at her. He hadn't heard a thing. Six years before, while he was still a constable, he'd taken a blow on the ear that left him partially deaf. The best the doctor could offer was that his hearing might return in time. But in the last few months, since autumn began, it had grown a little worse. Sometimes he missed entire sentences, not just words. His ear simply shut off for a few seconds. He'd never told anyone about the problem, scared that it would go on his record.

'On the stairs.'

He listened. Still nothing. Then someone was knocking on the door. Before he could move, she rose swiftly to answer it.

'It's for you.' Her voice was dark.

He recognized the young constable from Millgarth station. One of the new intake, his uniform carefully pressed, cap pulled down smartly on his head and face eager with excitement. Had he ever looked as green as that?

'I'm off duty—' he began.

'I know, sir.' The man blushed. 'But Superintendent Kendall told me to come and fetch you. There's been a murder.'

Harper turned helplessly to Annabelle. There'd be no visit to her sister for him tomorrow.

'You go, Tom.' She kissed him on the cheek. 'Just come home as soon as you can.'

TWO

The cold clawed his breath away. Stars shone brilliantly in a clear sky. He huddled deeper into his overcoat and pulled the muffler tight around his neck.

'What's your name?' Harper asked as they started down the road.

'Stone, sir. Constable Stone. Started three month back.'

'And where are we going, Mr Stone?'

'The Leylands, sir.'

Harper frowned. 'Whereabouts?'

'Trafalgar Street.'

He knew the area very well. He'd grown up no more than a stone's throw from there, up on Noble Street. All of it poverty-scented by the stink of malt and hops from the Brunswick Brewery up the road. Back-to-back houses as far as the eye could see. A place where the pawnbrokers did roaring business each Monday as housewives took anything valuable to exchange for the cash to last until Friday pay-day.

In the last few years the area had changed. It had filled with Jewish immigrants; almost every house was packed with them, from Russia and Poland and countries whose names he didn't know, while the English moved out and scattered across the city. Yiddish had become the language of the Leylands. Only the smell of the brewery and the lack of money remained the same.

'Step out,' he told the constable. 'We'll freeze to the bloody spot if we stand still.'

Harper led the way, through the memory of the streets where he used to run as a boy. The gas lamps threw little circles of light but he hardly needed them; he could have found his way in pitch blackness. The streets were empty, curtains closed tight. People would be huddled together in their beds, trying to keep warm.

As they turned the corner into Trafalgar Street he caught the murmur of voices. Suddenly he saw lights burning in the houses, and figures gathered on their doorsteps. Harper raised his eyes questioningly at Stone.

'The outhouses, sir. About halfway down.'

The cobbles were icy; Harper's boots slipped as he walked. Conversation ended as they passed, men and women looking at them with fearful, suspicious eyes. They were *goys*. Worse, they were authority.

They passed two blocks of four houses before Stone turned and moved between a pair of coppers, their faces ruddy and chilled, keeping back a small press of people. Someone had placed a sheet over the body. Harper knelt and pulled it back for a moment. A young man, strangely serene in death. Straggly dark hair, white shirt without a collar, dark suit and overcoat. The inspector ran his hands over the clothes, feeling the blood crusted where the man had been stabbed. Slowly, he counted the wounds. Four of them. All on the chest. The corpse had been carefully arranged, he noticed. The body was straight, the arms out to the sides, making the shape of a cross. Two bronze pennies covered the dead man's eyes, the face of Queen Victoria looking out.

Harper stood again and noticed Billy Reed talking to one of

the uniforms and scribbling in his notebook. The sergeant nodded as he saw him.

'Do we know who he was?'

'Not yet.' Reed rubbed his hands together and blew on them for warmth. 'Best as I can make out, that one found him an hour ago. But I don't speak the lingo.' He nodded towards a middle-aged man in a dark coat, a black hat that was too large almost covering his eyes. 'He started shouting and the beat bobby came along. They called me out.' He shrugged. 'I told the super I could take care of it but he wanted you.' His voice was a mixture of apology and resentment.

'It doesn't matter.'

It did, of course. He didn't want to be out here with a corpse in the bitter night. He'd rather be at home with his wife, in bed and feeling the warmth of her skin. But Kendall had given his orders.

The man who'd found the body stood apart from the others, head bowed, muttering to himself. He scarcely glanced up as Harper approached, lips moving in undertone of words.

'Do you know who the dead man is?' he asked.

'*Er iz toyt.*' He's dead.

'English?' the inspector asked hopefully, but the man just shook his head. He kept his gaze on the ground, too fearful to look directly at a policeman.

'*Velz is dayn nomen?*' The Yiddish made the man's head jerk up. What's your name?

'Israel Liebermann, *mayn ir,*' the man replied nervously. Sir. Growing up here it had been impossible not to absorb a little of the language. It floated in the shops and all around the boys that played in the road.

'*Ikh bin* Inspector Harper.'

A hand tapped him on the shoulder and he turned quickly to see a pair of dark eyes staring at him.

'What?' He had the sense that the man had spoken; for a moment he hadn't heard a word. He swallowed and the world came back into both ears.

'I said it was a good try, Inspector Harper. But your accent needs work.' The voice was warm, filled with kindness. He extended his hand and Harper took it.

'I'm Rabbi Feldman.'

The man was dressed for the weather in a heavy overcoat that extended almost to his feet, thick boots, leather gloves and a hat pulled down to his ears. A wiry grey beard flowed down to his chest.

A gust of wind blew hard. Harper shivered, feeling the chill deep in his marrow.

'If you think this is cold, you never had a winter in Odessa.' The rabbi grinned, then his face grew serious. 'Can I help at all?'

'Someone's been murdered. This gentleman found him.'

Feldman nodded then began a conversation in Yiddish with Liebermann. A pause, another question and a long answer.

He'd heard of the rabbi. Everyone had. Around the Leylands he was almost a hero. He was one of them; his family had taken the long march west, all the way to England, when the pogroms began. He understood their sorrows and their dreams. In his sixties now, walking with the help of a silver-topped stick, he'd been head of the Belgrave Street Synagogue for over ten years. He taught in the Hebrew school on Gower Street and met with councillors from the Town Hall. He was man of *mitzvahs*, good deeds. Portly and gentle, with quiet dignity, he was someone in the community, a man everybody respected.

'He says he needed the outhouse just before ten – he'd looked at his watch in the house so he knew what time it was. He put on his coat and came down.' Feldman smiled. 'You understand, it's cold in these places. You try to finish as soon as possible. When he was done he noticed the shape and went to look. That's when he began to yell.'

'Thank you,' Harper said, although it was no more than they already knew.

'Murder is a terrible business, Inspector.' The man hesitated. 'Is there anything else I can do?'

'We still don't know the name of the dead man.'

'May I?' Feldman gestured at the corpse. Harper nodded and one of the constables drew back the sheet again.

'*Mine Got.*' He drew in his breath sharply.

'Do you know him?'

It was a few seconds before the rabbi answered, staring intently at the face on the ground. Slowly he took off the hat and tugged a hand through his ragged white hair.

'Yes, Inspector,' he said, and there was the sadness of lost years in his voice. 'I know him. I know him very well. I gave him his *bris* and his *bar mitzvah*. He's my sister's son.'

His nephew. God, Harper thought, what a way to find out.

'I'm sorry, sir. Truly.'

The man's shoulders slumped.

'He was seventeen.' The rabbi shook his head in disbelief. 'Just a *boychik*. He was going to be the one.' Feldman tapped a finger against the side of his head. 'He had the smarts, Inspector. His father, he was already training him to run the business.'

'What was his name, sir? I need to know.'

'Abraham. Abraham Levy.' The rabbi rummaged in a trouser pocket, brought out a handkerchief and wiped his eyes. 'Why?' he asked quietly. 'Why would someone kill anyone who was so young?'

Harper didn't have the answer. Why was anyone murdered?

'Where did he live?'

'On Nile Street.' Feldman straightened suddenly. 'My sister. I have to tell her.'

'I'll come with you.'

'No,' the man answered, his voice firm. 'No, Inspector, please. It's better from me. I'll go and see them. Tomorrow you can ask your questions. Tonight's for grieving. You come in the morning.'

'Of course,' he agreed quickly.

He waited, but the rabbi didn't move, staring at something no one else could see.

'You know, where I grew up, they murdered Jews for fun,' he said after a few moments, his eyes wet with tears. 'They did it for sport. So we ran, because running was the only way to stay alive. Then, when we came here, we wondered if we'd run far enough or fast enough, whether it would be the same again. We had children and we built lives. But always, we keep our eyes open and a bag close by.' He turned his eyes on Harper, the tears shining on his cheeks. 'Is this the way it is now? Do we have to run again?'

'No, sir,' he promised. 'That's something you'll never have to do any more.'

From time to time he'd heard people, talking in the pubs after a few pints loosened their tongues. Jew this and Jew that. Hatred and fear. But it had never been more than words. Until now.

He watched Feldman shuffle away, exchanging a few solemn words here and there as he went. He stopped to talk to a young woman, and gently touched her shoulder as she put her hands over her face.

'Did you hear all that?' he asked. Reed nodded and lit a cigarette, smoke curling into the air. He looked down at the corpse.

'It's the position he was left in that worries me.'

Harper agreed. A mockery of the crucifixion, out on the cobbles. 'And the time. Christmas Eve.'

'What do you think?' the sergeant asked.

'I don't know yet, Billy.'

'The pennies?' Reed asked. 'What do you make of them?'

Harper shook his head. It was a strange touch, a ritual from long ago. Money to pay the ferryman for the crossing into the afterlife. He'd read about it years before. But it seemed curious. A way to emphasize death? That connection some people seemed to make between Jews and money?

'I'm not sure. It could be something or nothing.'

'I'll tell you another thing, too. Look around him. There's hardly any blood. He wasn't killed here.'

Harper nodded; he'd noticed. What it all meant was anyone's guess.

'Talk to everyone in the houses round here and find out if they saw anything,' he ordered. 'Start the bobbies on that. One or two of them must speak Yiddish. And have a word with that girl over there.' He pointed at her, surrounded now by others trying to give some comfort. 'It looks like she knew Abraham Levy.'

'Do you think she'll speak English?'

The inspector glanced at her. No more than sixteen. Probably born in Leeds. The place where her parents had lived would be no more than horror stories to her.

'I'm sure she does,' he said.

'What about the body?' Reed wondered. 'Do you want me to send it over to Hunslet for Dr King?'

'No,' Harper said slowly. With Christmas, the police surgeon wouldn't be there for the next two days. There was little he could tell them that they couldn't see for themselves. He knew the

Jewish way, burial before the next sunset. He could give them that, if nothing else. 'They'll have an undertaker along soon. And Billy . . .'

'What?'

'Once they've all gone, take a look through his pockets. And have them start searching for the knife that killed him. It might be around somewhere. I'm going to Millgarth and write up the report.'

THREE

The women moved away like a wave as he approached. It was always that way, Reed thought. As if they didn't want to be too close to a copper. As if they were all guilty of something.

'Miss,' he said, and the girl stared up at him. The first thing he noticed was her eyes, dark and deep, then the marks of tears on her cheeks. She had a headscarf knotted under her chin and a shawl gathered round her shoulders on top of a thin coat. The hem of a black dress trailed over the top of her button boots. 'Miss,' he repeated, 'did you know Mr Levy?'

She opened her mouth then just nodded.

'How did you know him?' Reed asked.

'He . . . we . . . we'd been courting.' She sounded hoarse, stunned, as if talking was an effort, but her accent was pure Yorkshire.

'Do you know what might have happened?'

Anger flashed across her face. 'They killed him.'

'They?'

'You.' She almost spat the word. 'The English.'

It took him half an hour to learn it all as they stood and shivered. Someone brought out hot, sweet tea, and Reed cupped his hands gratefully around the mug. Her name was Rachel Wasserman. She'd grown up in Nile Street, just three doors from Abraham Levy. From the very first there'd been an understanding between the families that the two of them would marry once they were old

enough. It seemed a fair bargain. He'd give her a good life and
in exchange she'd be a loyal wife. But a year before he'd started
attending meetings and coming home with ideas. About Jews.
About a homeland in Palestine. Their birthright. The land promised
to them in the Bible. Ideas that caught fire in both of them.

'Did he want to go and live there?' Reed asked.

Rachel shook her head. 'Not us,' she told him. 'We couldn't,
not with our parents here. But our children.' She turned silent for
a few moments at the thought of those who would never be born
now. 'A place they'd never have to leave. What Abraham wanted
was for us to be treated properly.' She stared at him defiantly.
'That's why they killed him.'

'Properly?' He didn't understand.

Three others had moved close, all of them under twenty. Two
boys and a girl.

'You don't know what it's like to be Jewish here,' the young
woman told him.

'No,' Reed admitted. He'd never even given it a thought.

'In a shop they'll serve everyone before me,' she continued.
'They'll make me put my money on the counter so they don't
have to touch my hand.'

'They spit at us in the street,' one young man said.

'They don't want us here,' the other boy told him, his voice
bitter. 'But we were born here, we're as English as they are.'

'You don't know what it's like not to be wanted somewhere,'
Rachel Wasserman told him. 'Abraham did. We all do.'

But he did. When he'd been a soldier with the West Yorkshires
he'd spent two years fighting in Afghanistan. He'd seen the looks
of hatred all over the country, known the natives only tolerated
him because he carried a rifle. And he'd seen what they did to
those they caught.

'What did Abraham do?' he asked.

'He made sure people treated us like everyone else.' Rachel
held her head up with pride.

'Did he belong to any organizations?'

'Why?' one of the young men asked angrily. 'What good do
they do? All they do is talk. Words.' He spat.

'Where did he go tonight?' Reed asked, looking around the
faces. 'Do any of you know?'

'Abraham liked to walk,' the other girl said. 'All over Leeds.'

'And you've no idea where he was for the last few hours?'

Rachel Wasserman shook her head and began to cry again.

Harper wrote up his report. Not that there was much. The wounds on the body, the fact that he'd been killed somewhere else. The bobbies on the house-to-house had nothing to add when they returned. If anyone had heard anything, they'd believed it was someone going to the outhouse. No one had looked. No one had paid attention. They'd been in their homes, simply trying to keep warm.

Reed came into the office, tossed his hat on the desk and stood by the fire, holding out his hands to the flames.

'Did the girl tell you anything?'

'Seems our Abraham was a bit of a firebrand.'

'Firebrand?' the inspector sat back. 'How do you mean?'

The sergeant explained.

'None of them knew where he'd gone,' he finished in exasperation. 'It could have happened any bloody where, Tom.'

'I don't think so.' Harper shook his head. 'No one's going to carry a body far. Never mind the weather. Someone would see them. Was there anything in his pockets?'

'Just a handkerchief, a packet of Senior Service and some matches. Nothing to help. We don't have much to go on, do we?'

Not a thing, Harper thought. Just a corpse and plenty of questions.

'I'll talk to his parents tomorrow. Maybe they'll know more.'

'I suppose leave is cancelled?' Reed asked warily.

'You can still take Boxing Day,' the inspector told him. 'I'll square it with the super.'

He wanted Billy to spend time with the widow in Middleton he'd been seeing since July. She was good for him. He was drinking less now, and his temper didn't flare or flicker so often. He was a good man, an excellent copper. But he was haunted; until Elizabeth, he'd kept people at bay. Somehow, almost effortlessly, she'd found a way through to him.

It was past four when he unlocked the door at the Victoria and eased his way into bed. Annabelle stirred and turned towards him.

'Bad?' Her voice was heavy with sleep.

'Bad enough.' He kissed her forehead tenderly. 'I'll worry about it in the morning. Happy Christmas, Mrs Harper.'

FOUR

B y eight he was back at Millgarth police station.

He'd given Annabelle her present before he left, the jet and silver pendant that had belonged to his mother. She let out a small cry of pleasure as she opened the wrapping, dashed off to the mirror to hold it against herself, admiring it as if it was the best gift she'd ever received, kissed him, put it on and kissed him again, leaving the kettle to boil and boil, filling the kitchen with steam.

'Do you know when you'll be home?' she asked as he pulled on his heavy gloves.

'No.' He sighed. 'I'm sorry. It's . . .'

'It's your job, Tom. I knew that when I married you. Dinner's at two if you can be here. Even for an hour, love . . .' There was hope in her eyes.

'I'll try,' he told her. 'I promise.'

The cold was bone-bitter as he stepped outside. No trams on Christmas Day, he thought grimly, just the frozen walk into town.

Superintendent Kendall was already at his desk, freshly shaved, his dark suit pressed, moustache waxed to pointed ends. A murder was enough to drag him into the station on a holiday. He let out a long sigh.

'I saw the report. Happy Christmas, eh, Tom?'

'I'm seeing the parents this morning. The boy was Rabbi Feldman's nephew.'

'I heard. We'd better clear this one up very quickly. We don't need him breathing down our necks.'

'Yes, sir.'

The superintendent tapped the papers on front of him. 'So what's not in here?'

'Billy Reed talked to Levy's friends. The lad was quite political.'

Kendall's eyes narrowed. 'Political how?'

'He thought Jews should be treated the same as everyone else. Quite outspoken about it, by all accounts. Talking about a Jewish homeland in Palestine.' He shrugged.

Kendall stroked his moustache. 'Outspoken enough to get him killed?'

'It's possible,' Harper answered carefully. 'I don't really know yet.' All the way into town he'd been weighing the possibilities.

'What does your gut tell you, Tom?'

'I think it was that way. That's how it feels at the moment.'

Harper remembered the way people treated the Jews when he was young. At first everyone had been wary of the outsiders with their dark eyes and strange language. But a year or two on and they'd become part of the neighbourhood, just a little different, with their odd ways and Saturday Sabbath.

Yet there were always a few who wouldn't accept them. The Andersons had been the worst. The wife was a shrunken shrew with a tongue as sharp as her teeth, never a kind word for anyone. And there was Joe, leering after the girls while he talked about dirty kikes. His son Jack had been as bad. He'd been in the same year at school as Harper. A natural bully, he'd deliberately pick fights with the skinny little Jewish lads just to punch them until they bled. Then more Jews arrived, a family or two at first, soon four or five a month, until it seemed as if they were coming on every tide. The Andersons moved away, flitting in the night with their rent unpaid.

'We can't afford to let this build,' Kendall said. 'The last thing we need is something simmering here. Find whoever did it and let's nip any trouble in the bud.'

'Yes, sir. One thing, though. He definitely wasn't murdered where we found him. We need men to look for the killing ground. It can't have been far away.'

'With Christmas, I can't spare any bobbies until tomorrow.' The inspector was just turning the doorknob when Kendall added, 'You haven't forgotten about the twenty-eighth, have you?'

'Twenty-eighth?' His mind was a blank.

'That French policeman's coming to look into the Le Prince disappearance. I told you last week.'

'But—'

The Superintendent took off his spectacles and polished them on his handkerchief.

'You're the same rank as him, Tom. It's protocol. Chief Constable's orders. You don't have to do anything, just help if he needs it. At least he's supposed to speak good English.' He searched for a crumpled note. 'He's arriving on the ten past twelve from London. You'd better meet him at the station.'

'What's his name?'

Kendall squinted, trying to make out the handwriting.

'Bertrand Muyrère.' He struggled with the word, then passed the paper to Harper. 'Something like that, anyway. See he finds a decent hotel. He's paying, mind. We're not picking up the bill.'

'Yes, sir.'

'And it's just a cooperation job, remember that.' He frowned. 'Odd case, though.'

It was. He'd read about it, front pages in the newspapers. Louis Le Prince was a Frenchman, an inventor, famous as the man who made pictures that moved. Harper had talked to a few who'd seen them; they'd scarcely been able to believe their eyes.

Le Prince had come over to Leeds, married his boss's daughter and dreamed up the camera; he'd filmed images in his father-in-law's garden and on Leeds Bridge. During the summer he'd gone back to see his family in France, taking the camera with him, before heading off to America to patent the device. But on the way he'd simply vanished. Boarded the train from Dijon to Paris and that was the last anyone had seen of him, as if the air itself had taken him.

'Yes, sir. I don't think he'll find his culprit here, though.'

'Nor do I, but we'll show willing. Look after him.'

'Anything more during the night?' Harper asked.

Reed shook his head wearily. 'Not a thing. No one's come forward. I have someone going back round the houses on Trafalgar Street. What do you want me to do?'

'Come along with me. I want to take a look at the place in the light.'

'After that?'

'We'll see. And happy bloody Christmas, Billy.'

*   *   *

There wasn't much to discover. Wind whipped along the road, swirling in eddies between the blocks of houses. The inspector kept his hands in his pockets, huddled tight against the cold. He stared at the ground and the outhouses. Here and there a woman's face gazed down at him, half-hidden in an upstairs window. Down the street he could hear the sound of a sweatshop, men crammed together in a single room making clothing. The sewing machines hummed at the edge of his hearing. No Christmas in the Jewish calendar.

He spotted something that might have been a bloodstain on the stones. He crouched, running a hand over it, fingertips checking the spaces between the cobbles. It was nothing.

'Did you look at his hands?' Harper wondered.

'No cuts or scratches,' Reed answered. So Abraham Levy hadn't put up a struggle. From the sound of him, that seemed unlikely unless the knife had taken him by surprise.

In his bones he was sure that no one from the Leylands had done this. But he'd been in the job long enough to keep an open mind. It was murder; anything was possible. He stood, thinking, then fumbled in his coat and took out his pocket watch.

'Time to talk to the parents,' he said.

He could have found his way around the house in a blindfold. The rooms were exactly the same as the home where he'd grown up, as every other place around here. They sat cramped around a table in the kitchen. The father, his eyes locked and uncomprehending in his pain. The mother, small and dumpy, all in black from the scarf around her head to the stockings that poked out from her long dress, kneading a handkerchief between stubby fingers. The rabbi, his back straight, his hand over his sister's. Three children, all boys, the oldest maybe fourteen. And Harper. Reed stood, his back against a wall.

The room was warm, the black range giving off enough heat for Harper to remove his overcoat. He'd asked his questions and received the answers, everything translated by Feldman from the rush of Yiddish.

'You didn't tell me your nephew was political,' he finally said to the rabbi.

'He was young, Inspector. Impatient. He didn't understand that changes takes time. He wanted everything now. Weren't you like that at seventeen?'

'I was rolling barrels all day at Brunswick brewery.'

'And reading at night.' He gave a quick smile at the surprise on Harper's face. 'I've been asking. There are people around here who still remember you.'

'Moishe Cohen?'

'And others,' Feldman said with a small nod. 'From what they tell me, you're quite political yourself.'

'I'm a policeman,' Harper answered.

'There's the policeman and there's the man,' the rabbi explained slowly. 'The head and the heart.'

'And there's a killer to catch. Every piece of information is important.'

Feldman stared at him. 'What do you want me to say, Inspector?' he asked slowly. 'Abraham wanted what we all want. He thought he should have that because he was a person like everyone else. He hasn't lived through worse. Most of us have.'

'How many think like him?' Harper looked at the boys.

'I do,' the oldest boy said defiantly. Samuel Levy. The rabbi raised a hand but the lad ignored him. English was his native tongue, without any trace of his uncle's heavy accent. 'We were born here. We're as English as you are.'

The inspector dipped his head in acknowledgement. 'Did your brother have any enemies?'

'Not round here,' Samuel Levy replied and Harper understood what he meant. Here, in the Leylands. Where they could all gather together, enough of them in one small place to feel safe and secure.

'Go on.'

'They don't like us in town.'

'Anyone in particular?' Harper asked.

The boy shrugged, all the bravado evaporating as his uncle glared at him.

'There are only a few who don't want us here,' Feldman said with a sigh. 'You know who I mean, Inspector. People who don't like the Irish or the Jews or anyone who's not from here. England for the English.' He raised his eyes. 'But they'll change in time, *imyirtseshem*.' God willing.

'Samuel,' Harper said. The boy stirred uncomfortably. 'Please, if there's anyone or any group, I need to know.'

But the lad just pushed his lips together and shook his head. The inspector wasn't going to discover anything right now. He pushed back his chair. From the depths of memory he dredged up a phrase.

'*Zayt moykhl oyf dayn onver.*' I'm sorry for your loss. He gave a small bow and left, Reed on his heels.

After the cloying heat of the kitchen, the bitter air was fresh and clean in his lungs.

'What did you make of that, Billy?' he asked as the sergeant lit a cigarette.

'No one from around here killed him. Think about it, Tom, the pose, murdered elsewhere . . .'

'Then we'd better find out about some of them. There must be some groups. Ask around at the station, someone might know something.' He drew the watch from his waistcoat. 'I'll see you there at half past one.'

Quarter past eleven. Harper knew exactly where the beat copper would be: warming himself in the shop at the bottom of Poland Street. It was a routine that had held for decades, already going strong when he was just a boy.

And Forsyth was just where he expected, putting the cup back on the old, scarred counter. The smells overwhelmed him as he entered. Sacks of sugar and salt and beans sat on the floor, spices in their jars, tins on the shelves. Twenty years before it had been Mrs Peters who owned the place. He'd been sent running down here often enough by his mother for a pennyworth of this or that, everything weighed out and packed in a paper cone. Now he couldn't read the strange writing on the notices and there were many items he'd never seen before. Different people, he thought, different tastes. The woman who stood there with hair neatly wrapped in a scarf and her shoulders covered by an old shawl, looked at him curiously.

'I wondered when you'd come looking for me, sir,' Forsyth said. He snapped the cap back on to his head. 'Do you fancy a stroll? I'll see you tomorrow, Esther.'

These were Forsyth's streets. He'd covered them for more than two decades, starting when he was fresh on the force. He'd grown into a portly man, his top lip covered by a ruddy moustache with streaks of grey.

'I surprised you're working today.' The constable had enough seniority to claim the holiday off.

'Dun't make no never mind to me, sir.' Harper remembered that Forsyth was widowed, with a daughter living in Holbeck. 'I'll go over to our Katie's later for me dinner.' He paused. 'Terrible about young Abraham.'

'How well did you know him?'

'So-so.'

'What was he like?'

The constable pursed his mouth. 'Bit of a hothead at times, sir, but a good lad under all that. I gave him a clip round the ear a few times when he was younger. I'm sure you remember what that's like.' Harper smiled; when he was a boy, he'd received one or two from Forsyth himself. Then the bobby would have a quiet word with his mother and there'd be more when his father arrived home.

'Any real trouble with him?'

'Nothing as you'd notice.' Forsyth strode with the easy grace of the beat policeman, eyes constantly glancing around, taking everything in and remembering it. But winter kept the streets empty as they walked. No children out running, no women gossiping in the doorways. The only sounds came as they passed the sweatshops, two of three of them on every street.

'What about people coming in here and stirring things up?'

The copper shook his head. 'Only now and then. They have a few drinks and come around shouting and yelling. We take care of it and they wake up in the cells. A fine or a few days of hard labour usually puts them off.'

'More in the last few years?'

'Mebbe,' Forsyth allowed after a little thought. 'You'll find words painted on the walls – Jews go home, things like that. But it's not bad. I'll tell you the truth, sir. This is an easy beat. There's hardly any problems beyond the odd domestic. They just work all the time. I've never seen anything like it.'

'What about Abraham? Were there people round here who didn't like him?'

'A few, perhaps. Happen one or two thought he was speaking

too loud, bringing attention to the place. Most of them here just want to be left in peace. But I suppose you can't blame the lad. I remember when he was born; this is all he's ever known, him and all the other young 'uns. Why shouldn't they be treated the same as everyone else?'

'Do you think there's anyone in the Leylands who'd kill him?'

'Here? No,' Forsyth answered without hesitation. 'I'm certain of that. Not him or that girl of his, or any of them. I went to see his parents this morning. Paid my respects.'

'Who do you think is responsible for his death, Mr Forsyth?'

'Me? I don't know, sir, and that's the truth. But I'm as sure as I can be that it wasn't anyone from round here.'

Reed hadn't learned anything at Millgarth. The few policemen working on Christmas Day didn't know much. Half the beat constables, the ones who kept their ears to the ground, were off for the holiday.

'Who's around?' he asked Tollman, the desk sergeant.

'There's Ash.' He glanced at the clock. 'Usually he'd be at the Royal about now, cadging himself a cup of tea. They'll be closed today, though.'

It took half an hour to find the man, tramping through the mean courts and yards between Briggate and Lands Lane. There was no joy of the season back here, none of the laughter and pleasure, simply another day of poverty and misery. He finally spotted the constable on Albion Street, outside the Co-operative department store, helping a drunk to his feet.

'If you don't go home, Albert, you'll bloody freeze to death out here. What would I tell your missus then, eh?'

He watched the man stumble off, barely able to stay upright, and waited until he was out of sight before turning to greet Reed.

'Another half an hour and I'll find him somewhere else.' He shook his head. 'Not often we see you in these parts, Sergeant. Happy Christmas to you.'

Ash was a big man, genial and intelligent, with warm eyes and a welcoming manner. He'd been more than a year on this beat, long enough to know it intimately. He'd hear every whisper and rumour that circulated.

'Busy today?'

Ash smiled. 'Quiet as church. Makes a change round here. I'll be done at two, anyway. Having me on shift gives the wife and that little one we took in a bit of peace from me. What can I do for you, sir?'

He listened closely as Reed explained, stroking his moustache as he thought.

'There's some nasty buggers around, and no mistake,' he said with a shake of his head. 'Round here I'd look at the Cork and Bottle, up on the Headrow. There's talk in there that would curl your hair.'

'About Jews?'

'Jews, Irish, you name it. It's not everyone who drinks there, mind. Just a few.' He raised an eyebrow. 'But that's enough, isn't it?'

'Any names?'

Ash shrugged. 'I've not paid much attention, Sarge. I can find out if you'd like. But I've heard that there's a place worse than that.'

'Where?'

'The Anchor, down on Mabgate. I've never been in myself, but that's what I've been told.'

'Who'd know?'

'Have a word with Terry Dicks. It's his beat, has been for years.' He leaned forward conspiratorially. 'I'm not so sure he doesn't believe things like that himself, if you know what I mean.' He tapped the side of his nose with his finger. 'Just a word to the wise.'

'Can you find out more about the people at the Cork and Bottle for me? Quietly.'

'Glad to. I should tell you, though, a lot of them up there spent time in the army. I know you served, too . . .'

'Thank you.' After the West Yorkshire regiment came back from the Afghan war he'd stayed in the army for a few months. But the bad dreams wouldn't stop, even in the safety of York barracks. He'd served long enough; it was time. He handed in his papers and came home. That was ten years ago. Nowadays the nightmares didn't drag him awake so often. He'd found peace of a sort in his life, a tenuous, uneasy beast. 'I'm off tomorrow; I'll be back on Saturday.'

'I'll leave a note on your desk, sir.'

*   *   *

Harper doodled on the paper. He'd finished his report, the station was silent, and he had time to think. The more he considered it, the more he believed that no one from the Leylands would kill Abraham Levy.

So who had? Whoever it was, they'd be the devil to find. And he'd already lost today because of Christmas. Everywhere was closed, people gathered around their fires. Good tidings to all men.

Meanwhile, with every hour that passed without finding the murderer, people in the Leylands would wonder if the police really cared, if they were even trying.

He glanced down at the page. He'd drawn arrows in pencil going in all directions. It was how he felt. Too many choices. Too many possibilities.

Reed arrived on the dot of half past one. Before he could even take off his coat, Harper was up, pulling on his muffler and gloves.

'We're going out.'

'Now?' he asked in astonishment. 'Where?'

The inspector just smiled. 'Come on.'

They walked out along Regent Street, exchanging information.

'Are you going to tell me where we're going, Tom?' the sergeant asked finally.

'Christmas dinner.'

'Where?' He looked around. No people, no carts on the road, no lights in any of the businesses.

'The Victoria,' Harper told him. 'Annabelle will kill me if I'm not there. And you need to eat.'

Harper opened the door and walked into the parlour. The pleasure that lit up Annabelle's face when she saw him made it all worthwhile. She was dressed to the nines, her hair swept up, the jet pendant hanging from her neck, wearing a bustled burgundy gown that swept across the floor as she came to greet him.

'I was hoping you'd be able to come home,' she whispered in his ear. 'It wouldn't have been right without you.'

'I brought Billy,' he said, moving aside to let the sergeant enter.

'I should hope you did, too,' she told him and turned to Reed. 'Find yourself a chair, love. There's room if we all squeeze up.'

It was a full table. There was Dan the barman, wearing a suit for once, with an old wing collar and tie, his hair greased down. Kitty and Emma, the servants, both looked slightly ill-at-ease out of uniform. Old Mrs Derby from Manor Road whose husband had died back in March. Christine and Wilhelmina who ran the bakeries, and Will, who helped out when the drays delivered the beer. Someone had already tapped the barrel in the kitchen and everyone was talking nineteen to the dozen, glasses half-empty in front of them.

'Are you off out again later?' Annabelle asked as Harper settled next to her.

'I've only popped back for an hour.'

'I'm glad you did.' She squeezed his thigh and smiled. 'Is Billy working, too?'

'Yes.' He glanced down the table to see Reed look longingly at the beer, knowing he daren't drink while he was on duty. A ten-shilling fine for the first offence, a pound for the second. The third time you were kicked off the force.

'I'll put the kettle on.'

The goose sizzled as Harper carried it in, fat spattering off the golden skin. Reed offered to carve the bird, using the knife with a skill no one suspected, each slice thin and even. He smiled shyly as they applauded his work.

Talk, laughter and food, Harper thought. For one afternoon, at least, they were all a family. The women cleared the plates. He heard shrieks of happiness from the kitchen, then they returned with the plum pudding, the brandy lit and burning soft blue.

'Right.' Annabelle tapped her spoon against the wine glass for silence. Her eyes glistened. She stood and looked around. 'I've known most of you for a long time. You've all been good friends to me.' She reached out and took Harper's hand. 'Now I've been lucky enough to find this one – lucky as long as you ignore the fact that he's a copper.' She gave him a broad wink. 'Anyway, I just wanted to say happy Christmas to you all and thank you for coming. And you'd better eat up.'

She had gifts for them all under the tree, even Billy. Just little baubles, but everyone oohed and aahed as they unwrapped the presents.

'I'm saving yours for later,' Annabelle told him as she gave him a kiss, fingers toying with her necklace. 'And I'm wearing the one you gave me. It really is lovely, Tom. Thank you.'

Finally he took out his watch and nodded to Reed. Half past three. Time had slipped past; they needed to be on their way.

'Will you be late?' she asked as she unlocked the door of the pub.

'I'll try not to be.'

Annabelle pushed herself into his arms. 'Just make sure you look after yourself, Tom Harper.'

'I will.'

'And you, too, Billy,' she said. 'Your Elizabeth must be looking forward to seeing you tomorrow.'

They walked back into Leeds along the empty road. Not even four and it was already full darkness. The bleak midwinter, he thought.

'Where are we going?' Reed asked.

'I'm going to talk to Abraham's brother. He knows something, I could see it in his eyes.'

'Where do you want me?'

'Back to the station. You're the duty detective today, remember?'

FIVE

In the end, Reed was almost late. He had to dash for the train, sprinting along the platform and clutching the packages tight against his chest. In the empty carriage he gave a sigh of relief and let everything tumble on to the seat: the presents he'd bought for Elizabeth and each of her children.

He'd had no idea what to buy them. Years had passed since he'd given a woman a gift. And children? Never. Finally he went to the Grand Pygmalion, the towering department store on Boar Lane to wander and weave through the Christmas crowds. Four floors and so much on sale. How did anyone ever decide?

Eventually a shop girl took pity on him. He gave her the ages and sexes of the children and let her choose. A whip and top, a doll, a book of adventure stories and something he couldn't even remember now. She wrapped them then guided him up the stairs to the women's floor. He watched her move confidently among the bottles of scent, selecting one and holding it up.

'She'll love this one. It's not the most popular but I think it's the best.'

He took it and thanked her. He just wanted to be out of there; with so many people about and so many things to see, he felt overwhelmed. The presents took almost half his pay, with just enough left over for his lodgings and a drink or two.

Ten minutes later the squeal of the brakes woke him from a doze as the train pulled in to Middleton station. Elizabeth was standing at the end of the platform, beaming at the sight of him, the children lined up politely behind her. She always seemed so happy to see him, so warm. God knew he enjoyed their time together; he just didn't understand what she saw in him.

'Hello, love,' she said, pushing up on tiptoe to hug him. 'Happy Christmas.'

He'd met her when he'd come to Middleton on a case, seeking directions to one of the pits. She was a widow who worked in a shop, so forward he could hardly believe it. But he came out again to walk with her. Then, almost without him noticing, it had become a regular thing. Whenever he had a day off they'd spend it together. A fortnight had gone by since he'd seen her last; she'd brought the children into Leeds and he'd taken them all to the pantomime at the Princess Palace, laughing just as hard as they did at the show.

She slid her arm through his as they walked, squeezing it gently and smiling up at him.

'Me mam's gone to see me sister today so it's us and the little ones. I've made a big dinner. I hope you're hungry.'

'I'll manage,' he told her with a grin. She knew his appetite.

He felt different when he was with her. All the anger inside him seemed to melt away. He was still wary around her children, never sure quite how to act. But with Elizabeth he seemed to be part of a family for the first time since he was a boy.

They opened the presents after the meal. The children loved what he'd bought. John, the oldest, stood straight and said, 'Thank you, sir,' giving a sharp salute. His younger brother tried to imitate him and the girls made graceful curtseys before they all dashed off to play, leaving Reed alone with Elizabeth at the table. He pushed a package towards her.

'I didn't know what to get you,' he admitted as she unwrapped it. With eager fingers she removed the stopper.

'Oh Billy, it's wonderful.' She dabbed perfume on the inside of her wrists and in the hollow at the base of her neck. 'Smell it. It really is,' she told him and he saw she was close to tears.

Reed watched as she brought a small package from the pocket of her dress and shyly placed it in his hand. He was careful, unknotting the ribbon then laying it and the paper aside. In the box was a pair of cufflinks with the crest of the West Yorkshires, his old regiment. Something he didn't even know he'd wanted, but he'd cherish them for the rest of his life.

'They're . . .' he began, but he didn't have the words for what he felt inside. 'Thank you,' he managed finally and kissed her.

'Tom,' Annabelle said tentatively, stirring him from his thoughts. 'I've been thinking.' He finished chewing his breakfast bread and butter and looked at her. She'd been up since four, wearing her old dress and apron, and out in the big kitchen in the back garden, first working with the bakers, then supervising the boys as they loaded the handcarts to push the loaves and pies and pastries to the shops. He reached across and brushed a flour smudge from her face.

'What?'

'About opening another bakery.'

'Another one?' he asked in surprise. 'What for?'

She already owned two, both of them local, as well as the pub. During the autumn she'd begun lending a little money to local families. He'd told her the interest rates the Shylocks charged and she'd been horrified, determined to do better for those who needed it. Harper hadn't been happy at the idea, but he knew that once a thought came to her she never let it drop. So far she'd done well enough, everyone paying back on time. She charged them a half-penny a week on five bob. People were grateful and eager. He just didn't want her to come a cropper.

'There's plenty more opportunity out there. I was over in Burmantofts last week. A lot of folk around, what with all those factories and industry, but not many shops to serve them. I only saw one baker.'

'It'll mean more work.'

'Not really.' She poured a cup of tea from the pot. 'We already bake for two shops. A third wouldn't take much more, at least to begin with. And we'd only start small. What do you think?'

He loved the way she wanted his advice, although he knew nothing about business. She trusted him, she truly wanted to know what he thought. She wanted him to be a part of it all. Annabelle had money. More than he knew, most likely. By any standards, she was a woman of means. Compared to those who lived in the streets around the Victoria, she was rich.

Annabelle could buy or sell most of the self-important men he met, but she had no desire for the big house, a carriage or any of those trappings. She was content in the rooms above the pub. She spent some money on clothes, new gowns to fill her wardrobe, but most went into the bank.

'Have you found a place there yet?'

She shook her head. 'I've not even started looking. I'm going to walk around over there in a day or two. It has to be right.'

'You really think it'll make money?' Annabelle had that glimmer of determination in her eye.

'I do. It should be a good little earner,' she said thoughtfully. 'And it's close enough.'

That much was true, he thought as he drained the cup of tea and stood. Burmantofts was little more than half a mile from the Victoria.

'If it's you, you'll make it a success.'

As he pulled on the overcoat, she straightened his tie.

'That suit looks just right on you,' she said approvingly.

It did; a perfect fit, the trousers tight across his thighs and tapering over his boots, the jacket cut just right, four buttons, expensive dark grey worsted. It was her Christmas present to him, a whole outfit, with shirt, a set of the new-style fold-over collars and a silk tie, all of it waiting when he returned home the night before.

'I went to see that man who made your wedding suit,' she'd explained as she held the clothes up for him. 'That Jewish one.'

'Moishe?' he said, then gave the English: 'Moses?'

'That's him. He did such a good job on that, I told him to make one like it but better.' Her smile turned shy. 'I hope you like it.'

It was the costliest thing he'd ever owned. The material felt smooth and luxurious under his fingers. It fitted as well as a pair of rich leather gloves. Now, staring in the long mirror, he could see just how perfect it was. Moses had performed his magic well. And the new fashion in collars was comfortable. They didn't rise up and press against his throat. Looked better with a tie, too.

Annabelle cocked her head. 'Are you poorly?'

'No,' he answered in surprise. 'Why?'

'You're very pale this morning, that's all.'

'I'm fine,' he said, giving her a quick kiss before he left.

His breath clouded the air as he strode out. He should have known better than to think he could fool her.

He listened carefully for noises as he walked. Everything was fine now. But when he woke, he hadn't been able to hear anything in his bad right ear again. Not a sound. He'd panicked, full of fear as he dressed.

It only lasted for five minutes. Then the hearing suddenly returned, no worse than it was before. Just like the day before. But the time seemed to stretch out forever. It was long enough to imagine himself always like this, half-deaf, and it terrified him, his very worst fear made real. A blasted future. Made to leave the police, back to a lifetime of pushing barrels every day at Brunswick's Brewery.

He breathed deep, icy air in his lungs. It was over, he told himself, it had passed. He needed to focus on Abraham Levy, not his own problems.

The night before, he'd gone back down to the Leylands, seeing the constables on patrol. Apart from them the streets were empty. On Nile Street he knocked on the door and waited. A rush of voices and then the rabbi was standing there, the long grey beard majestic, his eyes filled with sorrow, pain and a touch of anger.

'Inspector.' He sighed. 'This isn't a good time. You know we've just buried my nephew.'

He knew. In the ground before sunset the day after death.

'I need to talk to Samuel.'

'Not now, Mr Harper,' Feldman said. 'Please.'

'It's important, sir,' he insisted. 'Don't you want Abraham's killer caught?'

The man bristled. His mouth became a thin line.

'Come in, then,' he said grudgingly.

'No, sir. I'd like to see him in private.'

For a few seconds they stared at each other until Feldman turned away. Light spilled from the house. Harper waited outside in the cold and dark. Finally Samuel Levy appeared, still in his good suit, a wary look on his face, pulling on a battered overcoat two sizes too large for him.

He was tall for his age with thick, curly hair and full lips. In a year or two all the girls would be after him. For now, though, he was still lean, caught between boy and man. A scared lad who'd lost his brother.

They walked the streets for the better part of an hour. The talk was stilted at first, Levy keeping his secrets close. Bit by bit it eased and things began to spill out. Samuel had looked up to his brother. He'd followed him, listened closely and taken the words to heart.

'Did he have run-ins with people?' Harper asked.

'Sometimes,' Levy admitted, then quickly added, 'but it was usually nothing more than words. If people started something, Abraham wouldn't back down. None of us would.' He stared at the inspector with youthful defiance. 'Why should we?'

'Was there anyone in particular?'

'Not really. If any of them came out here, we'd try to chase them off.'

'No fighting?'

Samuel hesitated. 'Not often.' Pride came into his voice. 'Most of them ran fast enough as soon as we fought back.'

'The girls fought as well?'

'Of course.' He seemed astonished at the question. 'Why not? This is their home, too.' For a few seconds he was silent, eyes assessing the inspector's face. 'Come with me. I want to show you something.'

He led the way along the streets into town, moving quickly and purposefully. He stopped outside a rooming house on Vicar Lane, pointing at a sign in the window. 'Take a look at that.'

Roughly written on a piece of cardboard were the words NO JEWS.

Harper glanced at the boy. 'Are there many more like this?'

Levy walked away and the inspector followed. The lad paused outside businesses and lodging houses, simply pointing at the notices that read NO JEWS WANTED.

There were only a few of them, but even one was too many, Harper thought. He'd never seen them before.

'How long have those been up?' he asked as they walked back to the Leylands.

'Long enough,' Levy answered darkly. 'A few months.'

How had he missed these, Harper wondered? Why hadn't anyone mentioned it? He waited before broaching another question.

'Tell me, Samuel, do you know about any groups?'

'Groups?' There was a bitter edge to the boy's voice. 'What do you mean? What kind of groups? Gangs? Ones that hate us?'

'Yes.'

'There's really only one that causes much trouble. They've come down here a few times. Do you know what they call themselves? The League for the Defence of the Realm.' Levy snorted with disgust.

'I've never heard of them.'

'We've chased them off whenever they've come into the Leylands. But if they see any of us in town they'll follow us. Insult us, spit on us. Abraham—' He stopped suddenly.

'What? What was your brother going to do?' Harper waited, hoping for an answer. 'What?'

'He wouldn't tell me.' The admission sounded like defeat. 'He said it was better if I didn't know.'

He sat in Kendall's office at Millgarth station, recounting the conversation. The superintendent looked rested, as immaculately turned out as ever; the knot on his tie was neat, sideboards carefully trimmed along the jawline, the smell of pomade filled the room.

'The League for the Defence of the Realm?' the superintendent asked with a frown. 'Doesn't mean anything to me.'

'Nor me.'

'You think they could be behind this?'

'I've no idea yet,' Harper said. 'But at least we have somewhere to start now.'

'What do you want to do, Tom? Bring them in?'

'We have to find out who they are first, sir.'

'Then get the word out,' the super ordered.

'I will.' But carefully, he decided. Some of his snitches could be members. 'I do have one idea.'

'What is it?'

'After we find them, we put one of our men in the group.'

Kendall let out a slow hiss of breath. 'No. We don't have months to spend on this, Tom. I need someone in court as soon as we can.' He shook his head. 'Find out the names and pull them in. Force some answers out of them.'

'Yes, sir.'

'With luck we'll have this closed by the time the Frog comes on Sunday.'

Harper was at the door, already turning the knob, when the superintendent asked, 'Is that a new suit?'

'A Christmas present from my wife.'

'It looks good on you,' Kendall said approvingly. 'Very smart.'

The pubs were busy. Harper moved quickly from one to another. The Rose and Crown, Whitelock's, the Pack Horse, the Leopard Hotel; he went from Great George Street down through town. He saw some familiar faces, but no one had heard of the League. Finally he stopped in the Old Nag's Head on Kirkgate. The sign outside promised Pure Yorkshire Ales, but he doubted there'd ever been anything pure in here.

It was a single, low-roofed room, scarred and stained by years of abuse. The gas mantles hissed, but even with the faint light it always held a deep gloom, as if the price of entering was giving up hope. He gazed around; no one he knew.

Outside, the cold seemed to burn against his skin. He glanced up at the sky. Smoke from the factory chimneys rose, acrid and dark. Christmas was over and Leeds was back at work. Finally, rubbing his hands together to warm them, he crossed Kirkgate to the office of the Gasworkers and General Builders' Union. Maybe there was someone who might be able to help him.

A fire blazed in the hearth, warming the man who sat at the

desk. His wing collar was grubby, his tie was awkwardly knotted and his suit had seen better days. But there was a grin under the red beard.

'Seasonal visit, Inspector?' He gestured at a chair and Harper sat gratefully, unbuttoning his coat. 'Spirit of goodwill?'

'And good wishes to you, Mr Maguire.'

Tom Maguire was a union organizer, a socialist, a speaker at meetings and a poet when he wasn't earning his wage as a photographer's assistant. He'd been at the heart of the gas workers' strike a few months earlier and seen them beat the council.

'You're looking dapper.'

'My present from Annabelle.'

'She's a generous woman,' Maguire said. He'd known her since he was a baby, growing up Irish, just a street or two away from her family on the Bank. 'Good taste in clothes, too. But you've not come just to show off your tailoring.' He smiled. 'Too chilly out there for you?'

'I'm looking for some information. Have you ever heard of the League for the Defence of the Realm?'

'Not an organization that's likely to ask me to join.' He leaned back in his chair, eyes sharp, an amused smile playing across his mouth. 'Why are you interested in them?'

'They might have something to do with that killing in the Leylands.'

'Abraham?' Maguire pursed his mouth and shook his head slowly. 'Now that's a sad loss. He was a good lad, I met him a few times.'

Harper wasn't surprised that the pair would know each other. 'What did you make of him?'

'Clever.' He thought. 'He was angry but I could understand that. It's not just the Jews, you know. They're new here. The English have hated the Irish for centuries.'

'And the League?'

'They'd have us all out of here if they had their way.' He toyed with a pencil, turning it over and over in his hand. 'Anyone who comes here is stealing their jobs and taking their charity. Not that such a thing exists,' he added.

'Who are they? Do you know?'

Harper pursed his lips. 'Find one of them on his own and he's a very scared little man. Put a few of them together and they become bullies. You know the type, Inspector.'

He did. He'd arrested enough like that in his time. 'Any names?'

'You know that normally I wouldn't help the police.' Maguire continued quickly before Harper could interrupt. 'But in this case it's a service to my country.' He counted them on his fingers. 'John Godfrey, Rob Woods, Daniel Warner, Peter Lawton and Richard Boyd. Those are the ones I know.'

'Where will I find them?'

'That's your business, Inspector. I'm not here to do your job for you.' But his eyes were twinkling as he said it.

Harper stood and glanced out of the window. A thin sleet had begun to fall. Maguire followed his gaze.

'That good suit's going to get wet.'

At Millgarth the inspector asked Tollman about the names. If anyone would know it would be him; the desk sergeant had a memory that ran as deep and long as a river.

'Boyd, Woods and Warner,' he said after some consideration. 'We've had them in before now. Drunk and disorderly. Three times for Woods, if I remember right. Nasty piece of work.'

'Where did we arrest them?'

'Cork and Bottle, I believe, sir.'

That surprised him. Back when the public house had been part of his beat it had been a peaceful enough place. But times changed.

He assembled the constables carefully. Ash, bemused as ever; he'd arrested the men before, he knew them. And four other uniforms, all of them big men.

'Any problems, use your truncheons,' Harper ordered, waiting until they all nodded. 'I want them back here. Separate cells.'

'Are you going to question them tonight, sir?' Ash asked.

'No. Let them stew till morning. Right, any questions?'

Reed took the last train back to Leeds. Elizabeth left John, the oldest, in charge of the others, still happily playing with their presents.

'My mam'll be home in a minute,' she said as she put her arm through his. 'You know, I can't remember when we had any time just to ourselves.'

The platform was empty, no other passengers waiting. She put her arms around him rested her head on his shoulder.

'When do you have a day off again?'

'I'm not sure yet,' he answered. 'We have a murder case.' Tentatively, he stroked her hair and heard her sigh with contentment.

'Are you going to come out here when you're free?'

He nodded. It had become habit. When the shifts were long he clung to the thought of seeing her again, the same way he used to look forward to a drink. And still did, from time to time; just not so often any more. She was open, loving, generous. She'd chosen him and he couldn't understand why.

He heard the train approaching. Her eyes were sad as he kissed her.

'Make sure you take care of yourself,' she told him.

'I will.' He knew what she hoped, that some day he'd pop the question. But how could he take responsibility for her and the children when he could barely look after himself? He didn't want her jerking awake in the night when the bad dreams came to him. He didn't want them there when his temper roared.

SIX

Robbie Woods was still wearing handcuffs when the officer brought him into the interview room. Harper nodded and the constable removed them. He drank his tea and waited as the man rubbed his wrists.

'You didn't seem too happy last night,' the inspector said.

Woods glared at him and found his voice. 'Why the bloody hell would I? I wasn't doing anything, just having a drink with my mates.'

'Do you know why you're here?'

'No.' He was a heavy man, already run to fat, a tattered coat over a shirt with no collar. His face was sullen, heavy overnight stubble on his cheeks and dark, ratted hair under a checked cap.

'I hear you're involved with the League for the Defence of the Realm.'

'What's that, then?' Woods asked, but there was cunning in his eyes. He knew.

'You tell me.' Harper took another sip, watching Woods follow his movements. Let him feel the thirst.

'Never heard of them.'

'Funny, that's not what I was told.'

'Oh aye?' The man cocked his head.

'After last night, we're going to charge you with assaulting an officer and resisting arrest.'

Woods shrugged. He'd done time in Armley before. The sentences were badges of honour. 'It was your lot attacked me. We hadn't done anything.'

'No? You killed someone on Christmas Eve.'

'Who?' he challenged, hands gripping the chair arms. 'Who?'

'A young man called Abraham Levy. In the Leylands.'

'A Jew?' He leaned back and laughed. 'Good riddance, but nowt to do with me.'

Under the table, Harper bunched his fists. He wanted to lean across and take Woods by the throat, to shake a confession out of him.

They went round and round for an hour. The man was cautious as a miser, not giving up a thing. Finally Harper called for the constable to take Woods back to the cells.

'What about something to eat or drink?' the man protested.

'Maybe they'll have something in the cells at the Town Hall.' He nodded, and the bobby pulled Woods away. Perhaps he'd have better luck with the others.

But they only gave him silence and short answers. No wedge he could use to pry for more. By noon the inspector's throat was raw from asking questions over and over and he marched down to the office.

'Come on,' he said to Reed. 'Let's find some dinner.'

They walked in silence over to the Old George Hotel on Briggate. Advertisements were pasted across the brickwork outside the building, for bedmakers, cobblers, cures for this and that. Nothing he wanted to buy. Reed stayed quiet and Harper wondered how long the sergeant would last without saying anything.

They were sitting, eating their way through sausages and mash before he spoke. Trains passed outside the walls every few minutes, making the building shake.

'Why didn't you let me interview them, Tom?' He didn't sound angry, more hurt than anything.

'I didn't want them to see you.'

Reed raised his head sharply, suddenly curious. 'Why not?'

Harper sighed and put down his knife and fork. 'Kendall told me to pull them in. He knows we don't have any evidence, but he wants results, so people see we're doing something.' He saw the sergeant nod. 'All they needed to do was deny it and we were stuck. That's exactly what they did. The only thing we got from it was sending two of them to Armley for a few months. Had to let the rest go. It was a waste of bloody time.'

'I still don't understand what that has to do with me,' Reed said.

'I suggested to the super that we plant someone in this League for the Defence of the Realm.'

'Me?' he asked in surprise.

The inspector nodded. 'He turned me down, said it would take too long. Instead we've played our hand and come up with bugger all.'

'What are we going to do now?'

'I don't know yet,' Harper answered in frustration. 'But I wanted to keep you back, just in case I can persuade him.' He smiled. 'I was just thinking ahead. Did you have a good day with Elizabeth?'

'Nothing at all?' Kendall asked. He banged a hand down angrily on his desk.

'Two of them for assaulting a police officer,' the inspector told him. 'That's the best I could do. What did I have to use against them, sir? We've got nothing to tie them to the killing.' He could feel the colour rising in his cheeks.

The superintendent ran a hand through his hair, face set hard. 'Question them again.'

'It won't make a blind bit of difference. They'll just keep denying everything.' He hesitated for a moment. 'Sir . . .'

'Are you going to suggest putting Billy Reed in with them?'

'Yes, sir.' He paused for a moment. 'It's a good idea. Three of the ones we brought in were ex-army. And you know what Billy's like. He doesn't look like a copper, he doesn't carry himself like one.'

'They'd be too suspicious,' Kendall warned after a long silence.

'Two of them are off to Armley for the next few months. They're going to need some new recruits.'

Kendall nodded and rubbed his chin thoughtfully. 'It'll be dangerous.'

'Then let Billy decide if he wants to do it, sir,' Harper pleaded.

The superintendent sat for well over a minute, chin resting on his knuckles.

'Bring him in,' he conceded finally. 'Let's see what he has to say.'

'What do you think?' Harper asked Reed after he'd gone through it once more.

'I'll do it, sir,' the sergeant answered. He looked eager, ready to begin.

'The slightest suspicion, and I mean anything at all, I want you out,' Kendall ordered, his expression stern. 'We already have one dead body. I don't want any of my officers injured. Do you understand?'

'Yes, sir.'

'Good. And while all this is going on, I don't want you anywhere near the station. You two will have to find some way to communicate. Don't take any chances,' he added firmly. 'That's an order.'

After they left the office, Harper guided Reed outside.

'I'll be at the Midland railway station at noon every day. Come and report to me.' He paused. 'It's not too late to back out, you know.'

'I told you, Tom, I'll do it.'

Three hours later, in the room in his lodgings, Billy Reed stared at himself in the mirror. A worn shirt, no collar, a ratty waistcoat and trousers and his old army boots. But the real change was in his face. He'd gone to the barber's shop and told the owner to shave off his beard.

He didn't recognize the man staring back at him. His skin was too pale, too open, and his mouth was too thin. He'd worn the beard for so many years that he'd forgotten who was underneath. But no one would know him like this.

SEVEN

The inspector returned to Millgarth a little after three, and Tollman beckoned him over to the desk. It was growing even colder outside, he was certain of it. He stamped his feet and rubbed his hands together.

'Got something for you, sir.' The sergeant held up a brown paper bag.

'What is it?' He unfolded the top and drew out a butcher's knife. The handle was worn, the blade long, the steel shiny from years of use. Harper ran the ball of his thumb along the edge. Still sharp.

'They found it?' he asked. 'Where?' Two policemen had spent the previous day searching around the Leylands for the killing ground, with no luck; they'd been back out since early morning.

The desk sergeant shook his head. 'Maitland brought it in. He's covering Forsyth's beat today. It was behind a privy on Copenhagen Street. Someone at the house found it and told him.'

Copenhagen Street was just two minutes from where they'd found Abraham Levy.

'Where is he now?'

'Back on his rounds. He said he'd be where he found the knife at four.'

'Right. Have the bobbies who are out looking meet us on Copenhagen Street.'

'I'll pass the message, sir.'

He was there early, seeing the freezing, miserable constables shivering under their capes. Maitland was already waiting, grinning at them and saluting as the inspector approached.

'That was good thinking,' Harper told him.

'You reckon it could be the weapon, sir?'

'There's a good chance. He definitely wasn't killed where we found him. Where was it?'

'Down there, sir.' He pointed to a set of outhouses at the bottom of the hill. 'A woman was sweeping up around it. As soon as she found it, she sent her son to look for me.'

'Let's take a look.' They walked down in single file. The privies were out of sight of the houses. Harper glanced up. No one would be able to see from any of the windows. 'Where exactly did she find it?'

'Around the back, sir.'

'Right.' He turned to the constables. 'Search there. I know it's already dark, but use your lamps. I want blood in the dirt, anything you can find.' If someone had been sweeping there might not be much, but it was still worth looking. 'Did you check?' he asked Maitland.

'Just a glance, sir.'

'Anything?'

'Not as I saw. I wanted to get the knife to you.'

Harper knelt, rubbing a gloved hand over the ground. Frozen, hard as iron.

'Well?' he called out.

'Maybe, sir,' a thin voice answered tentatively.

The uniform stood aside, pushed against the wall. The inspector squinted, making out dark patches on the earth. Two of them, both large. They could be blood, but they could be so many things. Still, he thought, with the knife here, too, it seemed likely that this had where Abraham Levy had been killed. Now he knew. Harper looked around; no one from the houses would have been able to see a thing.

'Good work,' he told Maitland. The young man beamed. Harper ordered the constables to keep on looking and bring anything they found to the station, then walked off.

At his desk he stared at the knife, moving it around in his hands. There was nothing distinctive about it, just an ordinary wooden handle, long worn smooth, held together with brass rivets. The blade had been honed again and again. It had seen years of work. Someone had used it every day.

He read through his notes. None of the men from the Cork and Bottle had worked as butchers. Harper put on his overcoat and gloves, wrapped the knife in an old cloth and marched out into the cold.

Leadenhall Carcass Market stood behind an arch next to Smith's Tailors and Outfitters, on one of the thin lanes that ran between Vicar Lane and Briggate. It was late in the day but they were still at work, oil lamps glowing everywhere. The flagstones were slippery with frozen blood but the men working under the overhangs walked around easily, laughing, joking and shouting as they wielded their knives and carelessly hauled around sides of beef. There was a sharp tang to the air, and the flesh steamed as men sliced it open to gut and joint the carcasses that hung from iron hooks. Harper felt himself starting to gag as the bile rose in his throat. He stood still for a moment, hardly daring to breathe until the feeling passed.

The inspector watched, picking out the faces of those in charge. They were dressed just like the others, all of them down to their shirtsleeves in spite of the weather, stained leather aprons covering their chests and bellies.

'Do you run things here?' he asked a man who pointed and yelled out orders.

'Who wants to know?' He had sharp eyes set in a hard face. Luxuriant sideboards grew along his jaw, joining up with a bushy moustache. His hands and forearms were so dark with blood they looked almost black.

'Detective Inspector Harper, Leeds Police.'

'Oh aye?' The man's eyes flicked quickly around the yard. There were probably all manner of fiddles going on here, the inspector thought wryly.

'I'm wondering if you know who this belongs to.' He produced the knife, looking for any sign of recognition.

'That's Seth's,' he answered without any hesitation. 'Where did you find it?'

'Who's Seth? When did he lose it?'

'Wait a minute.' He called the name and a man came hurrying over, face worried as if he'd done something wrong. 'This fellow's found that knife of yours.'

'Really?' The man smiled as he turned to Harper. He was young, no more than middle twenties, brawny, with thick wrists and a cap jammed down over wild brown curls. He took the knife from the inspector's hands. 'I wondered what the bloody hell had happened to it,' he said gratefully. 'Had it since I was an apprentice. Where did you find it?'

'I'm Inspector Harper, Leeds police. Where did you lose it?'

'Lose it?' He laughed. 'I'd never lose this. It was stolen.'

'When?'

Seth slid the blade into one of the leather scabbards ranged along his belt. A perfect fit. All the others were filled with knives of different sizes, the tools of a butcher's trade. A sharpening steel hung from a metal ring.

'The day before Christmas. We knocked off at dinner time and went off for a drink or two.'

'Where did you go?'

'The Anchor, down in Mabgate. Some of the lads live over that way.'

Harper nodded. 'You had the belt with you?'

'Course I did,' Seth answered, as if the question was stupid. 'Only place I take it off is at home.'

'What happened?'

'Someone stole the knife. Took it right there in the public house.'

'Were you wearing the belt?'

'Course I were. Whoever it was, he lifted it out of here.' He tapped the knife hilt. 'Never felt a thing. Didn't even know it was gone until I was home. Can do some damage, that knife.'

'I think it did.'

Seth frowned. 'How do you mean?'

'Did you hear about that murder in the Leylands?' Both the men nodded. 'I think your knife was used in the killing.'

'Oh Christ. Are you sure?'

'I'm not certain,' Harper admitted. 'But I'd say it's very likely.'

Seth blanched and lifted the knife from the belt. He stared at it before holding it out by the blade.

'You might as well take it.' He shook his head. 'I can't use this again. Not now. Bloody hell.'

The inspector replaced it in the cloth.

'Do you know who did it?' Seth asked.

'Not yet.'

'Aye,' the man said slowly. He shook his head and started to walk away.

'Did you recognize anyone in the Anchor?' Harper called out.

'Just us. I don't usually drink down there.'

'Thank you.'

The Anchor, he thought as he walked back to Millgarth. And Mabgate lay right next to the Leylands. He needed to know more about the public house and the area.

'Who covers Mabgate?' he asked Tollman.

'Dicks, sir.'

'Where would he be now?'

The sergeant gazed at the clock and calculated.

'Somewhere near the top of Regent Street, like as not. Why, sir?'

'I just need a word with him about a place on his beat.'

'The Anchor?' The man's eyes twinkled with amusement.

'Bad, is it?'

'Rough as you please, sir, and you can believe me on that.' He hesitated. 'I'd best tell you, sir. Dicks drinks there. He's pals with the regulars, if you know what I mean. He's been fined twice for drinking in uniform. Just to tip you the wink.'

The people there were his friends. Harper wasn't likely to get any information from him.

'Anyone else who'd know?'

'Most of the men who work at night; they've been called out there often enough.'

The inspector took a piece of paper and scrawled a note.

'I need someone to deliver this to Sergeant Reed's lodgings straight away.'

'Yes, sir.'

He wrote a few words – the discovery of the knife, the information about the Anchor – and finished with a warning: *Don't go there. PC Dicks is a regular. He might recognize you.*

Harper closed the curtains in the parlour and sat in the chair. A moment later he was up again, on his way to the kitchen to put the kettle on the range.

'You're up and down like a jack-in-the-box,' Annabelle told him. 'What's wrong?'

'I just can't settle.' Reed should be at the public house by now, he thought, hoping all was fine.

'Well, come over here and listen to my plan.'

She was at the desk, account books open in front of her. Her dress rustled around her ankles as she shifted on the seat.

'I took another walk around Burmantofts today. I wanted to see if there were any shops to rent.'

'Any good prospects?'

'Three that have possibilities. One's small, but it's very cheap.'

'What about the others?'

'Bigger,' she answered slowly. 'That's the problem. They're too big for what I need at the start. But if the bakery does well I'll need somewhere that size.' Annabelle looked up at him. 'You see?'

'I do. But you must think you can make money. You wouldn't bother otherwise.'

'I will,' Annabelle said confidently. 'It'll take time, though. Nothing happens overnight. You have to build a business up, Tom. People aren't going to be flocking round as soon as I open the doors.'

'Word of mouth?'

She smiled. 'Best advertising in the world, and it's free. Give them good value and they'll come back and bring their friends. There's brass to be made. You know what? It's lovely to have someone to talk to about it all.' She reached and squeezed his hand. 'Do you know what I mean?'

'I do.' He wrapped his hand around hers.

'I'm so glad I finally persuaded you to propose. I'd been waiting ages for you to make an honest woman of me.' She smirked. 'It took you long enough.'

'Cheeky.' But he was grinning. She shrieked as he pulled her close and started to tickle her.

In bed a little later, she lay in the crook of his arm, her hair spread out across the pillow.

'I have to meet the French copper tomorrow,' he said.

Annabelle stirred a little and placed a hand on his chest, right over his heart.

'Is this that Le Prince thing?' she asked.

'For whatever it's worth. I doubt there's anything for him to find here.' It was all going to be a waste of time, he felt sure of that.

'I met him once, you know.'

Harper raised his head. 'Le Prince? You never told me that.'

'There's plenty you don't know about me yet, Tom Harper.' She was lost in thought for a few moments. 'It must have been four or five years back now. His wife was involved with some charity. They were having a do up at the cavalry barracks and I was invited.'

'You? Why?'

She shrugged. 'I gave them a little money. Anyway, he was there with her.'

'What was he like?'

'Pleasant enough, I suppose. We only exchanged a couple of words. He was very French. I liked his wife, though. No side on her at all.'

'Did you ever see the moving pictures he made?'

'No. I wanted to. Old Charlie Turner – you know, the one who owns Hope Foundry – he offered to take me, but I don't know, there must have been something else I had to do. He told me he couldn't believe his eyes.' She shifted slightly in the bed. 'What time does this fellow get in tomorrow?'

'Just after twelve.'

'Why don't you bring him back here for his dinner? I've got a nice piece of beef. I'll give him some Leeds hospitality if you like.'

EIGHT

Reed sat on his own in the Cork and Bottle, nursing a glass of beer, his eyes and ears sharp. No one had given him a second glance as he entered. No sign of recognition; he breathed a little more easily.

A group of five men talked intently around a table on the other side of the room. Some had been in the army, he felt certain of that. There was something in their bearing, the straight backs. And more in their eyes, the shared knowledge of what they'd seen abroad. Something time couldn't disguise.

He waited, drinking slowly, until one of them stood to buy more beer, then drained his glass and joined him at the bar. He had to start somewhere. All he could hope was that these were the right people.

'West Yorkshires?' Reed asked. The man was leaning on the bar and turned his head, eyes suspicious.

'What?'

'Just asking, were you in the West Yorkshires?'

'Aye,' the man answered warily. 'What about it?'

'You just look familiar, that's all. I thought I knew you.'

The man studied him then shook his head. He was in his thirties, scrawny, with curly hair that needed cutting. But he still held himself tall, the way it had been drummed into him. 'Never seen you before. When were you in?'

'I left in 'eighty.'

'Afghanistan?'

Reed gave the hint of a nod.

'I served with a few who were there,' the man said. 'In the Second?'

'Yes. Kabul.'

The man extended his hand. 'Peter Lawton. I was in the First. Beer?'

'Billy Reed. Thank you.'

The man nodded at the group over by the wall. 'Half of us were in. What do you do now?'

'This and that.' He shrugged. 'It's been hard to settle.'

'Aye, I know what you mean. I doubt I've had a job for more than three month at a time since I came out.' The drinks arrived. 'Give us a hand with these, Billy. Come over and sit down.'

He found a stool, gazing at the stony faces.

'He's all right,' Lawton assured them. 'He was in Afghanistan.' He introduced the men, Dick Boyd, John Godfrey and two others. Reed smiled inside. He'd seen the names of the men pulled in the night before; Lawton, Boyd and Godfrey were all on the list.

'Oh aye?' Boyd asked sharply. 'Who was your sergeant?' He was older, unshaven, with stubbly grey hair under a cap, his eyes hard, face wreathed in smoke from a pipe.

'Dufton till he bought it in '79. After that it was Clark.' He didn't even need to think. The images of them sprang straight into his mind.

Boyd nodded with satisfaction. He'd passed the test.

Reed sat back and let them talk. For a while there was nothing to it, rugby, the cold weather, one of them moaning about work. Then Godfrey said, 'Think the rozzers will be back tonight?'

Lawton gave a dark chuckle. 'Got Robbie and Daniel, didn't they? But bugger all else.'

'What happened?' Reed asked.

'Coppers came in here, full of piss and vinegar.' Lawton sounded outraged. 'Right here, in our place. Dragged us down to the nick, told us we'd killed some bloody Jew. Then they kept Rob and Daniel, all because they put up a fight. We was just sitting here, having a drink, not doing anything. No trouble.'

'Sounds wrong to me,' Reed told him.

'Course it's bloody wrong!' Lawton raised his voice for a moment before shaking his head.

'No respect,' Godfrey said. 'We served our country.'

'We're out of uniform now and that's it. We're on our own. You know what I mean, Billy?'

'I do,' he agreed.

'No jobs that pay owt to live on,' Lawton continued. 'You know why, don't you?'

'Bloody Irish and Jews,' Boyd said as if it was a litany, his voice quiet.

'That's it,' Lawton said. 'Everyone knows they'll work for nothing, so why would the bosses pay a real wage?' He looked around the table as the others nodded and stared at Reed. 'Right, Billy?'

He nodded. 'It's true enough. Seen it myself.'

Lawton smiled. 'See? Everybody bloody knows it.'

That was as far as they went but he hadn't expected more. It was a start. He was in.

'Do you go down to the Anchor at all?' Reed asked.

'Where's that?' Boyd wondered.

'Mabgate. They only like the English there,' Reed said.

'No, but it sounds like somewhere we'd like,' Lawton laughed.

Reed sat with them until ten, then stood up.

'Had enough?' Godfrey asked with a laugh.

'Got to be up early and look for work.'

'Come back tomorrow night,' Lawton told him. 'We'll be here, won't we, lads?'

'Happen I will.'

Harper stood in the Midland station. Wind howled down the platforms, scattering papers and rubbish like leaves. The place was filled with noise: the engines, voices, a train moving off, another arriving with a scream of brakes.

He glanced around. No sign of Reed, and just coming up to noon, according to the clock. He felt a thin twinge of fear, hoping that nothing had happened to him.

'Penny for them,' a voice said and he turned quickly. At first he couldn't place the face, then he saw and began to laugh.

'No danger of anyone recognizing you. Quite the baby face there, Billy boy.'

Reed snorted. 'I keep taking myself by surprise whenever I glance in the mirror.'

'Happen Elizabeth will like it.'

'Oh, she will. She's always complaining about the beard. Itches, she says.' He grinned. 'She'll be over the moon.'

'How was it last night?'

'Met them easily enough. It's what you'd expect. All Jews and Irish taking the jobs so there's nothing left for an honest man.'

'Did they . . .?' Harper asked.

The sergeant shook his head. 'Early days yet. But they seemed to accept me. I'm going back tonight to see what else I can find out.'

'Did you ask about the Anchor?'

'They don't know the place.'

So much for that idea, the inspector thought. 'Just watch yourself. Don't go and do anything daft.'

'Don't worry. But they know something. I can feel it.'

Harper hoped he was right. It was all they had and it was precious bloody little.

'We need the one who used the knife,' he said. Down the track he heard a whistle and the slow intensity of noise as the train approached. 'That'll be my Frenchman. Be here tomorrow. If you need me sooner, send word to the Victoria.'

The passengers alighted. The men first, some in elegant frock coats and striped trousers, others in shorter, modern suits. Then the women, helped down from the carriage with a hint of ankle and stocking as they trod carefully down the steps.

Couples and families moved away from the platform. A pair of businessmen with shiny top hats and determined frowns passed him. All that remained was a man on his own, carrying a valise and shambling along.

His hair was long, all the way to the collar of his heavy great-coat, and a battered hat was pulled down tight on his head. He looked around, curiosity in his eyes. Harper lifted a hand in greeting and the man began to stride towards him.

'Captain Muyrère?'

'You're Inspector Harper?'

They shook hands, Muyrère's as big as a bear's paw. His moustache was shaggy, as unkempt as the rest of him. But he seemed perfectly comfortable with himself.

'Call me Tom, please. I'm here to help you.'

'Bertrand. Muyrère. From Dijon.'

He spoke English clearly and fluently, the accent no more than an undertone. He stood a good four inches taller than Harper and at least three stone heavier. But he carried himself well, his gaze seeking out all the sights around him.

'I can take you to your hotel.'

'Good.' Muyrère smiled. 'But first, please, a cup of tea. Train journeys always make me thirsty.'

'Of course.'

Sitting in the Express Tea Room on Wellington Street he was surprised at the way the man seemed to relish the drink, sipping deeply then lighting a cigar. His eyes twinkled with amusement.

'You're wondering, Tom. I can see it on your face. All those questions. Why do I speak English well, why do I like tea?'

Harper laughed. 'That obvious?'

Muyrère cocked his head. 'We're policemen, we read people, monsieur, it's our job. I lived in London for three years after the war. I learned the language and I came to appreciate your drink.' He raised the cup in a toast.

'War?' He couldn't remember a war.

'Twenty years ago, Inspector.' He smiled kindly. 'You were no more than a child then. I was in the French army. The Prussians beat us.' His eyes clouded at the recollection. 'So many men died. Good men, some of them. I decided it was best to leave France for a while.' Muyrère shrugged. 'I went back and became a policeman. And now I'm trying to find out what happened to Monsieur Le Prince.' He finished the tea. 'I'm in your hands, Inspector.'

Harper had booked the captain into the Old Hall Hotel on Woodhouse Lane. As they entered, he glanced back to look at the Cork and Bottle on the Headrow.

The hotel room was small but comfortable – a good mattress, clean, the bedding fresh and aired. Muyrère nodded his approval and left the case on the bed.

'What now, Tom?'

'My wife wondered if you'd like to join us for Sunday dinner. She thought you might not know England.'

The Frenchman bowed his head slightly.

'I'd be honoured, of course.' He patted his belly. 'I have a rule, never refuse a meal.'

'Have you just come over from Dijon?'

'No.' The man grinned. 'I have friends in London. I spent Christmas with them. I needed to talk to Scotland Yard.'

'Have you learned much yet?'

Muyrère shrugged once more, a gesture that seemed to say everything and nothing.

'Time will tell.' He pulled out his pocket watch. 'And now . . . your wife will be expecting us?'

A hackney took them out along North Street. Muyrère stared with eager curiosity at the factories and the cramped back-to-back houses, saying nothing but taking it all in. He gave a quizzical look when the cab stopped outside the Victoria, then followed Harper inside and up the stairs.

Annabelle bustled out of the kitchen when she heard them, removing her apron and tossing it on the back of a chair. She was flushed with the heat of cooking, but dressed in her favourite gown, the dark red and blue that set off her features. Her hair was up, elaborately pinned, and she was wearing the jet pendant.

'Madame Harper,' Muyrère said, taking her hand between both of his and kissing her lightly on the cheek. 'Thank you for your invitation. It smells delicious.'

She smiled. 'Sit yourself down. The Yorkshires are almost done. Tom, take his coat and pour him a drink. I've even got a bottle of wine. I thought you might like that, being French.'

They talked about life, about France and Leeds. About everything but work. Muyrère was charming and funny, praising the food and the cook, clearing his plate of the Yorkshire pudding with onion gravy, then the beef, potatoes and vegetables. He only shook his head when Annabelle suggested pudding.

'Madame, you've filled me. No more, but thank you.'

He drank slowly, savouring the wine and smoking another cigar as the others ate.

'Annabelle met Le Prince,' Harper said.

'Really?' He stared at her with interest. 'I never had the chance. What did you think of him?'

She reddened a little. 'About all we said was "How are you?". He seemed nice enough. I liked his wife, though. Poor thing must be sick with worry.'

'He really just vanished?' Harper asked. 'That's what I read.'

Muyrère nodded and lit a thin cigar. 'His brother claims he saw him on to the train in Dijon. When it arrived in Paris, no Le Prince, no luggage.' He raised his eyebrows. 'Other people saw someone board, too. I talked to porters at the stations on the line. No one remembers him getting off.'

'Are you sure the brother's telling the truth?' Harper asked. It was the obvious place to start.

'No one can say it was definitely Louis who boarded. No one else talked to him.' The man chose his words carefully.

'No sign of a body in Dijon?'

'Nothing. We searched the brother's house, his business. And no sign of the camera.'

'Very strange,' the inspector admitted. 'Have you talked to the passengers on the train?'

Muyrère moved his head from side to side. 'The ones I could find. No one saw anything.' He gave a small, wry smile. 'Of course.'

Harper understood. Finding witnesses was always difficult. Reliable ones were even rarer.

'Was he on his way back here?' Annabelle asked.

'No, madame. To America.' Muyrère sighed. 'Now we come to the difficult part. Two years ago, Le Prince was granted patents on his moving picture camera over here and in America.' He held up a single finger. 'That was for his camera with sixteen lenses. But he's developed a new camera with just one lens, and he wanted a patent on that.'

'But if he's invented it, what's wrong with that?' Annabelle asked with a frown.

'Nothing,' Muyrère agreed. 'But there are others seeking a patent on cameras that do the same thing. Powerful men in France and America.'

'That's enough to make you wonder,' Harper said.

'It is, Inspector.' The voice was slow. 'I've never come across anything like this before. Have you?'

'No.' He didn't envy the man his job. Three countries and business rivalries? How could anyone solve that? He was on a hiding to nothing.

'And I hope you never will,' Muyrère chuckled. 'Believe me, monsieur, you don't want it. Theft, burglary, murder. Those I understand. But this . . . I don't think we'll ever know the truth. Not the whole truth.' He gave his shrug once more and stood. 'Now, if you'll forgive me, I'm tired. Trains might be fast but they're not so comfortable. Madame, thank you again. Tom, we'll work tomorrow?'

'I'll come to the hotel at eight.'

'*Merci.*'

Harper waited on the corner with the captain until a hackney passed, on its way back to town from the suburbs. It was already dark, the cold biting down hard. Gas lamps illuminated small patches of ice.

'Until tomorrow, Inspector.' Muyrère offered a wry smile and shivered. 'I like England, but I wish Louis had gone missing in the spring.'

'Sleep well.'

Harper reached Millgarth a little after six. The day shift had just taken over; Tollman stood behind the desk, leafing through the night ledger. The inspector hung up his coat and laid a fire in the office, twisting paper, then piling on kindling and coal before lighting it. He'd seen his mother do it so often when he was a boy that it felt like second nature. He scraped ice from the inside of the window and gazed out into the darkness.

There were papers on his desk, interviews with Abraham Levy's neighbours and friends. He went through them all, finding nothing he hadn't already discovered.

He was still reading when Tollman entered. 'Something that might be of interest, sir.'

'What's that?'

'There was a fight last night by Jews' Park on North Street.'

'Oh God.' He sat upright. It was what everyone called the scrubby patch of grass on the edge of the Leylands. 'Anyone hurt?'

'No, sir. Two lots of youths involved. They scattered as soon as our lads arrived. Can't identify anyone. I thought you'd better know, what with the Levy business.'

'Thank you,' he said and heard the sergeant's large boots march away.

He was still thinking about it when Kendall bustled through, waving Harper into his office. His cheeks were pink and shining from a shave and the cold. His frock coat was freshly pressed, the wing collar of his shirt crisp and sharp. The man was always immaculately turned out.

'Did you meet that Frenchman?'

'Yes, sir. We had him over for his dinner. He's in the Old Hall. I'm seeing him in an hour.'

The super nodded. 'Any word from Reed?'

'He's made a start.'

Kendall sighed. 'I hope you're doing the right thing, Tom. I've already had the chief constable wanting to know what's happening. He needs someone in custody.'

'Sir . . .'

'I know. I'm sorry.' He held up a hand. 'I shouldn't have made you pull them in. Not without a scrap of evidence.'

'Tollman told you about the fight last night?'

Kendall nodded. 'There are going to be more,' he said. 'The longer this drags on, the more tempers will fray. It'll be harder to keep a lid on things. Four days, Tom. That's all I can give you. We need an arrest by then.'

'Yes, sir.' It was as much as he could hope for, he knew. 'But it'd be faster if I didn't have to look after this French captain, too.'

'Orders from the top.' His voice was firm. 'You'll have to make time for him.'

'Yes, sir.'

'Just bring me results.'

Muyrère was waiting for him, bundled into his coat but still shivering as he finished his breakfast.

'How did you sleep?'

The man gave a rueful smile. 'Not so well,' he said. 'I had the blankets and my coat and I was still too cold.'

'Who do you need to see while you're here?'

The Frenchman pulled a notebook from the pocket of his suit, fumbled with a pair of spectacles and found the page he needed.

'Madame Le Prince, of course. They live with her parents. Her maiden name was Whitley, and Louis works for the family business. He has a workshop, too. All of those.'

Harper glanced at the addresses. 'The workshop's very close. Just up the street.'

'Then we should see it first, *non?*'

Their breath plumed as they walked, wearing hats, mufflers, gloves and overcoats, the armour of winter. The inspector could taste the soot in the air. Muyrère raised his eyebrows.

'Is it always this dirty here?'

'Yes.' It had been that way as long as he'd been alive. Skin and clothes were always grubby. Women hung out the wash and took it in with a layer of grime. People coughed all winter. It was the season, it was Leeds.

The house on Woodhouse Lane was stone, darkened by the years. He knocked and looked in the windows, seeing a shadow flit across at the edge of sight. Then the door was opened by an older man wearing a buff apron over his jacket, a cap jammed down tight on his head.

'Hello, sir. I'm Detective Inspector Harper, Leeds Police. This is Capitaine Muyrère from France.'

'You'll be here about the gaffer. I was wondering when someone would come.'

His name was Frederick Mason. He'd worked for Le Prince for

three years, he said, a woodworker who fashioned the cases for the cameras.

'When did you last see Monsieur Le Prince?' Muyrère asked.

'Back in August. 'Fore he went to France. We built new cases for moving the camera. He was going on to join Mrs P. in America and see about the patent.' Mason glanced up with sad, heavy eyes. 'You know about the patent?'

'I do,' the captain assured him.

Harper was content to let the other man ask questions. It was his business, he knew what information he needed. His eyes wandered around the workshop with its smell of fresh wood. Everything was neat, the floor swept, workbench empty, items stacked on the shelves, an old, worn tool case sitting on the floor. There were boxes in different stages of completion and a device standing in the corner.

'Is that the camera?' he asked.

Mason chuckled. 'No, sir. It was.' He pointed. 'You see that? Sixteen different lenses. That was Mr P.'s first effort. We keep it in here to remind us.'

It looked like drawings he'd seen showing the eye of a fly.

'What's the camera like now?'

'Just the one lens now.' The man smiled. 'Have you seen the moving pictures?'

'No,' Harper replied. Muyrère shook his head.

'You should. You really should.' He spoke with the enthusiasm of a disciple. 'You'll never see anything like it. It's like looking through a window. He's done something unbelievable, has Mr P. It'll change the world, you mark my words.'

'Tell me, Monsieur Mason, what do you think happened to him?' the captain asked.

The man shook his head slowly. 'I don't know. I wish I did. He doesn't make enemies, doesn't Mr P. Never even gets angry.'

'Did he work here or at the foundry?' Harper asked.

'Here, mostly,' Mason answered. 'If he needed something casting he'd go over to Hunslet; they have the equipment there.'

'His father-in-law and brother-in-law still work there?' Muyrère wondered.

Mason nodded. 'Mr John and Mr Theo, the pair of them together, but Mr John isn't there so much any more. He's getting on a bit.'

'Thank you.'

Outside, in the frigid wind, they walked back into town.

'Was that helpful?'

'I don't know.' Muyrère sighed. 'I need to go to that foundry in Hunslet.'

'Can you manage by yourself? A hackney can take you there and back.'

'Of course. You have work.'

'A murder.'

He saw Muyrère wince. 'You should have said. That's far more important than my wild . . .'

'Goose chase?'

'It feels like it.' He smiled sadly. 'So far I've been all over France and I've had the chance to come back to England. When I leave here I have to go to America. It's too many miles to go for nothing.'

'Too many mysteries?'

'Yes.' He gave another deep sigh. 'And my wife insists that I buy her an American gown in New York.'

Harper grinned. 'You'd better do it, then.'

'Yes.' The man's expression was doleful. 'But she didn't say what colour or style. Tell me, Tom, would you buy your Annabelle a gown?'

'I wouldn't dare.' He laughed. 'You can only hope.'

'Indeed, monsieur.' He sighed. 'Tomorrow I need to see Madame Le Prince.'

'I can come with you for that.'

Muyrère hesitated before he continued, 'I wondered . . . since your wife knows her, if she might accompany me instead. Maybe it would put Madame Le Prince more at ease. I know it's very forward, but you understand, perhaps?'

For a moment the idea shocked him. He'd never imagined involving Annabelle in his work. It was his, he kept it separate from home. Policing was a man's job. But Muyrère was right; Annabelle would be a familiar face for Mrs Le Prince. And she'd never given a fig for convention.

'I can ask her,' Harper agreed finally.

'Thank you.' The man sounded truly grateful. 'I wasn't certain if you'd allow it.'

Harper burst out laughing. Muyrère stared at him in confusion.

'I'm sorry,' the inspector said. 'You've met Annabelle, Bertrand. She does exactly what she wants to do. I've learned it's best to let her.'

Muyrère raised his thick eyebrows. 'That's rare, monsieur. A woman like that.'

'I knew who she was when I proposed.'

'And you seem happy.'

'I am, believe me. Very happy.'

At noon Harper was back in the Midland railway station, hands deep in the pockets of his coat. He paced up and down, eyes darting around to spot Reed, praying that things had moved along swiftly.

Suddenly someone was keeping step next to him. From the corner of his eye he saw the sergeant, so different without his beard. It made him look younger. Plainer.

'Got anything for me?'

Reed grimaced. He smoked a cigarette held cupped in his palm, and he was dressed in a threadbare jacket and trousers, a dirty shirt with a grubby kerchief tied round his neck. An old overcoat hung loosely on him.

'Nothing worthwhile. They were moaning about the two you arrested. About money, Jews, Irish. You name it.'

'But?'

'But none of them are saying they killed anyone,' he said with frustration. 'They haven't even mentioned the bloody murder.'

'We're running out of time, Billy,' Harper told him. 'I need something. I need the murderer.'

'I'll try,' Reed promised. 'Have you managed to find anything else?'

The inspector shook his head. What was there to find? 'You're sure they don't suspect you?'

'I think they're cautious,' the sergeant answered after a moment. 'They don't trust me yet.'

Harper stroked his chin, feeling the bristles under his fingertips. 'Is there a weak link in the group?'

'Boyd,' the sergeant said without hesitation.

'Then get him alone and work on him,' the inspector ordered. 'But any bad feeling at all, get out of there.'

'I can look after myself, Tom.'

'Don't get too bloody cocky,' he warned and glanced across. 'Where did you get those clothes, anyway?'

'I went down to the second-hand stalls on the market.'

Harper grinned. 'I'd steer clear of the uniforms. Dressed like that, they'll be taking you in for vagrancy.'

The freezing wind blew directly into Harper's face as he walked along North Street. He hunched down into the coat, plodding along until he reached the shop. The bell tinkled lightly as he entered and he breathed in air warmed by a small stove in the corner.

A man bustled out from the back room, tape measure flapping against his chest, then stopped and grinned.

'Tom.' His mouth turned downwards in disappointment. 'You're not wearing your new suit.'

'I wore it on Christmas Day.' That seemed an age ago now. 'It's a work of art, it really is. How are you, Moses?'

'Good, good.' He rubbed his hands and rolled his eyes. 'Oy, that wife of yours. She must love you, Tom. Only the best for you, doesn't matter what it costs. Please, send me a hundred more like her.' He started to roar with laughter.

Harper and Moishe Cohen had grown up together on Noble Street, just four doors apart. They'd played together as children and gone to the same school.

The man stared at him. 'You haven't come to thank me for the *schmutter*, Tom. I know you, you're here about Abraham. He was a good boy. Loud, sometimes, but who's to say he was wrong? These young ones, my Isaac, my Israel, they were born here. All they know is England.' He shrugged. 'What do they care about an old country they'll never see? They want to be part of this one.'

'So I've discovered.'

'Have you seen the signs people are putting up?'

'Samuel Levy showed them to me,' the inspector told him sadly. 'It's not my Leeds, Moses, you know that.'

Cohen gave a helpless nod. 'Maybe it will all change in time. God willing.'

'What about your boys? How do they feel?'

'Isaac's happy enough. He's quiet, goes to temple every week.'

'And Israel?'

'Israel.' Cohen pronounced the name very slowly. 'He was a friend of Abraham's, did you know that? He does his work every day, but he's out every night except Friday.' He shook his head. 'We've had one death around here, Tom. I'm scared there might be more.'

'I need to know what's happening around here, Moses. What people are saying and doing. Maybe it'll stop anyone else being killed.' He needed *something*, and he needed it soon. With each step in the Leylands, he felt he could taste the tension and the fear. He had to find the killer.

Cohen gave a wan smile. 'And you want me to help you?'

'I hope you can.'

'Tom,' he sighed, 'we might as well be *zeydes* for all we matter to these children. We're old, we might as well be grandfathers. I can keep my eyes open, I can listen. But it doesn't mean I'll hear anything. They're young, they don't talk to me. They talk to each other.' He paused. 'But if some little bird sits on my shoulder and tells me secrets, I'll let you know.'

'Thank you. I have to know what people are thinking round here.'

'I can tell you that very easily, Tom,' Cohen told him seriously. 'We're very angry. And very, very scared.'

Harper pulled out his pocket watch. After four, already dark. The air was growing thicker; he felt smuts of soot in his throat as he breathed. He was close enough to walk home to the Victoria. There was little more he could do; he'd put in a long day. For now it was all up to Billy.

Annabelle was in the bar, an apron over her work dress as she filled a small bucket with beer for a boy whose head barely reached above the bar.

'You watch out for yourself going home. Try not to spill too much.' She watched with a smile as the lad walked carefully. 'Honestly, some of them are too lazy to come for their own drink. They send the little ones out instead.'

He kissed her cheek. 'What are you doing down here?'

'I had to send Dan home. He was coughing so hard I thought

his insides were coming out. It's this weather. I gave him some chlorodyne and sent him on his way.'

'No one else to cover?'

'I don't mind.' She shrugged and ran a damp cloth over the polished wood of the bar.

'I was back over in Burmantofts this morning. The chap who owns one of those larger shops I was looking at has offered me a good price on rent.'

'Are you going to take it?'

'I said I'd let him know tomorrow.' She was smiling. 'Mind, if he's that desperate I should be able to get him down a little more. Let him wait.'

'You're an evil woman.'

'That's why you love me, Tom Harper.' She darted close and gave him a kiss. 'You look perished.'

'I swear it's getting colder out there.'

'There's a good fire upstairs. Go and get yourself warm, and have Kitty make you a cuppa.'

'What about you?'

'I'm going to look after things down here for a bit.'

'You work too hard.' He put his arms around her.

'Someone has to. It won't run itself.' She rested her head against his shoulder and sighed with pleasure.

'I was out with Captain Muyrère this morning.'

'Oh aye? Has he found anything yet?'

'He's off to see Le Prince's widow tomorrow.'

'Poor woman.'

'He asked if you'd go with him.'

She pulled back suddenly and looked at him with astonishment. 'Me? Whatever for?'

'You know her. He thought it might help if there was a woman there.'

For once Annabelle seemed stuck for words. 'Is that how they do it in France, then?' She stared into his eyes. 'Do you honestly think it might do some good, Tom?'

'It could make her feel more at ease.'

She stood, arms folded, staring at the floor, thinking. 'I suppose I could ask Arthur to help for a few hours if Dan's not back,' she began. 'He was serious? You're sure of that?'

'I'm positive,' Harper told her gently.

She grinned. 'I don't know. I've never helped a copper before. Might ruin my reputation.'

'I'll keep it quiet.' He winked.

'You'd better if you know what's good for you, Tom Harper.' She paused. 'Do you really think it's a good idea? It's five years since I met her.'

'That doesn't matter. At least you'll be familiar.'

'All right,' she decided with a nod. 'Tell him I'll do it. What time?'

'I don't know yet. I'll see him in the morning and let you know.'

NINE

People hardly gave them a second glance as they sat on the bench. The trains sighed, whistles blew, steam and smoke billowed under the ceiling of the station. Reed looked down at the ground, a cigarette cupped in his hand. He'd found an old bowler hat somewhere, the shine all gone, dents dotting the crown. Unshaved, he looked down-at-heel, a man adrift. Next to him, Harper wore his new suit and gazed out at the swarming crowds. He picked hot chestnuts from a bag and chewed them slowly, the warmth filling his belly. For all the world they looked like two strangers forced close to each other by circumstance. The sergeant was speaking intently and quietly.

'Boyd didn't arrive on his own last night. But they did say they had friends who like to attack Jews and Irishmen.'

'Any names?' Harper asked urgently.

Reed shook his head. 'They don't trust me enough yet. But Boyd knows, I'm sure. I'm going to get him on his own tonight.'

'Kendall was after me again today.'

'I'll do my best, Tom.'

'I know.' He held out the rest of the chestnuts. 'Do you want these?'

'Had enough?'

'They're going cold.'

'You're all heart, Tom.'

Harper grinned. 'Just looking out for the poor.'

He finished the working day in the superintendent's office.

'He's getting closer, sir.'

'How close, Tom?'

Harper explained what Reed had found out. Kendall listened, hands steepled under his chin. His nails were clean and all evenly cut.

'Tomorrow.' The superintendent's voice was firm. 'If there's nothing by then, we'll pull in these men from the Cork and Bottle again and force names out of them. You understand?'

'Yes, sir.' He prayed Billy could come up with something. Any lead they could follow.

'Have you been back to the Leylands today?'

'This morning. It's quiet enough. No more fights.'

'For now,' the superintendent warned. 'Anything else and God knows what might happen. I've had to put two more constables up there, as it is. If trouble starts to flare, the Irish in the Bank might get ideas.'

'Has Rabbi Feldman complained?'

'All it takes is one thing, though . . .' Kendall shook his head. 'What about that Frenchman? What's he been up to?'

'He went to see Le Prince's widow today. He's been to the workshop and the foundry the father-in-law owns.'

'Make sure he tells you everything, Tom. This is our patch, we need to know what's going on.'

'I really don't think there's anything to find here, sir. He's just looking for background. He's off to America next.'

Kendall snorted. 'All right for some, isn't it?' He gave a warning look. 'Don't you start suggesting you go gallivanting all over for cases, either.'

'No, sir.' He smiled. Not that he'd ever have the opportunity.

The tram stop was at the bottom of Roundhay Road. He dashed across the street and into the Victoria. Dan was back behind the bar, cleaning glasses before the workers came in at the end of shift, thirsty and loud.

'Feeling better today?'

'Cough's not as bad. I bought some different medicine last night, it seems to have done the trick. Annabelle's back in the kitchen. Want me to tell her you're home?'

'If you don't mind. I'll just go up and get warm. It's bitter out there.'

By the time he heard her on the stairs he had tea mashing in the pot, and the fire in the parlour was burning bright. He took hold of her and gave her a long kiss. Arms tight around her waist, he lifted her and twirled her around until her face was flushed and she started to giggle.

'What was that for?' she asked when she regained her breath.

'I'm just happy to see you.'

She gave him a coy smile. 'If that's what I get, you can be happy to see me every day, Mr Harper.' She twisted in his embrace. 'Just be careful around the corset, these stays pinch like nobody's business. I hope you've got a cuppa ready. I'm parched.'

He poured for them both.

'Did you go and see Mrs Le Prince with Muyrère?'

'I certainly did.' Annabelle's eyes widened. 'I don't know what her father does, but he must have made a fortune. That Oakwood Grange is a mansion. When we pulled up in the cab I thought I ought to go to the back door. I could never afford a place like that.'

'Would you want one?'

'Well, no,' she answered immediately. 'I like it here. But even so.'

'How was she?'

'How do you think?' She gave him a look. 'Her husband's missing, probably dead. How would anyone feel? You're too much of a copper, Tom.'

'Did she have much to say?'

'She kept talking about some man in America called Edison. I've never heard of him.'

The name meant nothing to Harper. 'Who is he?'

'Some sort of inventor, or something. He came up with those bulbs for electric lights and the phonograph. A few other things as well, I think.'

He was impressed and surprised. 'What about him? Does she think he's involved?'

'She says he wants to stop her husband taking out a patent on that moving picture camera.' She paused for a second and he looked at her. 'She claims he had her husband murdered. She really believes it.'

'Did you talk to her at all?'

'Not really. Just when the captain went out to smoke a cigar. She's frantic. You can imagine. If you ask me, I'm not sure she really knows what she's saying.'

'Does she have any evidence about this Edison man?'

'He asked her that. She doesn't. She's just sure, that's all.'

'There's nothing anyone can do without evidence,' he said.

'That's what Muyrère told her.'

'What else did she have to say?'

'That was it, really. Their son's coming in a day or two. He's grown, he's been working in America. He might know something more.'

'Maybe Muyrère will find something in New York. He's off there the day after tomorrow.'

'Really?' Annabelle's eyes widened. 'He never mentioned that.' She glanced at him suspiciously. 'I hope you're not getting any ideas.'

'Don't worry,' he laughed. 'The force wouldn't pay.'

'If they do, you'd better take me, Tom Harper,' she warned. 'Do you think he'll find an answer?'

'Honestly?' he said. 'No. He probably knows it, too.'

'That must be hard.'

He shrugged. 'Every copper's had it. Doesn't mean we get used to it.'

'I'll tell you something, and you can pass it on to that chief constable of yours.'

'What?'

'You'd get a damned sight more out of people if you had women asking the questions. You men, you just don't have a clue.'

Reed stood hidden in a doorway on the Headrow, the cigarette cupped in his hand. Men moved past in the darkness, on their way home from work. He took his watch from the pocket of his waistcoat. A little after five. None of the others were in the Cork and Bottle yet; he'd checked through the windows before he took up his position.

He needed Boyd on his own. He was the one most likely to talk.

He waited, out of sight, as Godfrey and Lawton moved along the other side of the street, talking together as they entered the public house. Boyd should be along soon.

He spotted the man far enough away to catch him on the street.

'Bloody cold,' Reed said, rubbing his hands together. His breath made a small cloud.

'I've been walking for the last half hour.'

'Where were you?'

'Over in Armley. Had to see someone.'

'Any good?'

The man shook his head. 'Nowt.'

'I had some luck with the dice. You fancy something to warm us?'

'What about the others?' He nodded at the pub, just up the street.

'I don't have the money to treat everyone.' He jingled the coins in his pocket. 'Come on, I'll buy you a brandy, then we can join them.'

For a few seconds Boyd looked uncertain, then the thought of a drink sharpened his smile. 'Go on,' he agreed. 'Just a quick one.'

Reed had only been in the White Swan a few times. No one would remember him, especially without the beard. The place was hidden away on Swan Street, tucked between the music hall and Thornton's Arcade. He scoured the room for familiar faces but eyes simply glided over him.

The brandies were doubles. Enough to loosen the tongue a little, especially if a man hadn't eaten all day. They touched their glasses in a toast and drank in a single gulp.

'Better?' Reed asked.

'Aye, that hit the spot.'

'I have enough for one more.'

'I can't stand my round,' Boyd warned him.

'Doesn't matter.' He came back with two more glasses. 'All the others, they seem to be just talk.'

'They're good lads,' Boyd protested.

'You know what I mean,' Reed said. 'Those friends you were talking about, they sound like they know what they're doing.'

'They do,' Boyd agreed. 'You know what it's like.'

Reed snorted. 'I see it every bloody day. Hard for a man to make an honest living.'

'You ought to talk to Alfred.'

'Alfred?' He felt the hairs rise on his arms. 'Who's that?'

'It's what he calls himself.'

'Why Alfred?' Reed asked. 'Who is he?'

'It's just what he likes to be called, that's all.'

'I see. Interesting fellow, is he?'

Boyd nodded. 'He knows his stuff. All facts and figures. Bit of a toff.'

'Toff?'

'You know, he has money an' that. Educated, like, sounds posh.'

'I'd like to meet him,' the sergeant said.

'Ah.' The man tapped the side of his nose. 'He doesn't like too many getting close.'

Reed shrugged. 'Pity. I could probably get along with a man like that.' His voice hardened. 'I saw what the bloody natives did to my mates in Kabul.'

Boyd glanced around, suddenly uncomfortable. 'Keep it quiet,' he hissed. 'We don't need everyone knowing.' He hesitated, then said, 'I tell you what, if you're so eager for this, meet me at noon tomorrow. I'll take you to him.'

'All right,' Reed said, trying to sound as if it meant nothing.

Boyd shifted on his seat. 'We'd better go and join the others. They'll be wondering what happened.'

'Where tomorrow?'

'Victoria Square, in front of the Town Hall.'

Reed nodded his agreement.

In the end he only stayed an hour. His mind was racing. He made his excuses. But instead of walking along Woodhouse Lane, out to his lodgings, he ducked through the courts and yards, making sure no one was behind him, then down to Millgarth station.

He made the note brief, just what Harper needed to know, and left it on the desk. Now he could go home and sleep. And wait for the morning.

TEN

'Tom! Someone's banging on the door.' Annabelle lit a candle.

He blinked himself awake.

'What?'

'There's someone at the door.'

He sat up and listened. Oh God, he thought. No sound in his right ear at all. Again. Just emptiness.

'What is it?' She saw his face. 'Tom?'

'Nothing.' He shook his head. 'I'll go down.'

The floor was freezing under his bare feet. He banged his palm against the ear, hoping it might shift something and bring his hearing back. Harper drew back the bolts and pulled the door open.

'What?'

It was the same young constable who'd come on Christmas Eve, when they'd found Abraham Levy's body. The name fell into his mind: Stone. He cocked his head, left side facing the man.

'There's a fire, sir. At the synagogue on Belgrave Street.'

Harper glanced at the horizon. There was no sign of flames or smoke in the clear darkness.

'How bad?'

'They managed to put it out before there was any real damage, sir. Constable Maitland said you should know.'

The poor lad looked nervous, scared to be waking an officer in the middle of the night.

'What time is it?' the inspector asked.

'A bit after two, sir.'

'You go back to what you were doing. I'll be there as soon as I can.'

In the bedroom he groped for his clothes.

'What is it?' Annabelle asked.

'A fire at the synagogue.'

'I mean you, Tom. Something's wrong, isn't it?'

'I can't hear anything in my right ear.'

'What?' She sat up quickly. 'Nothing at all?'

'No.' He pulled on his shirt and trousers, and knotted his tie.

'It'll pass,' she assured him. 'You probably just slept on it.'

'It's not the first time.'

'Tom?' She paused for a heartbeat. 'What do you mean?'

'I have to go. I'll tell you later.'

He gave her a quick kiss, grabbed his overcoat and headed out into the night.

Harper crossed North Street, feeling the cold and ice through the soles of his boots. On Belgrave Street the fire engine was still there; the Fire Inspector stood under the street lamp, talking to Constable Maitland.

'Evening, Tom,' Inspector Richard Hill called when he spotted him. 'Sorry to drag you out, but this lad thought you'd want to know.'

'Hello, Dick.' The pair of them had joined the force at the same time. They'd both walked beats before Hill moved over to the fire brigade. It was still part of the police force, with the same ranks, but different jobs. 'Quick thinking, Constable,' he told Maitland. 'What happened?'

'I'm back on nights, sir. I was at the top of Trafalgar Street, sir. I saw something over here and came to investigate.'

'What did you see?'

'I thought someone had lit some rubbish to stay warm. A lot of them have been doing it in this weather, sir.'

'Go on,' Harper told him. He shifted to hear the man's voice properly.

'There wasn't anyone here, so I blew my whistle, sir, and called the brigade.'

'We were lucky,' Hill picked up the story. 'Got here before it could took hold. And whoever set this didn't really have a clue. If he had we'd still have the hoses running.' He raised an arm. 'Come with me.'

Hill walked over to the main door of the synagogue and knelt by a pile of soaked wood and paper. 'Smell that?' he asked. Harper nodded. Under everything was the faint odour of paraffin. 'If they'd used more of it, everything would have gone up. Be bloody grateful.'

The door was heavily charred, the wood still smouldering in places. It would need to be replaced. But Hill had been right, it could have been so much worse. Another few minutes, a little more paraffin . . .

'What do you think?' Harper asked.

'It's arson. There's no doubt about that. I'll take a closer look once it's light. There might be some clues.'

'Where's the rabbi?' the inspector asked Maitland. 'He should have been here by now.'

'Manchester, sir. Some sort of conference. He's back in the morning.'

'What about the caretaker?'

'In the infirmary, sir. Slipped on Boxing Day and broke his hip.'

'Right.' Harper was concentrating hard to hear them both. His right ear was still completely deaf. He tried to ignore it, to think about what was happening. 'You can go back to the beat, Constable.'

'Yes, sir.' Maitland saluted smartly and walked away.

'You have problems around here, Tom? I read about the murder in the newspaper.'

'Looks like it.' They began to walk back along Belgrave Street. Harper kept Hill to his left.

'You haven't found the killer?'

'Not yet.' Harper nodded back at the synagogue. 'What do you think about the fire?' Hill was experienced. He had a keen eye and a sharp mind.

'You really want to know? Thank God they were idiots. If they'd had a brain between them there'd have been plenty of damage. Burning a place like that?' He shook his head. 'Someone wants to start something.'

'We've put more bobbies on patrol, but they're all over there.' He nodded towards the houses packed together on the far side of North Street.

'I'm sending someone up to stand guard here.' Hill shivered. 'Poor sod, don't envy him when the weather's like this. You ever miss walking the beat, Tom?'

'Not really.' He'd enjoyed it at the time. He'd learned about people, about crime. About life. But this job, being a police detective, was the one he'd always wanted.

'I heard you got yourself wed, too.'

'Back in July.'

'Under her thumb yet?' Hill laughed. 'She runs a pub, is that right?'

'Down in Sheepscar. The Victoria.'

'It's all right for some, eh? I'll have to pop down sometime and see how you've done for yourself.'

Harper grinned. Hill had been married for ten years now, with four children, and was still desperately in love with his wife.

'You do that, Dick. I'll buy you a pint.'

After more than an hour out in the weather, Millgarth station felt deliciously warm. Harper pushed a poker into the fire, seeing the flames jump, and held out his hands to the heat. He stood long enough to soak it in before taking off his coat and walking over to the desk.

The note from Billy Reed sat on his blotter. He read it through three times. Alfred? Who the hell was Alfred? A real name or one the man had taken? Come noon he'd follow the sergeant. He needed to know.

Harper pulled out his pocket watch and wound it without thinking. Not even four yet. For a moment he considered going home, but it wasn't worth it; by the time he arrived, Annabelle would be up to supervise the bakers. She'd be full of questions about his ear and he'd only have an hour before he'd need to get himself ready to come back here. He could sleep in his chair; he'd done it often enough before. The questions would wait until evening.

He rubbed his ear gently. Still nothing. The last two times the hearing had come back after a few minutes. It had been a couple of hours now. What if it had gone forever? He knew they had deaf men on the force. There was old Andrew Watson; he'd walked the beat in Burley for forty years and heard no more than a post for most of that time. But never a detective. The force wouldn't want that.

Harper closed his eyes and prayed that when he opened them again he'd be able to hear.

He sat up with a start as the door slammed. Superintendent Kendall stood by the desk.

'Sleeping on the job?'

Harper glanced at the clock on the wall. Five minutes to seven. He'd finally dropped off close to five. His mouth was dry. He yawned and brushed a hand over his hair, trying to look present-able. Very carefully, he turned his head. There was still no sound in his right ear. He swallowed.

'I . . .'

'Don't worry. The desk sergeant told me.' The smile faded from his face. 'How bad was it?'

'Just some damage to the door. They caught it early.' He focused on Kendall's mouth, tilting his head to be certain to hear every word. 'Dick Hill says the people who did it were complete amateurs. He's going back this morning to see what he can find.'

'I'm going to put more men out there at night.' The superin-tendent pursed his mouth. 'It's too volatile. I need this tied up quickly, Tom.'

'Yes, sir.'

'I hope Reed's found something.'

'He might have.' The inspector pushed the note across the desk.

'Alfred?' Kendall asked, raising his eyes.

The inspector shrugged. 'I'm going to follow him.'

'Just make sure you spend some time in the Leylands first. They're going to be angry. I need them to see you there.'

'I will, sir.'

'Are you all right?' Kendall gave him a quizzical look.

'Sir?' He could feel the chill creep up his back.

'You have your head tilted. Crick in your neck?'

'Oh.' He moved. 'Must be.'

'Make sure you look after yourself.'

Before the Leylands, though, Harper walked over to the Old Hall Hotel. It was a chance to say farewell to Muyrère. He liked the man; the Frenchman was a solid copper on a thankless task. He was sitting at the breakfast table, an empty plate in front of him. The inspector poured himself a cup of tea.

'I hear Mrs Le Prince was talking about someone called Edison,' he said.

'Which may be something or another wild idea.' The capitaine shrugged. 'More questions to ask in America.'

'Much to do today?'

'Not really – a few more questions at the foundry, that's all. Then tomorrow morning it's the train for Liverpool and the ship to America.' He brought a cigar from his pocket and lit it. 'I've had enough. All I want is to be at home again.'

'How long's the voyage?'

'Too long,' he said with a wistful smile. 'Then there's New York, and the journey back to France. You know, Tom, I always felt so proud that I'd learned English well. Now it's beginning to seem like a curse. You're lucky, you see your wife every night.'

'I'm not sure she always thinks so.'

'But she does, Tom. I can see it in her eyes.' He finished his meal. 'I should go and work.' He extended his hand and Harper shook it. 'Thank you for all you've done. And please, monsieur, thank your wife, too.'

Suddenly, as he waited to cross Merrion Street, he felt it. He could hear again; it had come back. He stopped and held on to a lamp post to steady himself. Harper gently tipped his head from side to side, scared he'd imagined it. But it was definitely there, and no better or worse than it had been for months now. He gave a sigh of relief, rubbing his hands across his face.

He looked at his pocket watch; this time it had lasted more than six hours. It had vanished, yes, but the deafness might return at any time. He knew he needed to see a doctor again. Annabelle would insist.

But it was going to have to wait. He had too much to do. For right now he was fine.

He spotted Inspector Hill standing outside the synagogue with two officers from the fire brigade, all of them huddled deep in their greatcoats. The water from the hoses had turned to a sheet of ice that covered that road.

'Found anything, Dick?'

'Morning, Tom.' He introduced the others. 'I can tell you two things right off the bat.'

'What?' he asked with interest.

'First thing, this was done by a man.'

'I assumed it was,' he said, surprised at the statement.

'Most arsons are,' Hill agreed. 'Not all, though. But any woman would know how to build a better fire than this. They do it every day.'

That made sense. 'What's the second thing?'

'He hadn't been in the army. They learn how to make a fire, too. Out in the field you need that skill.'

'That's not a lot, Dick.'

'Best I can do,' he said. 'Honestly, Tom, there's not much more I can tell you. He used newspaper, pieces of wood, paraffin. There's an old rag. That's it. Nothing to give us any clues. They'll be able to replace the door easily enough and I doubt there's more than a little smoke damage inside. We were lucky that constable of yours saw it when he did.'

'So there's bugger all, really?'

'More or less. I'm sorry.'

'Better leave it to the real coppers, then, Dick. We'll find him for you.'

Hill grinned. 'A tanner on that?'

'You're on.'

'Just give it me when you're paid.' Hill turned serious. 'I'll warn you though, Tom, I wouldn't put it past him to try again. Maybe here, maybe somewhere else. Have your lads keep an eye out.'

'I will.'

He crossed North Street, his mind on the blaze, and started to walk into the Leylands. Somewhere in the distance he could make out loud voices. No, he decided, it was just one voice, raised. And he thanked God his hearing had come back.

The inspector followed the sound, coming out on Gower Street. There were ten or twelve in the crowd, he guessed, all of them young. He spotted Abraham Levy's girlfriend and his brother, listening intently to a man, his arms waving as he spoke loudly in Yiddish.

Twenty yards away a constable stood, watching them closely but doing nothing. He saw Harper and saluted.

'What's happening?' the inspector asked. 'Who's the man speaking?'

'Rabbi Padewski, sir. That's his synagogue behind him, the Polish one. Started a couple of years ago. It's *what* he's saying, sir.' The officer was young; he hadn't even grown into his uniform yet, and his cheeks were still very pink and smooth.

'You can understand it? A name clicked into his mind. 'You're Henderson, aren't you?'

'Yes, sir. I grew up on Star Street, heard the lingo as long as I can remember. He's telling them that after the killing and the fire they ought to fight back.'

Harper blew out a slow breath. This wasn't going to help.

Padewski looked to be in his early thirties. His wore his dark beard trimmed short in the English way, and his eyes blazed behind a pair of spectacles. He was a small, wiry man, and very animated, hands constantly moving. The thick overcoat seemed to engulf him and the hat was a size too large on his head, but the effect wasn't comic. The man had presence.

'They're a young crowd,' Harper observed.

'Most of his congregation is young, sir,' Henderson told him. 'They think he's got more about him than the old rabbi.'

That was obvious. Padewski spoke with real passion; it was impossible not to listen. And Feldman came from an older generation. He was a good man, but how could he hope to speak for the ones who'd grown up here, who'd lived a different life? They wanted someone with fire, with life. Someone like this.

Harper could pick out a few of the Yiddish words, but nothing more. The man spoke too quickly, his voice angry and bitter.

'What's he saying now?'

'More of the same, sir.'

'Tell me about him. Is he always like this?'

The constable looked at him and chewed a lip thoughtfully. 'He's been here about six months. A bit of rabble rouser since he arrived, sir. A lot of the older ones round here aren't too sure about him.'

Padewski raised his voice to the climax of his speech, then he was done. The inspector had heard the tone before, the same stridency in men addressing strikers or political meetings. A couple of the listeners gathered around him while others wandered away, stamping their feet and rubbing their hands.

'How's his English?' Harper asked.

'Good as yours or mine, sir.' Henderson chuckled. 'He grew up in Manchester.'

The inspector waited until the rest of the crowd had drifted away then walked over to the rabbi. He wasn't large but he towered over the man. Yet it was Padewski who seemed bigger, with his penetrating gaze and questions in his eyes.

'Rabbi, I'm Detective Inspector Harper.'

'I know who you are, Inspector.' The only accent in his voice came from Lancashire. 'You're investigating Abraham's murder.'

'And the fire.'

Padewski nodded. 'And you haven't caught anyone for either.' It came out as an accusation.

'No, sir, not yet.'

'Are you close to an arrest?'

Harper smiled gently. The man was trying to provoke him. 'You know I can't tell you that, sir.'

Padewski snorted. 'You've got nothing.'

'I can't tell you any details, sir, I said that.' He remained polite, vaguely official. 'But there is something you can do.'

'What's that?' Padewski asked suspiciously.

'All this talk, it's not helping us.'

'Talk?' the rabbi asked sharply, raising his eyebrows. 'You don't want us to talk now?'

'Sir, you're welcome to talk all you like.' He tried to keep his voice patient and pleasant. 'This is England, it's a free country. But stirring people up like this makes everything harder for us.'

'I'm not stirring anyone up.' The man was serious, his gaze concentrated on Harper's face. 'I'm simply reminding them of things. You mentioned England, Inspector. We might be Jewish but we're still as English as you. We were born here. All I'm telling them is that no one should treat us differently just because of our religion.' He paused for a second. 'Or perhaps you don't agree?'

'You said you know who I am, rabbi. You'll know my politics.'

Padewski gave a thin smile. 'I've heard.'

'I treat everyone equally.'

'That's good to know, Mr Harper. But then you shouldn't object to me talking to people. They need to hear the message that they're as good as everyone else. You've seen the signs around town?'

'I have. I know we have problems in Leeds, sir. We just don't need more of them.'

'Who's been causing the problems? It's not us. We haven't

murdered anyone or set any fires, have we? We're not putting up notices saying "No Christians Wanted."' The man was sharp and fiery, but that was his business. A scholar needed to be able to argue.

'You know the answer to that, sir.'

Padewski pursed his lips. 'Tell me, do you know much history, Inspector?'

'Not really, sir.' He wondered why the man had asked the question, what it meant.

'Go back through time, all the way to the Bible. You'll find it's always the Jews who suffer. Maybe it's time to say enough is enough.'

'Let the police take care of the law and order, please sir,' Harper said. 'That's our job.'

Padewski held up one gloved hand and counted on his fingers.

'One Jew dead, a fire at our great synagogue, both in a matter of days. Is that the police doing their job well?'

'If there are more problems between people, it's not going to make our job easier.' He tried to hide the tension he was feeling, to let his face and his words remain calm and reasonable.

'Find the killer, Inspector. Find the arsonist.'

'That's what we're trying to do. What we need is cooperation here.'

The rabbi gave him a sharp look. 'By keeping our mouths closed?'

'By not inflaming things. Violence breeds violence, isn't that what they say?'

Padewski smiled. 'In the Old Testament – *our* Bible, Inspector – they say an eye for an eye.'

'When we find the killer, he'll hang. That's the law here. You know that as well as I do. We don't want any more deaths on the way, rabbi.'

'No one wants death, Mr Harper. But tell me, would you rather we just sat here and became targets for everyone?'

'We've increased the number of officers around here.'

'For the moment.'

'And we'll find whoever murdered Abraham Levy,' Harper promised.

'I hope so, Inspector.' He tapped a gloved finger against his temple. 'We're Jews, we always remember. You understand?'

'Perfectly.'

'But we're English, too. This is ours.' He pointed at the ground. 'All of it. Just as much as it's yours. We've been running for centuries, Inspector. Tell me something, what's the most common profession around here?'

'Tailor,' he answered. It seemed that almost every man made clothes.

'And do you know why?' Harper shook his head and the rabbi smiled again. 'Because all a tailor needs is his needle. He can run and keep his skill. These young ones, the clever ones, their parents want them to become doctors. Can you guess the reason?'

'A doctor can work anywhere.'

The rabbi nodded approvingly. 'Very good, Inspector. This is our land, we want to be here. But before anything, we're Jewish. Deep inside, we know we might always need to run again. Nowhere is ever safe.' He paused. 'Do you know why the Jewish tailors all work around here?'

'Why, sir?'

'Because none of the big firms will hire them. They don't want Jews. Only as outworkers. Did you know that?'

Harper nodded. He'd always thought it foolish not to employ men with real skill, like cutting off your nose to spite your face. And now the signs were going up. What was happening to Leeds?

'The police don't care where you come from or what religion you are,' the inspector insisted. 'We'll look after you, sir. The same way we look after everyone else.'

Padewski shook his head sadly. 'I hope so. But if you don't, we'll look after ourselves.' The words sounded like a threat. 'Good day, Inspector.'

Harper watched as the rabbi disappeared into the synagogue. The man was going to cause problems unless they solved this very quickly. Kendall was right; time was against them. The only good thing to salvage from this morning was the return of his hearing.

ELEVEN

Before noon, Harper was waiting on the Town Hall steps. He stood, tucked behind one of the wide stone pillars, watching as Reed paced around the open space, smoking and moving to keep warm.

As the clock struck the hour another man approached, a wiry figure with a sharp, rat-like face. He was familiar, one of the lot they'd pulled in from the Cork and Bottle. The pair began to walk and Harper followed, trailing them to Wellington Street until they joined the queue for the omnibus out to Kirkstall.

He needed to make a quick decision. Wait with them for the bus or begin walking? One thing was certain: he wasn't going to let Billy disappear with the man, not knowing where he'd gone. After a moment's hesitation he strode out, passing the stop quickly and seeing Reed's small nod as he went by. He'd gone almost half a mile before he heard the clop of hooves and the vehicle passed, the horses dull in their traces. The sergeant and the other man shared a seat inside.

At least walking kept him warm, breath wreathing his head as he moved. The omnibus was slow enough to keep in sight without much effort, and the rhythm of his steps gave him a chance to think. His hearing. How long until it happened again? What if it didn't return next time? A chill ran through him that had nothing to do with the weather. He tried to push the idea from his head. Half a mile became a mile, then two, until he could see the ruined tower of old Kirkstall Abbey down by the river. Cramped streets of houses poked like fingers up the hill, most so new that the bricks were still rosy red.

As Reed and the other man alighted he hung back. They crossed the road and entered the Cross Keys public house. Now he needed somewhere to wait.

'This Alfred lives all the way out here?' Reed asked as they walked into the warmth of the pub. 'It's bloody miles.'

'Worth it,' Boyd told him. 'Wait and see.'

'I will. What are you drinking?'

The men were waiting in a back room. Six of them gathered around a small table in the middle of the day, Reed thought. Working men with no work, grime ingrained in their skin, anger and frustration in their eyes. Boyd nodded, said hello to one or two, getting grunts in return. But no Alfred. No one who looked like a toff.

Reed waited and wondered for five minutes. The others kept a sullen silence. Then a man burst in, closing the door behind himself and looking around the room. He was in his twenties, in a clean, dark suit, the jacket cut halfway to his knees, trousers tight against his legs. His dark, curly hair shone with pomade, a thin moustache and bushy sideboards showing off a handsome face. He carried himself confidently, a glass of whisky in his hand. So this was Alfred, Reed thought. Boyd had been right; the man looked like a toff. But there was definitely something about him. He had the sense of a man who expected people to please him.

Before Alfred took the empty chair, he went around the table, placing a silver florin in front of every man except Reed. He sat and took a drink before he cleared his throat.

'Who's this?' he asked Boyd.

'Billy Reed. Used to be in the West Yorkshires.' A couple of men nodded their approval. 'He's one of us.'

'Mr Reed.' Alfred uttered the name slowly, as if he relished it. He had a cultured voice, educated, exactly as Boyd had said. But there was a mocking look in his gaze, as if he could see beneath the skin, all the way to the truth. It was eerie, and left the sergeant uneasy.

'I was told there'd be men like me here,' Reed said.

'And what kind of man are you?' Alfred sounded amused.

'One who believes England should be for the English.'

'Very good,' Alfred turned to Boyd again. 'You vouch for him?'

'Yes.'

The man dipped his head briefly. 'Then welcome, Mr Reed. You can call me Alfred. You're among people who have the same feelings as you.'

'Billy,' the sergeant said.

Alfred stared at him. 'Tell me, Billy, which are you, a talker or a man who prefers action?'

'Action,' he replied quickly, and for a moment he believed it.

'Well, lads, we have someone who's not afraid.' He was smiling, an edge of disbelief in his voice. 'Have you ever killed anyone?'

'In Afghanistan.'

Alfred took another sip of the whisky, then asked, 'What would you do if someone ordered you to kill?'

'Who did you have in mind?' Reed asked.

Then man smiled again, a slight curve of his thin lips. 'I didn't say I had. It was just a question. But if it was an Irishman or a Jew, how would you feel?'

Reed shrugged. 'Wouldn't bother me.'

Alfred put his glass down on the table and stared at him, his eyes never blinking. 'All you have to do now is prove yourself. Come back tomorrow and I'll have something for you.'

Reed paused. 'All right,' he agreed finally.

'We'll see you tomorrow.' His gaze was intense and piercing as Reed stood up and left.

Harper was frozen, trying to remain still and out of sight. He moved around and pushed his hands deep into his pockets, his muffler covering his mouth and nose. Finally he saw the sergeant emerge alone and start walking back towards town.

He waited, counting out three full minutes in case someone came from the pub to follow. Then the inspector marched quickly, constantly checking over his shoulder, until he was close to Reed. He trotted the last few paces. Billy turned, his hands clenched into fists, ready for a fight, before shaking his head.

'God, Tom, I thought they were coming after me.'

'You're safe, there's no one. So who's this Alfred? What did you make of him?' the inspector asked.

It took Reed a long time to answer, sorting through the thoughts in his head. 'He has an air about him.'

'What do you mean?'

'There's . . .' Reed fumbled for the words. 'I had the feeling he was just playing with me. Like he knew who I really was.' He paused. 'He scares me.'

He stared at the sergeant. 'Have you ever seen him before?'

'I don't think so. He didn't look familiar.'

'You don't have to go back if you don't feel safe.'

'No, I'll be fine,' Reed said after a long pause.

'If you think there's any danger, I want you to run.'

'Did you see anyone go in that pub after me?'

'No one,' Harper answered. 'Why?'

'We'd been there at least five minutes before Alfred arrived.' He raised an eyebrow.

'So he was either already there or he came in a different way.'

'Yes,' the sergeant nodded. 'And he doesn't live round here. He's far too posh for Kirkstall.' They covered another block. 'He's dangerous. Slippery.'

'And he paid them?'

'Two shillings. Just for being there.'

It was a good day's wages. For a man without work, it could be a lifeline, Harper thought. 'We'll arrest Alfred after he gives you your task tomorrow.'

Reed shook his head. 'Don't. He's the type who'd have a lawyer at the station in an hour, Tom. Let's see where it goes.'

'We don't have time, Billy.' Tomorrow was the deadline the superintendent had given them.

'We need it to stick,' Reed reminded him, and the inspector knew he was right. They had to be certain of a conviction in court. Solid evidence that couldn't be doubted.

'Go back to the Cork and Bottle tonight,' Harper told him. 'It would look strange if you didn't.'

'And tomorrow?'

'Come back out here. I'll be around.'

'What are you going to do?'

Right now, he wasn't sure.

It was almost five o'clock and full, gloomy dark when Harper alighted from the tram at the bottom of Roundhay Road. With dusk, the freezing fog that had been threatening all afternoon had clamped down hard. The air was thick, and left the acrid taste of soot and dirt in his mouth. He could only see about ten yards along the street, and heard coughing as people walked past with wet lungs and raw throats.

The lights of the Victoria glowed soft and welcoming. Inside, the fire was warm and embracing, burning bright in the hearth. The bar was full, men standing and talking in groups. He slipped through and up the stairs.

Annabelle was sitting at the table, waiting, a teapot and empty cup in front of her. He kissed her forehead and slowly took off his scarf and overcoat.

'Turned bad out there.'

'Tom,' she said.

'What?'

'Sit yourself down.'

He'd hoped he could glide past the subject. But he should have known better. She didn't forget. Harper pulled out a chair and faced her.

'How's your ear?' Annabelle asked.

'Fine now. My hearing came back during the morning.' He smiled at her.

'It scared you. I saw it on your face. And you said it wasn't the first time.'

'That's right.' He kept his voice low, staring down at the table-cloth, feeling her stare.

'I'm your wife, aren't I, Tom? We got ourselves wed back in the summer, didn't we? I didn't imagine it?'

'You know you are.'

'Then you'd better tell me what's going on.' It wasn't begging, it wasn't a request; it was a demand. She put a small hand over his. 'I love you. I married you. But I can't help you unless I know what's happening, can I?'

He nodded. He'd kept the secret for so long that hiding it had become second nature.

'It's happened twice. The last was a couple of days ago. Just for a few minutes.'

She waited, then said, 'Go on, Tom. All of it. Please.'

He took a deep breath, glancing up at her face.

'About six years ago I was chasing a thief. I was still in uniform back then. He started fighting when I brought him down and hit me on the ear. Hard.' Without thinking, he raised his hand and rubbed his right ear. 'I don't know what happened, but I've not been able to hear properly since.'

'Just the right ear?'

'Yes.'

'Have you seen anyone? A doctor?'

'Three of them.' His voice was bleak. 'The best any of them could say is that my hearing might fully return in time.' He shrugged. 'I'm still waiting.'

'What about it growing worse? What did they say about that?'

'That it could happen,' he admitted.

She sighed. 'Why the hell didn't you tell me, you daft sod?'

'Because . . . because I've never told anyone. If they find out at the department they might sack me. You can't have a deaf detective.'

'You've managed so far, haven't you?'

'Yes,' he agreed.

'Then we'd better see what can be done to get your hearing back.'

'I told you—'

'Tom.' Her voice overrode his. 'When was the last time you saw anyone about it?'

'Three years,' he admitted quietly.

'Then you need to have it checked again. Look,' she told him, 'I have money. We can afford the best. Let him take a look and see what he says.'

He twined his fingers through hers. 'Thank you.'

'Who's the top man at this in Leeds?'

'Dr Kent.' He kept an office on Park Square, expensive, prestigious surroundings. His services were beyond anything the inspector could afford on a policeman's salary.

'Make an appointment.' She smiled. 'We might not be as rich as those Whitleys and Le Princes but we're not on the streets just yet.'

'Are you sure?'

'Course I am. I'm your wife. Go ahead and arrange it. I'll come down with you.'

'Don't tell anyone, please.'

Annabelle closed her mouth and grinned. 'Schtum, don't worry.'

'Thank you,' he repeated. What more could he say? 'What about you? Anything more on that shop?'

'Oh aye.' She pulled a shawl from the chair back and wrapped

it around her shoulders. 'He came down a little more on the rent,
so I said yes.'

'The big shop or the smaller one?'

'Big.' She gave a small laugh. 'In for a penny, in for a pound.'

'What next?'

'I'm meeting the carpenter there tomorrow. The same fellow
who did the other bakeries for me. He does good work and he's
reasonable.' She scrabbled in the pocket of her gown, bringing out
a notebook and the stub of a pencil before scrawling a note. 'I
need to talk to the printer, too. Get some notices up about the
opening.'

'When is it?'

'I'm planning on the twenty-sixth of January. It'll give them
time to anticipate so they'll be waiting when we open.'

'Interesting idea.'

'It'll work,' she said with confidence. 'I did it with the other
bakeries. Then I'll give them good quality at a fair price. That's
what keeps them coming back.'

'As long as they do.'

'They'd better, for what I'm spending on this place.' She
shrugged. 'Open a business and you take your chance. I'll know
more in six months.'

'That long?' Harper asked. It seemed like forever.

'You have to give it a chance to build,' she explained. 'Offer
customers what they want and they come back and tell others. By
July I'll have a good idea if it's going to make money or not.'

'And if it's not?'

She shrugged. 'I'll close it. There's no point throwing good
money after bad. I'll look around and try somewhere else. But I
wouldn't be opening the place if I didn't think it couldn't make a
bob or two.'

There were times he realized that she was beyond his understanding. Capable, ambitious, a businesswoman in a man's
world. Around Sheepscar they loved her. She was generous but
always practical. He'd spend the rest of his life trying to keep
up with her.

TWELVE

'In my office,' Kendall said as he marched past. Fog swirled against the windows, as if Millgarth police station stood on its own, apart from the rest of Leeds.

Harper waited while the superintendent removed his overcoat, muffler and hat, coughing up the soot that filled the air outside.

'I had to see the Chief Constable yesterday. Rabbi Feldman had a word with him.'

'About the fire?'

'The fire, the murder.' He sighed. 'The Chief wants someone in the cells.'

'Reed met Alfred yesterday. He has to go back today.'

'Then it had better be good. I mean it, Tom With all the men I've put in the Leylands we're stretched so thin we're going to tear.'

'Yes, sir. But we still need evidence.'

'Then find it, Inspector.'

'Yes, sir.'

'We have to convict someone for this. And we can't afford to fail.'

Before twelve Harper was out by the Cross Keys in Kirkstall. In town the fog had felt thicker than ever, like a blanket around his face, heavy and choking. Out here it was lighter, wispy. He found a place to watch the public house. Close enough to see everything but far enough not to be noticed. A cloud of mist drifted over the river in the distance. Every sound was deadened, muffled.

He saw men arrive in ones and twos, then finally Reed on his own, trudging out from Leeds, still wearing the battered old bowler hat, head bowed against the weather. But there was no one who looked as if he had money. No Alfred. They were all working men with their heavy boots and steady pace.

He ran a hand along the tree trunk that hid him; it was damp from the fog. At least it wasn't as frozen as yesterday. Cold, but bearable to stand and wait. Time still dragged, though. He imagined them inside, by the warmth of a fire.

Eventually they came out again. A gaggle of them together, vanishing along the road. But no Reed. Harper tensed, hands pressed into the pockets of his overcoat, pushing on to the balls of his feet.

Then the sergeant was there, alone, moving slowly back towards Leeds. The inspector let him go. Alfred would show himself soon enough.

Reed heard the footsteps approaching quickly. He tensed and turned, ready. If they were coming for him, he'd give them a fight. The figure approached quickly, like a ghost, a dark outline against the fog. The man was close before he could make out the inspector and he breathed again.

'God, you scared me there, Tom.'

'What happened?'

'They're planning something, that's all I know.'

'What?' he demanded.

'They wouldn't tell me.' He could hear the frustration in the sergeant's voice. 'I had to stand outside the room while they talked. I'm meeting them tonight at the top of Briggate. Ten o'clock.' He paused. 'You were going to follow Alfred.'

'He had a chaise waiting at the back of the pub. I couldn't even get a glimpse of his bloody face.'

'What are they planning?' Kendall asked.

'I don't know, sir,' Reed answered. The sergeant had come back to Millgarth with the inspector. 'They wouldn't tell me. I think it's a test.'

The three of them were sitting in the superintendent's office, the door firmly closed.

'I don't want Billy there, sir,' Harper said. 'It's too dangerous.'

'What are you going to do, then?'

'Nab them. If they're really planning something, they'll have weapons and tools on them. The top of Briggate is only a few hundred yards from the Leylands and the synagogue.'

'I know exactly where it is, Inspector,' Kendall told him coldly. 'But we need them committing a crime.'

'Yes, sir,' Harper agreed.

'Meet them,' the superintendent ordered Reed. 'We'll have men around.' He thought for a few seconds. 'Go with them. Find out what they're doing. As soon as you get where you're going, run. We'll take care of the rest. Understood, sergeant?'

'Yes, sir.'

'Good. Be there on time tonight and ready.' Kendall waited until Reed had left, closing the door behind him.

'You didn't see this Alfred? Not even a glimpse?'

'The chaise was right behind the pub and he had his head down. Took off up the hill. I wouldn't have been able to keep up.'

'When you arrest these man tonight, make sure you ask about him. I want to know who he is.'

'So do I.' Harper's face was grim. 'I want him in the dock, right beside them.' The man had been too quick and too clever for him, almost as if he'd guessed someone would be watching. He wasn't going to be bested by someone like that.

'You know what to do, Tom.' Kendall picked up his copy of that morning's *Yorkshire Post*. 'Have you seen this?

'Not yet, sir. Why?'

The superintendent gave a long sigh. 'Councillor May again.'

May was the bane of every copper's life. He'd made sure he became head of the Watch Committee, which made every decision about the force. But he hated the police, in the same way as he seemed to despise the poor, all the immigrants, everyone who didn't have money and lived in a way he approved.

'What's he saying this time?'

The superintendent pushed the newspaper across the desk.

'Bottom left corner.'

Harper read it quickly. For the most part, it was May's usual bombast. But there was one new twist: a threat to cut the police budget, 'so they can learn to live the way honest people do, not profligate with money.'

'Considering he's rich, it doesn't mean much,' the inspector said when he'd finished.

'He was talking to the chief about it yesterday.' He gave a brief grin. 'The way I heard it, the chief didn't mince words telling May what he thought. We'd better watch out; he's going to want the axe to fall. Fewer constables. We'll maybe have to close one or two stations.'

'It hasn't happened yet, sir.'

'It will if May has anything to do with it.' He shook his head and tipped the *Post* into his rubbish bin. 'Just make sure you do it right tonight. We can't afford any mistakes.'

'I'll need men in plain clothes.'

'Five enough?' the superintendent asked.

'Yes, sir. I'd like Ash among them.'

Kendall nodded. 'I'll arrange it.'

'You should look at him for promotion, sir.'

The superintendent raised an eyebrow. 'You think so? He's barely been on the force a year or so, hasn't he?'

'Yes, sir. But I've worked with him and he can think. That's more than you can say for most of them.'

The superintendent lit his pipe. 'He has your old beat off Briggate, doesn't he?'

'He's put it in good shape. It took me a lot longer than that.' He'd had to spend several years in uniform before becoming a detective. But Ash was ready. There was no reason for him to wait.

'I'll consider it.'

He'd planned it carefully. Everything was riding on this. If they took the men cleanly, they could wrap up Abraham Levy's murder.

Harper's small force was scattered around, close enough to watch but not near enough to arouse suspicion. They'd wait for his signal, ready to shadow the group wherever they went.

He'd briefed them a few minutes before, smelt liquor on the breath of one man and sent him home. He wanted everyone alert, ready to go whenever he gave the word.

They were all in place before ten. Harper kept his distance, a scarf pulled up over his mouth. With the fog clinging, no one would think it strange. He kept opening and closing his fists in his pockets. Come on, he thought. Bloody come on.

Finally they gathered, four of them, dim shapes in the thick mist, standing, talking, smoking. Reed arrived, striding quickly down the Headrow to join them. A few quick words and they began to move off together. One man seemed to be in the lead, squat, a cap jammed down on his head

No toff, no Alfred, but he'd never really expected it. He sounded like the type to give orders and keep his distance, never to get his hands dirty. The inspector raised a hand in a signal and his men followed.

He could just pick out the group as they walked through the fog, haloed by the gas lamps. Past the Grand Theatre and out towards North Street. His heart was beating faster. They were going into the Leylands.

He held back until they disappeared down Trafalgar Street. Then the inspector waved his men on. He dare not lose track of Reed and the others for long.

The area was quiet, the mist clinging low. People slept early here, up before dawn to work for twelve or fifteen hours. Harper kept to the shadows, treading lightly. He was close enough to make out someone bend, pick something up and throw it. A window broke with the brittle shatter of glass. The group strolled on, careless, as if they owned the area.

One window. Criminal damage, but it wasn't enough. He wanted them for a real offence, and he could feel it coming. Another stone, another window broken further down the street. Then they were running like a small mob. A yell; they must have seen someone. He waited three seconds, then whistled loud.

The inspector sprinted with the others, round the corner on to Bridge Street. They were there, a clump of men gathered around something.

Harper was on them before they could scatter, grabbing someone by the collar and pulling him to the ground, jumping on his back and putting handcuffs around his wrist as he tried to wriggle free.

There were shouts and punches, but they never had a chance. The policemen were trained, cold and angry. An old man lay on the cobbles, a pair of spectacles smashed by his side, his hat a few yards away. The inspector knelt beside him.

'You're safe now. I'm Detective Inspector Harper. The men who attacked you are under arrest.'

Then man blinked slowly. He had a withered face filled with sorrow, his eyes watery, his beard soft and almost white. He'd be bruised and sore in the morning but there was no blood; they'd arrived in time. Harper extended a hand and gently helped the man to his feet.

'Where do you live?' he asked, then '*V ton leben?*'

'Back Nile Street,' the man answered in halting, heavy English.

A pair of bobbies had arrived on the run, drawn by the sound. He spotted Maitland.

'Help this man home,' the inspector said. 'I want you to talk to him and his family. Tell him we're very sorry, but that the men who did it will go to jail. And make sure you get his statement.'

'Yes sir.' The constable picked up the hat and glasses. '*Komm, los uns heym geyn,*' he told the old man with a smile, lightly taking hold of his arm. 'I'll look after it, sir.'

Harper could still feel the blood pulsing in his neck. He took a moment to steady his breathing.

'This one's got a knife,' Ash called out. 'Nasty looking bugger, too.'

'Take them down to Millgarth,' the inspector ordered, watching as they were marched away. No Reed. Good. He must have scarpered before everything started.

Harper waited, standing alone in the road, the fog all around him. The cobbles were shiny and slick in the faint light from the gas lamps. Two full minutes passed before he heard the footsteps.

'We got them all,' he said.

Reed halted beside him. 'They were going to attack anyone they saw,' he said. 'They wanted me to be part of it. An initiation.'

'At least we stopped them before there was any real trouble. They'll be going down for a while.'

'Alfred didn't come.'

'I'll get that from them.' The inspector's voice was hard. 'Was Boyd there?'

'Yes.'

'Who's the leader?'

'He's called Tom Blake. Little fellow, strong, got a tattoo on his right hand. Seemed to think he was cock o' the walk.'

'Any other names?'

'Peter, Bernard.' He shrugged. 'I'm not sure who's who.'

'It doesn't matter. I'll find out. I'll need your report first thing. Everything that happened tonight.' He saw Reed nod. 'I don't want you around the station tomorrow, Billy. Let them think you ran off and we didn't catch you. Go and see Elizabeth. Surprise her.'

He brightened. 'She'd like that.'

'Give her a treat, then. You've done a good job here.'

He watched the sergeant walk away then began to stroll to the station. After a few paces he turned. The questions could wait until morning.

'What time is it?' Annabelle stirred as he climbed into the bed. He tried to be quiet, but his weight on the mattress woke her.

'A bit after midnight,' he said, putting his arm around her.

'How's your ear?' Her voice was full of sleep, inviting as she rolled into him, curling against his body.

'No more problems.' With everything else happening, he'd forgotten about it.

'Make the appointment tomorrow, Tom.' He heard her breathing slow as she fell back to sleep.

THIRTEEN

The inspector sat and read. God only knew when Reed had written it, but the pages were waiting on his desk when he arrived shortly after six. It was much as he'd imagined. The group had gone hunting in the Leylands, looking for anyone on his own. No one had talked about murder, but if it happened, they wouldn't lose sleep over it. Maitland had taken a statement from Solomon Shavitz, the victim. He'd simply been in the wrong place at the wrong time, on his way home from seeing an old friend. At least he'd escaped any real injury.

Blake had been in command of the men. There was little more to tell. They'd spotted Shavitz and chased him, not that he could move quickly. The sergeant had vanished before the attack.

No one had mentioned Alfred.

'Have someone bring Blake to the interview room,' he told Tollman.

It was no more than a table and two chairs, with a single barred window that looked out over the yard. The glass was frosted over.

Harper scratched at it, clearing enough to see officers exercising the police horses on the hard, icy ground.

He turned as the door opened and a constable brought the man in, pushing him down on to one of the chairs. Tom Blake was stocky, with short, bandy legs. Wide shoulders under an old jacket, a small body full of strength. He had heavy beetle brows and angry eyes; a moustache covered his upper lip. A crude Union Jack tattoo, probably done in jail, covered the back of his right hand.

In his old shirt, a waistcoat that sat snug against his large chest, torn moleskin trousers and working man's boots, the man looked like a labourer.

'Your name's Thomas Blake.'

The man stared directly at him with hatred. 'That's right.'

'Do you deny attacking a man in the Leylands last night?'

Blake straightened his back and pulled his shoulders back, at attention while he sat.

'No,' he said with pride.

'How long had you been planning it?'

'We had a few drinks and we decided to have a little sport.'

Harper slammed his hand down on the table. The sound filled the room. 'Do I look like a bloody idiot? I know you've all been in the Cross Keys in Kirkstall.'

For a moment he saw a flicker of fear in the man's eyes. Good.

'It's not the first time you've attacked someone in the Leylands, is it?' the inspector continued.

'Never been there before.' Blake smirked.

'I don't believe you.' He opened the desk drawer and brought out the knife Ash had discovered the night before. 'Look familiar?'

'That's mine,' he admitted, a hint of pleasure in his voice.

'Going to use it, were you?'

'It's for protection. Nasty out there. Dangerous.'

'It's for killing,' Harper told him. 'It's like the knife that killed Abraham Levy on Christmas Eve.'

'Wasn't me.' Blake folded his arms.

'Where were you on Christmas Eve?'

'Drinking with the rest of the lads.'

'Where?'

'Cross Keys until it closed. Then my house. Ask any of them. Ask my missus, she'll tell you.'

Harper had no doubt they all would. He decided to change tack, to try to take the man off guard. 'What about the fire at the synagogue?'

'You what?' Blake asked, and his surprise seemed so genuine that the inspector believed him. That was a dead end.

'Who's Alfred?'

'Someone we know. A rich man. He helps us out. A bob or two here and there when we need it.'

'He arranged last night.'

Blake kept his mouth shut and shrugged.

'What's his name?' Harper asked, his voice low.

'Alfred. You bloody know that.'

'His full name. His real name.' He waited a moment. 'Might go easier on you when you're in Armley jail if you tell me. I know the warders there. They can make a sentence seem like a long, long time.'

'He's Alfred,' Blake said. 'That's all I know. It's God's honest truth. It's all he ever told us.'

'So you were willing to kill for a man you didn't even know?' Harper asked.

'He only wanted us to rough someone up a bit, to keep all the bloody Jews scared. He'd promised us ten bob for it.' It was a great deal of money for a few minutes' work. But Blake sounded earnest, almost believable.

'How much did he pay you to kill Abraham Levy?'

'I told you, we didn't have nothing to do with that.'

'What about the fire at the synagogue?'

'No,' Blake insisted.

'What work do you do?'

'Nothing. Can't find anything.' The man's face hardened again.

The inspector didn't believe him. There were jobs. Probably he'd been sacked for drunkenness or idling, and no employer was willing to take him on.

'How did you meet Alfred?'

He had to drag it out. Alfred had come into the Cross Keys one day at the beginning of December. None of them had ever seen him there before. He'd bought them drinks, begun talking to them, asking how they felt about this and that before talking about the Jews and the Irish and how they were ruining England.

He'd arranged to meet them again the following week, and asked them to bring friends who thought the same way. One of the men invited Boyd. Alfred arrived, placing two shillings in front of each man there. That night he had them go out and paint words like Jews Go Home around the Leylands. At the next meeting he gave each man an extra shilling for the job. The week after, it had been breaking windows, and the same pay.

But not murder, Blake insisted. And not arson. The night before had been the first violence.

Two hours later Harper had had enough. He yelled for the constable to take the man back to the cells and bring up the next. No murder, nothing more on Alfred. None of his threats or promises worked.

He asked questions all morning, going through each of the other men. Dinner time came and went. Harper drank cup after cup of tea to keep his throat wet. Every time, the story was the same. The only name they knew for the man was Alfred, and they did what he wanted because he paid them. They all admitted the attack, but they hadn't murdered Abraham Levy or set the fire. They'd all been drinking together until late on Christmas Eve. The inspector sent out a man to check the story. Blake's wife and the landlord at the Cross Keys said the same thing.

And no one knew the toff as anything more than Alfred.

Finally he had to admit defeat. They were telling the truth. He signed the paper to send them all off to the cells at the Town Hall and up before the magistrate.

'Tom,' the superintendent called. He entered the office, still fuming. 'Close the door.' The noise outside in the station was muffled. 'Did you get anything from them?'

'They didn't kill Levy or start the blaze.' He paced around the room, clenching and opening his fists.

'Do you believe them?'

'That's the problem, sir,' Harper admitted. 'I do.'

'Then we need to find out who did it.' Kendall's voice was cold. 'Where's Reed? Why isn't he with you today?'

'I told him not to show his face here while I was questioning them. I've got his report.'

'I suppose he's earned a day off,' Kendall agreed grudgingly.

'It was good work, Tom. Did that Frenchman get off without a problem?'

Muyrère. He hadn't even thought about the man.

'As far as I know, sir. He should be on his way to America by now.'

'Let's hope it's warmer there for him, eh?' He paused for a heartbeat. 'You'd better get to it, Inspector. The Chief wants answers. It's both of us on the line.'

The café on the far side of the market was filled with men in search of hot food and a little warmth. Harper found an empty table in the corner and ordered the sausage and mash. His belly growled. The tea was stewed, so strong the spoon could stand up in it, but it hit the spot, and the food took the edge off his hunger.

'Anyone sitting there, Inspector?'

He looked up to see Tom Maguire, a cup and saucer in his hand.

'Help yourself.'

'You look like the weight of the world is pressing down on you.' He was smiling, red hair tousled, his suit unkempt, waistcoat buttoned wrong.

'Long day.'

'I hear you had a long night, too.'

'Word gets around.'

Maguire shrugged. 'Leeds, Inspector. You know what it's like here.'

He knew. And all the gossip in town seemed to find its way to the union organizer.

'What about you, Mr Maguire. Keeping busy?'

'Every minute of every day.' The lightness vanished from his voice. 'The mills, Mr Harper. The way they treat the girls there . . .' He shook his head. 'Sitting for hours in the hope of work, not getting paid a penny. No dinner. And all the while, the owners grow richer. Do you see the fairness in that?'

'No.' It wasn't a new tale; things had been the same as long as he could recall. Strikes, government commissions; in the end he wondered if they made any difference at all.

'We fight. We educate.' He knew that Maguire had published poems about it all. He'd seen one in a magazine once. A fair effort, though he was no judge. Heartfelt, anyway.

'Do you think you'll win?' Harper asked.

'Eventually. Not in my lifetime, but it'll happen.'

'What happens then? Paradise?'

'Man lost Paradise, if you recall your Bible, Inspector. It can never last.'

Harper chuckled. 'You don't give much comfort, do you?'

'I'm honest. I want justice for everyone.'

'You don't think I do?'

'I know you do,' Maguire said earnestly. 'But you work for the law. That's not the same and you know it, Inspector. Laws are for those rich enough to buy them. The factory owners, not the mill girls.' Maguire drained the cup and stood. 'The only problem is that you work for the law and you believe in justice, too. Uneasy bedfellows. I'll bid you good day.'

Law and justice, Harper thought as he walked back to Millgarth through the fog. People appeared and vanished like ghosts. Only the sound of coughing made them real. Sometimes the two things could be the same. Maguire was right, though; all too often, they had nothing to do with each other. But he'd made his choice; he'd sworn to uphold the law. He'd find justice wherever he could.

Harper walked out along North Street, slipping into Cohen's tailor shop across from Jews' Park. The warmth from the stove was sweet relief after the bitter wind outside.

'It's New Year's Eve, Tom,' Moses Cohen laughed as he came through from the back. 'What is it for you tonight? A ball? A party?'

'I'd be happy with some hot food and an early night,' Harper said wearily.

'Is that wife of yours wearing you out already?' He grinned.

'Cheeky bugger.' But the inspector was smiling, the gloomy mood lifted for a minute. 'How about your wife? Still under her thumb?'

'Always,' Cohen said happily. 'She rules the home.'

'And the boys?'

'Ah.' Under his beard, the man's expression turned serious. His shoulders slumped and he seemed to age. 'I sent Isaac into town today, just a small errand. On his way back, a group of young men started to chase him. He had to run for his life. I had to stop

Israel going looking for them.' He looked up helplessly. 'This, the notices . . . What's happening here, Tom?'

He didn't know how to answer. On the way home through the small, dirty streets he heard the hum of sewing machines in the countless sweatshops. So many lives, all of them so desperate but hopeful, all of them on a knife edge. And no answers.

FOURTEEN

It had snowed out in Middleton; the better part of two inches covered the ground. Reed's boots crunched through it as he walked from the railway station, his breath clouding in the cold air. Night had fallen, gas lamps giving off a soft glow that reflected the white on the street. He passed the shop where Elizabeth worked. It was still open, still busy.

Down the street and around the corner. In the distance he saw a small fire burning off the gas at one of the pits, flickering bright against the darkness. He knocked on the door of a terraced house, hearing the voices inside, and he smiled at the thought of seeing her again.

On the way down he'd stopped at the barber in Hyde Park and told him to remove the stubble that had grown back on his cheeks. It was time for a proper change, to throw off the past completely. But when she opened the door and looked up at him, he wondered if he'd made a mistake. Her eyes were quizzical, suspicious; she didn't recognize him.

'Hello, Elizabeth,' he said and her expression opened. She reached up and touched his face, fingers sliding over the smooth skin.

'Billy. I . . .' He could see her redden with embarrassment. 'Get yourself in here. It's too parky out there.'

The kitchen was warm, a kettle sitting to the side of the range, steaming gently. Darning sat on the table, socks and stockings waiting to be mended.

'I didn't know you at first,' she apologized. She hugged him fiercely then stared at his face. 'I'd no idea who it was. You get that coat off, I'll make you some tea.' She bustled around, stealing glances at him.

'Where are the children?' he asked? He'd brought a bag of sweets for them to share.

'Already in bed. They'll be sorry they missed you. This is late for out here, you know.'

She put the cup in front of him with a pair of broken biscuits from the shop, then sat and stared.

'It suits you,' she said finally as she scrutinized his face. 'Makes you look younger.' Elizabeth shook her head and smiled. 'It's just going to take me a while to get used to it, that's all.'

'It was a shock to me, too.'

'Why did you do it?'

'Work.' He began to explain, reaching across to hold her hand. Her expression darkened as he told her about the men at the Cork and Bottle, then Alfred and his crew.

'What were they thinking of, asking you to do that?' Her outrage exploded when he finished. 'You could have got yourself killed.'

'I volunteered,' he told her gently. 'It was the only way we were going to find out.'

'You're more than they deserve, you are.' She leaned across and kissed him. 'I hope they appreciate you, Billy Reed. I know I do. I've missed you.'

For an hour they talked and spooned. She sat on his lap, arms around his neck. Finally Reed looked at the clock, sighed and said, 'I need to go. The last train will be leaving soon.' He didn't want to leave. He felt content here with her. Happy.

'Tell me something,' Elizabeth said. She seemed hesitant, almost reluctant.

'What?'

'We've been seeing each other a few months now,' she began. 'I know.'

'What are your intentions, Billy Reed?' She stifled a giggle as soon as she spoke, reddening at her own words. 'That's a terrible thing to say, isn't it?'

She was trying to make light of it but he knew she was serious. He'd thought about her over the last few days, aching to see her again. But she scared him. She was outgoing, able to chatter nineteen to the dozen while he was so often quiet. She embraced life in a way he never could. But he'd come to understand that he needed her. He loved her. It had taken time for him to realize it, and the feeling was disturbing. It left him off balance.

'We're courting,' he answered. His voice was husky. He didn't like having to give a name to it, to be put on the spot.

She pulled back to look into his eyes, searching for the truth there. 'Aye, we are.' She kissed him once more and stood. 'Come on, or you'll end up walking all the way back to Leeds.'

At the door she held him close, burrowing into his coat.

'Billy?' Her voice was muffled by the cloth.

'What?'

'I want someone who'll come home to me every night. I don't need a hero.'

Don't volunteer for anything dangerous. That was what she meant. He smiled.

'I think I've done my bit.'

She hugged him closer. 'Go on, you'll miss the train. I'd come with you but I can't leave the children.'

'It's fine.' He stroked her hair and let a sense of peace rise inside for a minute. But what she saw in him he couldn't imagine.

This time he heard the sound. Wood on wood, a truncheon banging against the door. Harper was out of bed, reaching for his dressing gown and making his way down the stairs before Annabelle could stir.

He drew back the bolts and turned the key. A different young constable this time, out of breath from running, and a blast of frigid air from outside. The lad saluted eagerly.

'What is it?' He folded his arms, tucking in his hands.

'Another body, sir. On Gower Street.'

For a second he thought he'd misheard the street. Christ. The Leylands again. It was like being caught in a bad dream.

'Another Jew?'

'I don't know, sir. They just said to come and get you.'

'Right.' He thought quickly. 'I'll be there as soon as I can. In the meantime I want every available man in the area.'

'Yes, sir.' The bobby scribbled in his notebook.

'Contact Woodhouse police station. Have them send someone to fetch Sergeant Reed.'

'Anything else, sir?'

'No.'

'Right, sir. And happy New Year, sir.'

January the first. 1891, he thought as he closed the door. And it was off to a bloody awful start.

Upstairs, he dressed hurriedly. An extra shirt and waistcoat, the heaviest trousers he owned. Two pairs of socks. With all those clothes he felt bundled and bloated, but he'd be warm out there.

'Tom?' Annabelle murmured.

'Just work.' He kissed her forehead above the blanket and quilt.

'Be sure you make that appointment with the doctor.'

'I will. I promise.' Trust her; even in her sleep, she never forgot.

He was there in ten minutes, breath steaming like a train. It looked as if half the Leylands was standing on Gower Street, men and women, young and old alike. A few were shouting, some wailing their grief, most of them just silent, eyes downcast, with too many memories of places where all this had happened before.

Harper pushed his way through the crowd. Four coppers in their dark blue uniforms formed a circle around the body to keep everyone back. Someone had placed an overcoat over the corpse. The arms were extended. The same mockery of a crucifixion as Abraham Levy.

Maitland was one of the ring guarding the dead man. He had one hand on his truncheon, eyes watching all the people around. He retreated as the inspector called him.

'What happened?'

'You'd better take a look at who it is first, sir,' the man said, his face shadowed.

Harper gave him a curious look then pulled back the coat enough to see the face. Rabbi Padewski. He let out a long, slow breath, replaced the covering and stood. No wonder the crowd had gathered. This was the worst thing that could have happened.

'What do you know?'

'Not much, sir.' Maitland kept his gaze outward, alert for any sign of trouble. The people were quiet for now, but the mood could turn in an instant, they both knew that. They could have a riot on their hands. 'The clock had just struck one. I was over on

Copenhagen Street and I heard someone shouting.' He thought for a second. 'Crying. I ran over and found him like this.'

'How long have they been gathering?'

'Started right away. They came pouring out. I've been keeping my eye on the young ones. I blew my whistle and the other lads came. I sent one of them to Millgarth to get a message to you.'

'Good job.' More men should arrive soon. Enough to disperse this lot, he hoped. He dared not take a proper look at the corpse with them all around; that would only inflame them. He needed to wait and hope the constables arrived quickly.

'Did any of you see anything tonight?' he shouted, then looked at Maitland to repeat it in Yiddish.

'We didn't see you,' someone yelled from the back, and the murmurs grew like a wave. No, Harper thought. This wasn't going to work.

'How many of them do you know?' he asked Maitland.

'Most of them, sir. By face, if not all by name.'

'Once they've dispersed I want you to talk to some of them. Quietly. See if anyone knows anything. I need fact, not rumour. Start with the ones who were here when you arrived.'

'Yes, sir.' He cocked his head. 'Reinforcements on the way,' he said with a relieved smile.

It was another few seconds before Harper could make out the tramp of boots marching over the cobbles. Then the uniforms arrived in their ranks. Ten of them; the night sergeant had done well to find so many.

It was by the book. They worked politely but insistently, slowly pushing everyone back. Five minutes and it was over, all of them dispersed, men on the street corners to stop the crowd flooding back.

Harper crouched and pulled the coat away again. Padewski's spectacles and hat were missing. He'd been carefully arranged, arms spread wide in the shape of a cross. Two pools of blood on his chest where he'd been stabbed, but little blood under him. Exactly the same as Levy. And once again, two bronze pennies covering the sightless eyes; did they mean anything? The rabbi had been killed somewhere else and brought here, right outside his own synagogue. Whoever did this knew exactly who Padewski was.

Normally he'd send the body over to Dr King, the police surgeon. The man usually managed to find something useful. But not this time. The body needed be in the ground before night came again, out in the Jewish cemetery on Gelderd Road; that was their way. He dare not argue the case, certainly not when the corpse was a rabbi's.

But unlike Levy, Padeweski hadn't gone easily to his death. There were the beginnings of bruises on his cheek and jaw, and his knuckles were scraped, blood dried on them.

'A terrible sight, Inspector.'

He looked up at the words and saw Rabbi Feldman standing there, the heavy coat, scarf and glasses making him seem larger. His body was stooped, resting heavily on his walking stick, eyes sorrowful behind thick spectacles.

'Yes.' He stood, feeling the cold in his knees.

'The same as Abraham, from the look of him,' Feldman said accusingly. Harper stayed silent; there was nothing he could say yet. 'And no killer.'

'We're doing everything we can, Rabbi.'

'Not enough, Inspector.' He shook his head. 'We need people like Piotr Padewski. They're the future.'

'I talked to him a day or two ago.'

'Then you know what he was like.'

'I had a glimpse,' Harper said.

'We were very different, but people listened to him. They respected him. And he believed what he said.' Feldman gave a small, sad shake of his head. 'I'd like a minute alone with him, Inspector.'

'Of course.' He walked away, pulling Maitland aside. 'Where does Padewski live?'

The constable tilted his head towards the synagogue.

'Above there, sir.'

'Married?'

'Wife and two young kiddies.' His mouth moved into a grim line. 'The little one's nobbut a baby.'

God, Harper thought. The woman would be able to see her husband's body from the window.

'What's the wife's name?'

'Sarah, sir. She's as English as he is. Was.'

'Right. I'm going to see her. You'd better arrange something for the funeral with Feldman.'

'Yes, sir.'

The door stood to the side of the building. Someone had taken care in painting it, putting on several coats to leave it shiny. Someone was proud to live here, to make it home. He hesitated before knocking, then let his knuckles fall softly on the wood.

She came down the stairs in a rush of footsteps, pulling the door back quickly. She held an oil lamp in one hand, the glow bright enough to show her eyes were red from crying.

Sarah Padewski wore a heavy black dressing gown drawn tight around herself, a dark woollen shawl gathered around her shoulders. Her thick, unruly hair was gathered into a braid that hung over her shoulder. In the faint light he could make out a small round scar on the olive skin of her throat.

'I'm Detective Inspector Harper,' he told her. 'May I come in?'

She nodded and turned, holding the lamp high and leading the way up the steps and leading him into a room filled with furniture. A desk on one side, over by shelves heavy with books. A dining table, papers stacked along one side. A pair of chairs gathered close to a fireplace. Closed doors led elsewhere.

'I'm sorry . . .' he began, but she didn't wait for him to continue.

'I heard people shouting. I got up to take a look.' The woman had a flat Lancashire accent, the words coming out empty. 'He was down there.'

Sometimes he felt that he spent his life speaking to the grieving or the guilty. Those were the faces that stayed in his mind at night. Theirs were the voices he heard when he walked.

He sat on a wooden chair, seeing the wet marks his boots had left on the swept boards.

'Tea,' she said suddenly. 'You must be frozen after being out there.' Before he could speak, she scuttled away, disappearing through a door. He heard her moving the kettle on the range, the light clatter of cup and saucer. He knew what she was doing. Every moment put off the time when he'd say her husband was dead. She'd seen his body, but until the words were spoken it wasn't real. If she kept moving the truth might not catch up to her.

He stood by the window. Rabbi Feldman was deep in conversation to Maitland. The light from the gas lamps formed a soft circle around them, with Padewski's body lying on the ground. From here she'd have been able to make out his face. There'd have been no mistake, no confusion. He tried to imagine how he'd feel, looking out from the windows above the Victoria to see Annabelle lying on the pavement.

'I put milk in,' Sarah Padewski said. 'No sugar. I hope that's fine.' The words were so normal, so everyday, but he could hear the note of fear at the edge of her voice. He had no choice but to say it.

'Mrs Padewski, I'm sorry. I have to tell you that your husband's dead.'

'We have two children, you know,' she continued, ignoring what he'd said as if she'd never heard it. 'David's four and Rebecca's almost a year old.'

'I'm sorry,' he repeated, looking into her eyes until she gave a small, defeated nod and pushed her lips together to stop the tears forming. 'I need to ask you some questions about your husband.'

'I . . .' He waited for her to speak. 'I need to see to his funeral.'

She began to edge away, hands fidgeting with a lace handkerchief. As long as she kept busy she didn't have to think. She didn't have to face the future.

'Rabbi Feldman's downstairs,' Harper said gently. 'I'm sure he'll come up to see you in a few minutes.'

'Yes.' It was a word, something to fill the emptiness.

The inspector cleared his throat. 'Mrs Padewski, where did your husband go tonight?'

It took a moment to focus her thoughts.

'He went to visit Mrs Cohen on Star Street. And he had a meeting with the youth group.'

'Where was it? What kind of meeting?' Harper kept his voice low and soft.

'They meet every week. Peter teaches and then they talk.'

'Where do they meet, Mrs Padewski?'

'There's a building on Poland Street. They use that.'

His mind pictured the road, trying to pick out the exact place. 'What time does the meeting usually finish?'

'They can go on very late sometimes.' She gave a sad, liquid smile. 'Peter likes to argue. He enjoys picking things apart.' He remembered the way the rabbi had been when they talked. 'I'm usually asleep when he comes home.'

Her gaze was turning distant. He was losing her to memories and sorrow.

'I'll have Rabbi Feldman come and sit with you,' he said, unsure if she heard.

Feldman stood in the cold, watching men wrap Padewski in a shroud before carrying him away in a handcart.

'She needs you,' Harper said, and the man bowed his head.

'Two men dead and a synagogue burnt. Find them, Inspector. Find them now.' His voice was deep and weary, his words a plea.

'I will.' But he didn't know how. Alfred's men were in jail. Someone else had done this. It had to be the same ones who'd killed Abraham Levy; the pennies on the eyes were like a calling card. And he had no idea who they could be.

'May God give you help.' The rabbi put a hand on Harper's shoulder and walked towards the synagogue.

The inspector took out his pocket watch and sighed. Five minutes to three; a bitter welcome to the brand new year. Harper saw Maitland down on the corner, talking rapidly with a young man. He strode towards them, hands deep in his pockets.

'This is Daniel Orbaum, sir,' the constable said. The short, skinny youth at his side gazed down at the pavement. He had pale blond hair under his hat, the light catching the faint down on his upper lip. 'He was with Rabbi Padewski tonight.'

'You were at the meeting on Poland Street?' the inspector asked.

'Yes.' The lad raised his head to show intelligent blue eyes. His shirt had a collar but no tie, and his overcoat was too large for him. He could almost hear the boy's mother telling him he'd grow into it in time. He was probably seventeen or eighteen, but he looked younger. Already a man in Jewish terms, but just emerging into real adulthood. It was easy to image him as the runt, bullied at school.

'What time did it end, Mr Orbaum?'

'After midnight. We wished each other happy New Year when the clock struck.'

The lad was clear and precise, better than most witnesses. From the corner of his eye, Harper saw Maitland give an approving nod.

'How much longer did it last?'

'Maybe ten minutes,' Orbaum answered. 'It might have been a quarter of an hour.'

So Padewski was still alive at quarter past midnight.

'When did the rabbi leave?' Harper asked.

'When all the others did. I stayed and helped put the chairs away with my cousin. We were gone before half past. The caretaker locked up when we left.'

'How many people had been at the meeting?'

'Twelve of us.'

The inspector tried to fix the times in his mind. They'd found the body a little after one. Say forty-five minutes to kill the rabbi and move him. That was ample time, but it couldn't have happened far away.

'Where do you live, Mr Orbaum?'

'St Thomas Row. By the steelworks.'

He knew it, a street filled with the constant clang of hammers and the heat of the furnace. 'Did you see or hear anything on your way home?'

'I heard noises on Copenhagen Street.'

Harper was suddenly alert. Copenhagen Street was where Levy had been murdered.

'What kind of noises?'

'It sounded like a fight. I thought someone had been celebrating the New Year and had an argument.'

'You didn't go and look?'

Orbaum shook his head. Harper understood; staying clear was safer.

'When did you hear about the rabbi?'

'The neighbour knocked on our door.'

The inspector thought rapidly. 'Tell me, when you were on Copenhagen Street, did you recognize any voices?'

'No. Nothing. I'm sorry.'

'Thank you.'

Orbaum nodded, then shambled away, the overcoat trailing around his ankles.

'What do you need me to do, sir?' Maitland asked.

'Talk to the others who were at that meeting. They might have seen something. Knock them out of their beds if you have to.' He gazed at the houses. Half of them still had lights burning. There'd be little sleep for many in the Leylands tonight.

'What about Copenhagen Street, sir? That was where—'

Harper cut him off. 'I know. We'll search there as soon as it's light.' To see if it had been the killing ground once again. 'I'll need people canvassing the houses. Find out if anyone saw or heard anything. It's going to be a long shift for you.'

'Doesn't matter, sir.' Maitland gave a grim smile. 'I liked the rabbi. Always had time for a chat. It's the same people who did for young Abraham, isn't it?'

'It looks that way.'

'Anything I can do to catch them, just tell me, sir.'

He understood the man's determination. This was his area, they were his people. He knew them, he had a bond with them. He'd felt exactly the same when he had his beat in the courts and lanes in the city centre.

'Don't worry, I will.'

On the way to the police station he walked along Noble Street, glancing at the house where he'd grown up. Curtains were drawn in the windows. Shards of his history lay all across the Leylands: childhood, school, his first job. He'd never manage to escape them all.

Reed was waiting in the office. He'd made tea; a cup was stewing on Harper's desk.

'They said there'd been another murder.'

'Laid out just the same as the Levy boy.' The inspector took a drink of the tepid liquid and pushed a poker into the fire to stir the flames. 'Happy 1891, Billy. Aren't you glad it's New Year?'

'Exactly the same?'

'Crucifixion pose, stabbed. Pennies on the eyes. But this time they murdered a rabbi.'

'What?' Reed stopped with cup midway to his mouth. 'They killed Feldman?'

'No, the young one, Padewski. We already have Alfred's men in jail, so it can't be them.' Harper tapped his fist against his chin. 'We're back to square bloody one.'

The sergeant swore. 'What can we do now?'

'Think. And look.' He ran his hands down his face. 'And we'd better start praying for some good bloody luck. Go over all the statements again, Billy. See if there's anything at all we missed before.'

Harper heard the sound of the day shift coming on duty at six, and an hour later Kendall swept in. They'd found nothing.

'My office,' he said. 'The pair of you.'

They waited as he removed his winter clothing and rested his shiny top hat on its hook.

'Right. What have you learned so far?'

It didn't take long.

'Maybe there'll be more when Maitland's taken the statements,' the inspector finished. 'We're going to search Copenhagen Street once it's light enough.'

'Ideas?' Kendall asked, staring from one face to the other. 'I need to know what you're going to do, Tom. The chief's going to ask me.'

'We're going back to the beginning.' He'd gambled, put the sergeant in with the men at the Cork and Bottle and Alfred's troop. And he'd lost.

'You can have Ash with you,' Kendall told him. 'See how he does in plain clothes. That's all, gentlemen. Tom . . .' he added as Harper was leaving.

'I know, sir.' Time. The one thing they didn't have. And it was vanishing quickly.

He pulled out his pocket watch. Half past seven. A few more minutes and they could leave. He pulled across another pile of statements. Before he could start reading, though, he heard the clump of boots across the floor.

'Ash, sir, reporting for duty.' There was a huge smile under the bushy moustache. He looked awkward, squeezed into his suit, the collar so tight that his face was red. His hand was extended, holding out a letter. 'Sergeant Tollman said to give you that, sir. It's addressed to that French copper who was here.'

Muyrère, Harper thought in surprise. Why would anyone write to him here? A Leeds postmark and flowing, feminine handwriting. He ripped open the envelope. There was a single sheet with the address printed at the top: Oakwood Grange.

Capitaine,

I thank you for your visit and the knowledge you will do all you can to find my husband. However, I have new information. My son arrived yesterday, back from America. He has talked to people in New York who claim that Mr Thomas Edison contracted two men to see that my husband's patent did not arrive before he had the opportunity to file his own.

I understand that you may already have left for America, but perhaps an officer from Leeds Constabulary can talk to my son and forward the information.

Yours sincerely,
Elizabeth Le Prince

Later. He'd go and see her later, once he had a spare hour. There were more important things on his plate than the disappearance of Louis Le Prince. He took out his watch once more.

'Right,' he announced. 'Let's get moving.'

As they walked he briefed Ash. The constable stood taller and broader than the others, a bowler hat perched awkwardly on his large head. He listened carefully, asking a few thoughtful questions, ready to work as soon as they reached Copenhagen Street.

FIFTEEN

'I hope you're ready to get mucky,' Reed said. They were standing by the privy on Copenhagen Street, cold to their bones. The air still stank.

'If I'd known, I'd have brought me apron,' Ash replied with a chuckle. 'At least it's frozen, eh, sarge?'

'Be grateful for small mercies. You wouldn't be able to breathe back here in summer.'

'What are we looking for?'

'A knife, if we're lucky. More likely we'll see patches of blood if the rabbi was killed here.'

It didn't take long to find a lake of blood, dried and cold on the ground. But no knife. They used sticks to poke and move piles of rubbish, all of it in vain.

'There's nothing else to find here, Sergeant,' Ash said finally.

'Doesn't look like it,' Reed agreed thoughtfully. The last time the killer had abandoned the blade. Why not now? 'We'd better widen the search a bit.'

They were thorough, another half hour in the area around the lavatory and down in the pans. But still no knife. Finally Reed stood with a long, weary sigh.

'It's not here.'

'We've found where he was killed, though,' Ash said.

'For whatever that's worth. It doesn't give us any clues.'

'What now, sarge?'

'We go up the road.' He saw the inspector standing there, checking with the constable who'd been on the house-to-house.

Reed followed Ash's long stride, eyes moving around, searching for anything they'd missed, any place where a knife could be hidden. The first time, the killers had stolen a knife and left it. Why would they take it with them now? The thought niggled at him.

They were halfway along the street when he stopped suddenly. 'Come with me,' he told the constable, turning back to the privy. He looked at the building again. It was solid brick, taller than a man, topped with a corrugated tin roof. 'Boost me up.'

Ash made a stirrup with his hands. Reed placed his foot in it and reached for the edge of the roof, holding on to the metal as he struggled to pull himself higher. He could see the top now. There. A knife with a long, thin blade, along with a hat and a broken pair of spectacles. He stretched out his arm, straining, but he couldn't come close enough; he was still a few inches away.

'More,' he said, gritting his teeth. He heard Ash grunt, then he could stretch a little further, enough to touch the handle of the knife. But he still couldn't grip it. His fingertips teased against the surface, tapping at it, trying to pull it closer. He held his breath. Half an inch at first, then another until he could grip it firmly. He used the tip of the blade to drag the hat and spectacles close and topple them on to the ground. 'Down now,' he ordered.

With both feet on the ground he brushed off the front of his overcoat and straightened his hat.

'Well done, sarge,' Ash said with real admiration. 'I'd never have thought of that.'

Reed held up the knife, studying it. The blade was long, the best part of twelve inches, blood dried on the steel, the handle made from bone. With the hat and glasses there was no doubt at all. The rabbi had died here.

'Take a look at the knife,' the sergeant said. 'Tell me what you see.'

Ash stared, frowning, bring his head close to peer at the blade. 'It's been used a lot,' he began slowly. 'And that bone handle won't be cheap.'

'Good.' Reed gave an approving nod. 'The knife that was used last time belonged to a butcher.'

'I'd say as this does, too.'

'Yes.' It felt good to be doing proper police work again. He'd enjoyed the assignment infiltrating Alfred's men. It had made his blood run faster, like the excitement he'd felt in the army before he went into a skirmish. But it was real, being a detective, and this was solid; it gave them the first step to finding the killers. 'Let's see what Mr Harper says.'

The inspector was still talking to Maitland; the young copper looked dead on his feet.

'Right,' Harper said as they approached. 'You've done a good job. Let Forsyth take over. Go home and get some sleep.'

'Yes, sir,' Maitland replied with relief. As he marched away, the inspector turned.

'What did you find?'

'That was the killing ground, right enough,' Reed confirmed. 'Plenty of blood, and these were on the roof of the privy.'

Harper took the knife, weighing it in his hand. 'You know what I think, Billy?'

'Same as me, I dare say.' He smiled.

'The last one was stolen from a man at Leadenhall. I'd start there if I were you.'

'I don't suppose anyone saw or heard anything?'

'It was New Year.' Harper shook his head. 'Too much noise around, a scuffle or three. No one seemed to notice anything unusual. It's the mood round here that worries me.'

'On the edge, is it, sir?' Ash asked.

'It will be, once the funeral's over this afternoon. I'm going to see Feldman, then I'll have a word with the super about having more coppers around here later.'

'Come on,' the sergeant told Ash. 'Let's go and earn our pay.'

Leeds was a wall of noise and movement. The roads were filled with omnibuses, carts and carriages, all the overwhelming noise of wheels and hooves, and men shouting as they worked. Reed watched them as they walked.

'Do you prefer this detecting to walking a beat?' Ash's question interrupted his thoughts.

'I do,' Reed answered. He'd done his stint in uniform. Every one of them had begun that way, all the way up to the chief constable. They all knew what it was like. His patch had been around Marsh Lane, the roughest part of Leeds. The coppers had to patrol in pairs there. It was the only way to stay safe. The streets were unpaved, mud that turned into bogs after the rain. Families crammed into cellar rooms with no water, no heat, damp running down the walls. After Afghanistan, the sergeant thought he'd seen how primitive and brutal life could be, but Marsh Lane had shocked him. As soon as the chance came to put on plain clothes, he'd grabbed it.

'Looks like there's plenty of thinking involved,' Ash said doubtfully.

'You have to use your brain,' the sergeant agreed. 'That's part of the pleasure.'

'I don't know, I'm used to my beat. All the problems, keeping everything in order.'

'You'll find this different.'

'I can see that.' He paused. 'You're not a married man, are you, Sergeant?'

'No, I'm not.' They passed by Lockwood's Hotel on Vicar Lane, the smell of beer wafting out as the door opened. 'Are you?'

'Yes, sir.' Ash beamed. 'Met her when we were at school, as happy as you please. We adopted that lass as went missing from Fidelity Court back in the summer. Bright as a button, she is.'

The arch led from the street into Leadenhall Carcass Market. They stood as a butcher took his cleaver to a carcass, opening it in deft strokes. Steam rose from the inside as he pulled out the guts and used another knife to cut them away.

The foreman bustled over, his face dark and suspicious. 'Who are you?'

'Leeds Police,' the sergeant told him.

The man spat. 'We had one of your lot here a few days ago.'

'Do you know this?' He held up the knife.

'That's what the other fellow asked. Different knife.' He frowned. 'This one kill someone, too?'

'It did.'

The man shook his head. 'It's not from here, I can tell you that. None of my lads has one of those bone handles.'

'Have you ever seen it?'

'No,' he answered brusquely. 'Try the butchers' shops.'

Back on the street, Reed could breathe more easily, away from the stench of meat and blood. 'How many butcher's shops in Leeds, do you think?'

Ash raised an eyebrow. 'No idea, sir. Fifty? A hundred? There are four on my beat and two close to where I live.'

Too bloody many to visit, the sergeant thought. They'd need to have the bobbies go round and ask. He stood, thinking.

'There's the fish market,' Ash suggested. 'They use knives, too.'

It was a good idea.

'Come on, then.' Reed began to walk. 'You might have the makings of a detective.'

The fish market stood no more than two hundred yards from Millgarth, a wide hall with light coming through a glass roof. The floor was slick, sparkling with scales, and the smell was overwhelming. But the men wearing leather gauntlets, tall rubber boots and big aprons didn't seem to notice. They worked at tables, slicing and gutting then tossing the fish into baskets.

Reed gazed around. Hardly anyone gave him a glance, all of them absorbed in their labours. Finally he'd had enough. He raised the knife and yelled, 'Anyone know this?'

It brought their attention. Heads turned quickly and peered.

'Anyone?' he asked again.

'That's Clem's,' one of the workers answered. 'Looks like his, any road.'

Two or three heads nodded.

'Where's Clem?' Reed asked.

'Didn't come in today,' the man replied with a chuckle. 'Probably still drunk. Not that he's worth owt when he shows up.' He blinked behind thick spectacles. 'Why, who are you, anyway?'

'Police. Where does Clem live?'

'Nay, lad,' he said, 'you want the office for that.'

'Where is it?' Ash asked.

'Down the end of the block. But that clerk's neither use nor ornament.'

They strode off. The office was a tumbledown wooden structure. An iron chimney belched smoke. The sign on the door had faded to nothing, words all gone. Reed turned the handle and entered. A man sat by himself behind a battered desk, a pile of invoices in front of him, scribbling away, fingerless gloves warming his hands.

Before he could open his mouth, Reed began to speak.

'We're with Leeds Police. You have someone called Clem working in the shed?'

'We do,' the man replied after some hesitation. 'Why?'

'I need his address.'

'What's he done?' The man sat dumbly, ink dripping from the nib of his pen.

'Just his address please, sir.' The sergeant was polite enough, but his voice was firm.

'Yes. Yes, of course.' He picked up a ledger and searched through it, copying the address on to a piece of paper. 'What's he done?' he repeated.

'Maybe nothing, sir,' Reed answered. 'We just need to talk to him.'

'That was a good thought,' the sergeant said to Ash as they walked away. He glanced at the paper. 'Manor Street. Do you know it?'

'Sheepscar, I think, sarge. Close to that pub where the inspector lives.'

The tram, Reed thought. A few minutes inside, out of the numbing cold. It wasn't warm, but any respite helped. By the time they alighted at the bottom of Roundhay Road, across from the Victoria, he felt a little better.

Ash led the way through the blocks of back-to-backs. Manor Street was all red brick, cobbles and empty dreams. Rubbish was scattered in the gutters and a thin, sharp wind blew against their backs.

They knocked and waited. A woman's face appeared at the

window for a moment, then a bolt was drawn back and a key turned. She was short, no bigger than five feet, cheeks sunk where her teeth had gone, the skin taut over her bones.

'We're with Leeds Police,' Reed told her. 'Does Clem Fields live here?'

'Mebbe,' she replied cautiously. 'Why?'

'We're looking for him.'

She folded twig arms across her chest and raised her chin. 'He's not here.'

'Do you know where he is, luv?' Ash asked. He smiled at her. 'We'd like a word with him.'

'He's only ever here to sleep and have his supper,' she answered grudgingly. 'And he didn't come home last night.'

'Do you know where he was going?'

The sergeant was happy to let Ash take over. He had the touch to draw people out, an easy manner that made them trust him.

'Didn't say. Probably found himself a lass. New Year, he might have got lucky.'

Ash produced the knife. 'Is this his?'

'Might be,' she allowed. 'He has knives for his work.'

The constable smiled patiently. 'Do you know who he sees, luv? His friends?'

The woman shifted from foot to foot. 'I don't, and no point asking me, neither.' She sniffed. 'I told you, all he does is eat and sleep here.'

'He's not much of a talker?'

'Hands over his money every week and that's it. He doesn't like to speak a lot. Has a bit of stammer.'

Reed listened as Ash teased out the rest of the description. He took his time, asking the woman about herself, her other lodgers, until her suspicions vanished.

At least the man should be easy to spot. Hair so fair it was almost white, very pale skin and blue eyes with spectacles. Medium height and thin. And a smell of fish that wouldn't leave, no matter how much he scrubbed.

'It's in his skin,' the woman confided. 'He'll never shift it.'

It took a quarter of an hour, standing as the wind whipped around, to discover everything, but Ash seemed satisfied, barely feeling the cold.

'We need to get a bulletin out to all the divisions,' Reed said as they walked back towards town.

The constable nodded his agreement, then said, 'What do you think, sarge? Did he do it? Kill the rabbi, I mean?'

'Maybe. Someone could have stolen his knife.' He shook his head. 'Too early to tell for certain yet.'

'Do you think it's worth going back to Copenhagen Street?' Ash asked after a little while.

'Why?'

'Well,' he began, 'Fields works at the fish market. All those men there, they have scales all over them.'

'You think he might have left some at the scene?'

'It's possible,' he said. 'It might let us know it was him. Worth a look, do you reckon?'

'Definitely.' The constable was a natural detective, Reed thought. He could think, he made connections and saw the possibilities. It would be a waste to send him back to the beat. A single morning and he'd already proved his worth.

Reed increased his pace, marching as if he was back in the army. Moving quickly had helped keep them warm in the Afghan winters. Over there the cold had been so raw they thought it would tug out their lungs. Ash was taller, with longer legs, and matched him stride for stride.

The air was thick, chimneys belching out their smoke all over Leeds. The sergeant coughed and spat. The streets were quiet in the Leylands, with only the sounds of sewing machines from all the sweatshops making clothes.

Behind the privy on Copenhagen Street they stood back a little, studying the ground again, watching the light play on it. At first they didn't see anything, then something changed; a shadow shifted or a cloud moved, and Reed could make out the tiny sparkles scattered across the dirt.

'There,' he said, seeing Ash nod. Plenty of them. He looked for another minute, concentrating, searching for patterns and finding none. But enough scales to convince him. Fields had been here. 'Right,' he said. 'Let's get to the station and get this bugger's description out.'

SIXTEEN

Harper hurried down the Headrow towards Park Square. He should have been at the Great Synagogue, talking to Rabbi Feldman, but first he needed to do this; he'd promised Annabelle.

The brass plaque outside the building was lovingly polished, engraved with copperplate script, the door painted a thick, glossy black. The inspector took a deep breath, turned the handle and entered. Inside, the atmosphere was as hushed as any church. A fire burned comfortingly in the grate and a thick Oriental rug covered the glistening floorboards. A single marble bust sat on a table, and in the corner an elephant's foot container held umbrellas and walking sticks. There were two paintings on the walls, a pair of naval scenes, all the subtle touches of wealth. But the people who paid Dr Kent's fees would expect nothing less. They wanted luxury and gentility, to feel exclusive. Two patients looked up for a moment and returned to their newspapers. He felt out of place here; he'd been up most of the night, and he was unshaved, his suit rumpled. Turn and walk out, he told himself. But he knew what Annabelle would say. *Don't you dare, Tom Harper. Our money's just as good as theirs.*

The clerk behind the polished desk was young and so well-groomed he seemed to shine. Harper could feel the man's eyes judging him and finding him wanting.

'Can I help you, sir?'

'I'd like to make an appointment to see Dr Kent.'

It was simply done. Saturday the third, two days away, at nine in the morning. Maybe the doctor really could help with his hearing. He hoped to God he could, anyway.

The burned doors of the synagogue on Belgrave Street had been replaced, and wood shavings still lay on the pavement. Harper entered, removing his hat as he looked around. Everything was clean, smelling of beeswax, seats like pews and a gallery above.

Feldman stood by a lectern at the far end of the room, a scroll opened before him. He glanced up at footsteps crossing the floor.

'Coming to the funeral, Inspector? It's at two o'clock.'

'I'm here to see what I can do to help, Rabbi.'

'Help?' Feldman cocked his head and his eyes hardened. 'The best help you can give is to find the killer.'

'I know.' He nodded slowly.

'People are scared, Mr Harper,' the rabbi continued. 'We've seen it all before. We know that this is how it all starts.'

'We'll look after you. I told you that. Every one of you.'

Feldman shook his head. 'You haven't, Inspector. You give us promises, but you haven't made us safe.' He raised a hand, pointing over to the Leylands. 'There are already people packing out there. They're ready to flee. Do you really want to see how people feel around here?'

'What?' he asked, hoping the rabbi had something useful to show him.

'Come back this afternoon. Take a walk around. You won't find anything open anywhere in the Leylands. No shops, no businesses. Everything will be closed.'

'I see.'

'No, you don't, Inspector, but never mind. It's our message. Now, if you'll excuse me, I have a service for the dead to prepare.'

Clouds and smoke hung low in the sky as he walked along North Street. The wind sliced at his face, and his eyes were tearing as he opened the door of Moishe Cohen's tailor shop. Moses came through as the bell tinkled, a tape measure fluttering from his neck.

'Tom.' He stopped, staring at the inspector. 'You look tired.'

'I've been up since the middle of the might.' He gave a deep sigh, trying to warm his hands by the fire. 'I'm sure you've heard.'

'There's no one round here who didn't know an hour after it happened.'

'What are they saying?' Harper asked. 'I need to know.'

'What do you think?' He frowned and shook his head. 'Who'll be next, why aren't the police doing their job?' Cohen shrugged. 'You can't blame them.'

'No,' the inspector agreed sadly. He knew how it must look to them, as if the force simply didn't care, that the people in the Leylands were fair targets. 'But I hope you know it's not true.'

'I know you're not that way, Tom.' Cohen chose his words carefully.

'We try to keep everyone safe.'

'Those aren't the right words for today.'

'I know. Just make sure they know that we're sorry. That *I'm* sorry. Please.'

'No, Tom, not today. A rabbi dying is bad enough. It means we lose a teacher. But a rabbi murdered . . .' He struggled for the right word. 'It's a desecration.'

'We're doing everything we can.'

Cohen came close and put his hand on Harper's shoulder, staring him full in the face.

'I believe that. But don't ask me to convince them, please.'

Reed and Ash were already in the office when Harper entered. The knife lay on his desk, along with Padewski's spectacles and hat.

'Clem Fields,' the sergeant said.

'Who?'

'He's the killer. One of them, anyway.'

He explained what they'd learned, the lodgings on Manor Street, the fish scales on the ground where the rabbi had died.

'It was Ash's idea to look for them,' Reed added, and the constable blushed.

'Good work.' Harper paced the room, trying to think. They had a name now, somewhere to start. They'd find him, he could feel it in his bones. 'Go back to the fish market. Find out about his friends.'

'We've already been back and asked questions,' the sergeant told him. 'No real friends, keeps himself to himself. He has a stammer and he doesn't talk much. Most of the time he's a sullen bastard from what they say.'

'Could they tell you anything at all?' Every way they turned, they hit a brick wall, he thought. They had a name, but they knew nothing else about him.

'Not as you'd notice, sir,' Ash told you. 'They didn't even know where he did his drinking.'

'The knife used to kill Levy was stolen at the Anchor in

Mabgate.' He exchanged a look with Reed. 'Go there, see if they recognize Fields. And search his lodgings. I want to know what's in his room.'

At least Harper was out of the wind in the hackney carriage as it rolled past the Victoria and up Roundhay Road. The horse trotted, head down. All the way to Harehills it was endless streets of houses, red bricks turned sooty black. Factories and forges, shops with their goods displayed in the windows. Men and women walking, faces grim against the cold.

Roundhay meant the park, acres of green. The cabbie followed the Wetherby Road where houses stood large, fields and farms out on the horizon. He turned down a long gravel drive and came to a halt by a set of solid steps.

The Whitley home was built from large blocks of Yorkshire stone, made to last for years, a testament to money and power. He rapped on the door and a maid dashed along the hall to answer. He only had to wait in the elaborate drawing room for two minutes before a woman swept in, a young man trailing behind her.

'Inspector Harper,' she said, extending a strong hand to shake his. 'I'm Lizzie Le Prince. This is my son, Adolphe. Thank you for coming. I believe it was your wife who accompanied Capitaine Muyrère.'

She was in her forties, a handsome woman wearing a grey woollen skirt with a small bustle, black button boots peeking from the hem. Her ivory blouse was closed at the collar with a cameo, and her hair was up in a simple bun. But there was an intensity in her stare that hardened her face. The young man had the look of her around his mouth, his dark hair parted neatly in the middle.

'It was,' Harper told her. 'You said you had some more information?'

She frowned. 'I'd hoped to be able to give it to the capitaine.'

'He's on his way to New York,' the inspector told her.

Mrs Le Prince made a small, annoyed sound. 'Adolphe's just come from there. It's been our home for a number of years.'

'So I've been told.'

'We have a business in New York. You're familiar with my husband's work, Inspector?' She spoke in clipped sentences, eyes darting around the room.

'Just the bare bones,' Harper said.

'He's a remarkable man. His camera and the moving pictures will change everything.'

'And make him a rich man, perhaps?'

'If he can obtain the patent on his new camera, yes,' she agreed. 'My son has some information that the capitaine should hear.'

The inspector looked at the young man and waited.

'I was talking to a couple of fellows in New York last month,' Adolphe began. There was a musicality to his voice, some of the words pronounced oddly. An American accent, Harper decided. 'They said that an agent working for Edison had made them an offer.'

'You know who Edison is?' Mrs Le Prince interrupted.

'Only his name.' The inspector smiled. 'He's a competitor of your husband, I believe?'

'Yes. He's very famous in America. He's made plenty of money and he has a great deal of influence.' She glanced at her son.

'What kind of offer, sir?' Harper asked.

'To prevent my father from filing his patent. Mr Edison is working on his own machine, but it's not ready yet. He's not a man who likes to be beaten.'

'I see.' The story seemed far too convenient. Adolphe Le Prince had handily managed to talk to a pair of men who'd been offered money for this. 'Do you have the name of the agent and what exactly he was offering, sir?'

'Five hundred dollars, Inspector.' Lizzie Le Prince took over. 'Believe me, that's a fortune. The agent wanted to be sure my husband never reached America.' Her eyes were blazing with anger and hatred.

'Sir?' He turned back to Adolphe.

'That's right. The man called himself Phileas Scott. The men told me he offered to pay their expenses and a fee if they succeeded. They turned him down. I suspect he found someone who agreed.'

'I see.' He thought for a minute. 'How reliable were these men you talked to, sir?'

'They'd have no reason to lie,' Le Prince said defensively.

'What about this Phileas Scott?' the inspector continued. 'What do you know about him? Does he work for Mr Edison?'

'I haven't been able to find out anything about him,' Adolphe admitted. 'I asked a few people. One or two said they'd heard of him, but no one seemed actually to know him.'

'Then, forgive me, sir, but what evidence do you have?' Harper pressed. 'Is there anything beyond what these two men told you? Anything in writing?'

'Well, no.'

'The men you talked to, what do you know about them? Do you have their names?'

'Jed Grainger and Bernard Van Duren. I met them in a bar down on the Bowery.'

Wherever that was, the inspector thought. It meant nothing to him.

'How did you come to find them, sir? And do they have a criminal background, do you know?'

'Someone told me about them, that they'd been telling this story about being offered a lot of money to do something.' He drew himself up. 'Yes, Mr Harper, they're criminals. What else would they be?'

'We have names now,' Lizzie Le Prince insisted. 'A trail for the capitaine to follow. You need to get this information to him.'

'Of course.' He nodded. 'Is there anything else you can tell me?'

'I found them in a place called Blecher's Tavern,' Adolphe said.

'Thank you, sir. Mrs Le Prince.'

He began the long walk back towards town. In the distance it looked as if a heavy cloud lay over Leeds, a pall of smoke choking the place off from the sky. What he'd been told could be something or nothing. Still, it might be useful for Muyrère. But he had no way of contacting the man, no address for him in America. All he could do was send a letter in care of the police in Dijon. Tomorrow, though; there'd be time enough for that then.

Finally, in Harehills, he was able to take the omnibus. A spattering of rain left drops on the windows. If much more fell and froze, he'd be skating to work in the morning.

Millgarth police station was busy. Three people were waiting to talk to the desk sergeant as he listened to a complaint from a fourth. Kendall was bent over a pile of papers in his office, reading, then signing them with a flourish.

Reed and Ash were waiting in the detectives' room, standing together in front of the fire and absorbing its heat.

Harper took off his gloves, unwound his muffler and shrugged off his overcoat. 'Found much?'

'Nothing at the lodgings,' Ash replied. 'Some clothes, two or three pamphlets and that's it. According to the landlady that's all he's ever had, too. No letters, no books, nowt.'

'Right.' The inspector looked at Reed. 'The Anchor?'

'You know the place has a reputation?' the sergeant asked. Harper nodded. 'There are flags and a picture of the Queen behind the bar.'

'So?' Those were everywhere; Annabelle had a photograph of the queen flanked with Union Jacks at her pub.

'A dozen more flags all round the place and a big map of the empire.'

He raised his eyebrows. 'Did they know Fields?'

'They wouldn't say at first. I had to insist a bit.' He gave a thin smile. 'But they know him, right enough. He's a regular, in there every night.'

'Was he in last night?'

'They weren't sure.'

'They're not sure or lying?' Harper asked.

'It was New Year's Eve, everyone was drinking. I think they're honestly not sure.'

'Who does he drink with? Did you get that out of them, at least?'

'There are three or four of them.' He looked at his notebook. 'Tim Hill, Jack Anderson, Robert Briggs.'

'Anderson?' The inspector repeated the name.

'Jack. Why?'

'I used to know someone with that name, that's all.' Maybe it was the boy he'd known growing up in the Leylands, the one who bullied Jews. It would certainly fit.

'Well, this one's been arrested a few times. So has Briggs. Fighting, assault, public drunkenness. Hill's been in Armley for taking a bottle to someone.'

'What about Fields?'

'Nothing much. Fined a couple of times. Drunk, fighting.'

Harper snorted. 'A charming lot.'

'And don't forget that Constable Dicks drinks down there, too,' Reed said.

'Is he friends with them?'

'The landlord didn't say so. But he's bound to know them.'

Ash coughed. 'If I can say so, sir, not many of the lads like Terry Dicks. He's a lean streak of piss and nasty with it.'

'Is he on duty today?'

Reed shook his head. 'Day off. I checked with Tollman.'

'I'll want a word with him when he's back at work tomorrow, too.'

'Fields's description has gone out to all the divisions,' the sergeant said.

'Send uniforms out to where the others on that list live,' Harper ordered. 'Bring them in. I want some men to go into the Anchor tonight, too. I doubt we'll find them but it's worth a try.'

'I can take care of that, sir,' Ash offered. 'I know who we can trust.'

'Good.' He nodded. 'Any more thoughts, Billy?'

'The landlord at the Anchor told me something curious. Fields and his friends were never there on Thursday nights. He didn't know where they went.'

'We'll find out when we question them. Right, anything else?'

Reed watched the inspector leave for the night.

'You'll be fine with going into the Anchor?' he asked Ash.

The constable beamed. 'Don't you worry, sir. It's Thursday, they might not even be there. But if they are, we'll get them. And if anyone gives us trouble . . . it'll be their loss.'

'Right. I'll leave you to it. Bright and early tomorrow.'

'I'm looking forward to it, sir.'

A cart had tipped its load out towards Hyde Park. Traffic was at a standstill. Reed fidgeted on the omnibus. They'd been stuck for ten minutes and they weren't going to be moving anytime soon. At this rate he'd do better getting off and walking across Woodhouse Moor. Another five minutes passed. He stood and climbed down into the cold. Anything was better than just sitting there. In the distance, across the grass, he could make out the lights of the houses.

SEVENTEEN

'**N**ine on Saturday?' Annabelle asked as they ate. Tripe and onions, hot from the oven, a winter meal to warm the belly.

'We'll see what the doctor says,' Harper said.

'I want to come with you, Tom.'

He nodded. Part of him wanted to go alone, but she was his wife. Whatever the truth and their plans for the future, she had to be there.

'I saw someone you know today.'

'Oh?' she wondered. 'Who?'

'Mrs Le Prince.'

Her eyes were full of curiosity. She put the knife and fork down on the plate.

'Well,' she told him, 'go on. You can't leave it at that.'

He gave her the short version, Adolphe and the men he'd met in New York.

'Do you believe him?'

'I've no idea,' he admitted. 'But it seems unlikely to me. The word of a pair of criminals? It doesn't help. I'll send the French police a letter. That's all I can do.'

He was about to say more when they heard the tramp of feet on the stairs and a light tap on the door.

'Dan must need something,' Annabelle said, rising, her dress swishing across the floor.

'Someone for Mr Harper.' He heard the voice and stood.

Kendall walked into the room. His face was pinched and serious, the top hat clutched tightly in his hands.

'Mrs Harper, I'm sorry to intrude, but I need a word with your husband.'

'Of course.' She flashed Tom a look. He had no idea why the super had come. The only time the man had been in the Victoria was for their wedding reception. Whatever the reason, it must be important.

'Sir,' he said.

'I've just come from the infirmary,' the superintendent began and Harper felt his spine stiffen. 'I'd been called down there. There was a do for children at some place in Wortley and a fire started.' Harper heard Annabelle draw in a sudden breath. 'Half of them were badly burned. While I was there a copper found me. They'd brought Billy Reed in. He'd been attacked up on Woodhouse Moor. He's unconscious, Tom. He's in a bad way.'

'Christ.' The word slipped out.

'I have to go out and see where the fire happened. You're in charge until I'm back. Call in as many men as you need.' An iron edge entered into Kendall's voice. 'Do whatever you have to do. *No one* hurts one of my men.'

'Sir?'

'I can't stay, there's a hackney waiting for me outside. Get yourself to the hospital, then to the station.'

'Yes, sir.'

He was gone, and Harper was reaching for his overcoat when Annabelle said, 'Elizabeth.'

He turned to stare at her.

'She needs to know, Tom.'

All he remembered was that she lived in Middleton. No address. He couldn't even recall her surname.

'I'll have someone send a message to the Middleton police. They might know her.'

'No,' she said firmly. 'I'll go out there and bring her to the infirmary.'

'It's dark. You don't even know how to find her,' he objected.

'Then I'll knock on every bloody door in Middleton!' Her eyes blazed. 'For God's sake, Tom, you don't want a copper telling her. Ted Lomax was downstairs earlier. He'll take me to the railway station in his cart and I'll catch a train.'

For a moment he thought about saying no. He didn't want her wandering around a strange place at night. But Elizabeth would need some kindness, a shoulder to cry on. And if it came to the worst . . .

'Just look after yourself,' he said, giving her a swift kiss before vanishing out into the bitter darkness.

*   *   *

They'd put Reed in a room on his own. The constable guarding the door saluted as the inspector arrived.

A nurse stood by the bed, holding a thermometer up to the light.

'How is he?' Harper asked.

She turned to face him, a hawk-faced woman with large brown eyes, wearing a severe uniform with a crisp white cap and apron.

'The same as when he arrived,' she answered calmly. 'Who are you?'

'Detective Inspector Harper. I work with the sergeant. What can you tell me?'

'I'm Sister Richards. Your sergeant has been beaten very badly.' She bit her lip. 'There are bruises all over his body. We've no idea what damage there might be inside.'

'Has he woken yet?'

The sister shook her head. 'He took blows to his head, too. He's still unconscious.'

'Has the doctor seen him?' Harper asked urgently.

'As soon as he was admitted, Inspector.'

'What did he say?' He was desperate, pressing for any kind of answer. Something definite, something hopeful.

'We don't know,' she answered, her voice professional and calm. 'With injuries like this you can't tell for a while. I've seen people wake up as if nothing's happened.'

'And others?'

'Sometimes there can be serious problems.' She hesitated. 'Or he might not wake up at all.' The nurse stared directly at him. 'I'm sorry, but that's the truth.'

Harper looked down at Reed. His body was covered by a sheet and blanket, a bandage wrapped around his forehead. His jaw was swollen, eyes closed and sunken. But he was breathing steadily. That was something.

'Sister . . .' he began but she shook her head.

'No, Inspector,' Sister Richards told him. 'I'm not even going to guess. But I'd pray if you're a praying man. It might help, and it can't hurt.'

'There'll be someone coming later,' he said. What could he call Elizabeth? 'She's the sergeant's fiancée. Let her sit with him.'

She looked doubtful. 'I don't know. That's very unusual.'

'He's a policeman. You just said yourself that he might die. Let her sit with him, please.' Reluctantly, she nodded. 'And as soon as he wakes up, can you send word to Millgarth police station?' *When* Billy wakes up, he thought, not *if*. When. When.

'Of course.'

He placed a hand on Reed's shoulder before leaving.

With no carts or omnibuses on the roads the hackney made good time. He was at the station within five minutes. Inside, men were moving around quietly, all of them looking grimly determined. What had happened to Billy Reed could have happened to any of them.

The night sergeant looked at him, and the inspector shook his head. No news. He strode through to the office, finding Ash waiting, standing by the fire and smoking a cigarette.

'What are you still doing here?' Harper asked.

'I heard the news when I came back from that raid on the Anchor. I thought I'd stay around and see what I could do to help.'

'Thank you.' He was grateful; he'd need all the men he could muster.

'What's the latest, sir?'

'Nothing new. He's still unconscious. Someone gave him a proper going over.' He saw the constable frown. 'Did you find any of them at the pub?'

'Came up dry. But like the landlord said, they're never there on Thursdays.'

'What about the houses? Did the constables check there?'

Ash nodded. 'Looks like they've all scarpered. Briggs was in lodgings but the other two are married men.'

'Do we have descriptions?' the inspector asked.

'Better than that, sir.' His eyes twinkled. 'I told the coppers who went out to ask for a photograph. We have those on Hill and Anderson.'

'Well done.' It was a simple idea but one that wouldn't have occurred to him. 'What else?'

'That's it, I'm afraid, sir. We've put the word out to all the divisions.'

Harper nodded. 'Where's the constable who found Billy?'

'Changing room, sir. Dare say he's having a cup of tea.'

'Did anyone take his statement?'

'It's on your desk.'

The inspector read it through quickly. Out on his beat, Constable Gerald Harrison, 624, heard someone yelling on Woodhouse Moor. When he investigated, he found a man unconscious and he blew his whistle to summon assistance. The police sub-station was only a couple of hundred yards away; someone had arrived within a minute.

'Let's talk to Constable Harrison, shall we?'

He was an older man, close to fifty and running to fat, thick fingers curled around a mug of tea. He'd unbuttoned the collar of his uniform. Four cigarette butts littered the floor around his polished boots. Probably a lifetime as a bobby, Harper thought. Harrison's flabby face was pale, blue eyes staring somewhere ahead. He stirred as the inspector and Ash entered.

'How is he, sir? Do you know?'

'Still unconscious,' Harper told him. 'It says in your report that you heard someone yelling on the moor.'

'That's right, sir. With no lights out there, took me a little while to find him.'

'Did you get the name of the man?'

'Didn't need to, sir. It was old George Willis. Known him for donkey's years.'

'So you don't think he was involved?'

'Him?' Harrison looked astonished. 'Never, sir. He just found the sergeant, that's all.'

'When did you realize it was Sergeant Reed?'

The constable chewed his lower lip. 'Not until we had him in the station. I went through his pockets and found his identification.'

'His wallet was in his jacket?' the inspector asked in surprise. He'd thought it was a robbery that had gone badly wrong.

'Yes, sir, and coins in his pocket. So we sent a message down here straight away.'

'What time did you find him? I didn't see it in your report.'

'Must have been a little after seven,' Harrison answered after a little thought. 'It was twenty past when we got finally him into the light, I know that.'

Harper pulled out his pocket watch. Twenty-five past eleven.

How long had Billy been lying there before someone found him? And why had he been walking over Woodhouse Moor? He knew the man's routine. Reed always took the omnibus to Hyde Park Corner. All too often he'd stop for a drink at Mould's Hotel.

'Was there anything strange out there tonight?' he asked.

'Strange, sir?' Harrison frowned, then his face cleared. 'There was a cart that lost its load. Backed all the traffic up for a good half hour. Had to keep my eye on that. It happened about six o'clock.'

'What time did the sergeant leave here?' the inspector asked Ash.

'Probably about half past five.'

A few minutes to walk and wait for the bus. He'd have been trapped in the traffic. Billy was never good at waiting. He'd have alighted and walked home to his lodgings, taking the quick way across Woodhouse Moor. But with the wallet still there, this was no robbery. So it had been deliberate. Revenge. The only thing he had worked on recently was the Leylands killings. Harper's mind took a leap. The sergeant had said Alfred looked as if he could see through him. What if he really had known all along who Reed was?

'Thank you, Constable,' Harper said to Harrison. 'You can go.'

In the office he sat and thought, staring at Reed's empty desk. Billy would be back. He'd recover. He'd return. Please God.

Alfred. Bloody Alfred.

The desk sergeant poked his head around the door. 'Inspector, there's a woman to see you.'

A woman at this time of night, he thought, then he understood; Annabelle, on her way home. 'Show her through, please.'

It might have been late, but she still looked lovely. Composed and perfect, hands warm inside a fur muff, a hat with a feather perched jauntily on her head, a long wool cloak over her dress. It was the first time she'd been here and her eyes took in everything. The old paint, coloured by years of smoke, the shabby desks, the notices pinned to the wall.

'Elizabeth is with him now,' she said.

'How difficult was it to find her?' Harper asked.

'Easy as you like,' Annabelle said dismissively. 'Her mam's going to take care of the children until everything's sorted out.

I told Elizabeth she could stay with us. We have that spare room.'

'Of course,' he agreed. It was the least they could do. 'At the infirmary I said they should let her sit with him.'

'She's torn apart, Tom. She really loves him. Spent half the time crying. I told her she has to be strong when she's with him. I saw him in that bed. He looks bad.'

'He is,' Harper agreed solemnly. 'Not that the doctors know much yet.' From the other side of the room there was a cough. 'Constable Ash, this is my wife.'

'Pleased to meet you, Mrs Harper.' He gave a nod of his head.

'Ash, Ash.' She pursed her lips and narrowed her eyes. 'Do you have a sister called Dottie?'

'Aye. Our Dorothy. She's older than me.'

'She was a cook at the Victoria when I started on there as a servant. Went to work for some family up in Chapel Allerton.'

'That's her,' Ash agreed. 'Left when she got herself wed. Has five nippers now.'

Leeds was a large town, Harper thought. Hundreds of thousands of people. But sometimes it seemed no bigger than a village.

Annabelle turned back to him. 'Small world, eh?' The brief smile left her face. 'If you go back to the hospital and Elizabeth's still there, send her to the Victoria, will you, Tom? I'll pay for the cab.'

'Of course.'

She kissed him quickly, arms around him, then let her head rest on his shoulder for a few seconds. He knew the thought in her mind; it could have been him.

'I'm going home,' Annabelle said. 'I'm exhausted. Come back when you can.'

Then she was gone. In the silence, Ash said, 'Who'd have credited it?' He sighed. 'Right, sir, how are we going to find the bastards who attacked Mr Reed?'

Harper rubbed his hands down his face. 'Did he tell you about Alfred?'

'Yes, sir.'

'I think he has something to do with this.'

'How?' He frowned. 'Why, sir?'

The inspector explained his theory and Ash nodded slowly.

'I still don't understand exactly why he'd want to do it, though.'

'To pay him out,' Harper said. 'He probably knew all along that Billy was a copper. As soon as it's light we need to go and look up on Woodhouse Moor. I want to see where it happened. Maybe we'll have a little more idea then. In the meantime, I want every constable hunting Fields and his friends.'

'Is there any more word about those children in Wortley, sir?'

The inspector shook his head. He hadn't had time to give it another thought since Kendall had told him. He glanced at the clock on the wall. A few minutes past one.

'Go home,' he said. 'Get some sleep. There's not much more we can do tonight. Be back at seven.'

'Yes, sir. If anything happens . . .'

'I'll send for you.'

He talked to the desk sergeant, looking at the day roster and arranging to pull men from their beats. He wanted an urgent sweep through Leeds for Field, Hill, Anderson and Briggs, one that wouldn't stop until they were found. Until they had some more clues they couldn't begin the hunt for Alfred. They'd almost finished when the officer whispered, 'Just coming in through the door, sir.'

Harper looked up. A pair of reporters, one from the *Yorkshire Post*, the other from the *Leeds Mercury*. Juniors, both of them. All the best reporters would be out in Wortley or at the infirmary. Both of them were young, their sideboards nothing more than down dusting their faces. They looked so eager, hopeful for a story that would help to make them known.

'Sergeant, do you think we could find these gentlemen a cup of tea? They look cold.'

Todd and Reeve. He'd met them before on cases when they'd sniffed around with their questions. He took them into his office and let them warm themselves by the fire, gave them tea and found some old biscuits in a drawer.

They all knew which story would fill the front page, but this would demand space, too, and the inspector fed them just enough. A policeman beaten unconscious. That was an outrage. Add to it the fact that he'd been investigating the murders in the Leylands, and hints that this had been revenge, and it had everything. Hints that the force knew who was responsible and were undertaking a hunt across the town.

He was certain they'd make the most of it. They were hungry to make names for themselves. They'd follow this and try to turn it into a sensation. He hadn't named the men they were seeking, but once the story was out, everyone would be looking. By the time they left he could see that the reporters were desperate to write their articles.

Almost two o'clock. He bundled himself in his overcoat and muffler and left the station, walking through the night up the Headrow. The rain had frozen into dangerous patches of ice on the pavement, reflecting the light from the gas lamps. Fog clung in places, hanging low and thick enough to taste. He coughed and moved on. The streets were empty, the only footsteps his own.

Elizabeth was sitting by the bed, holding tight on to Reed's hand. She turned as the inspector entered. Her face was haggard, the tracks of dried tears on her cheeks.

'Any change?' he asked quietly.

'Nothing,' she answered in a husky whisper. 'He won't wake up.'

'He will,' Harper assured her, hoping it was true. 'Just be patient. Look, why don't you go to the Victoria and sleep?'

'I need to be here.' She squeezed the sergeant's hand again.

'You go,' he told her. 'I'll sit here for a while.'

'Do you know who did it yet?'

'I have an idea, yes. We'll find them. Billy's one of ours, we're not going to let anyone get away with that. Come on, I'll make sure you get a hackney.'

She was reluctant to leave. Gently he guided her out to the street and gave the driver of the single waiting cab the address, slipping him money to cover the fare.

'Knock hard,' he said to Elizabeth. 'Someone will let you in.'

Annabelle would look after her. A hot drink, a talk, and a bed for her rest. He made his way back down the corridor to the room, treading quietly, exchanging a wink with a nurse he passed.

Reed's breathing was low, even and steady. The inspector stood at the foot of the bed, staring down at him. It hurt to see him this way, like a fist in the gut, taking the breath from him. Billy was more than another policeman. He was a friend, too. Finally he had to force himself to turn away and leave.

Harper found a press of people outside the children's ward. They sat in sorrowful silence, families gathered together. Harper could hear the high, pained cries from beyond the closed doors. The worst sound any parent could endure.

He moved past them and found Kendall sitting in a room with Superintendent Cross from D Division and Chief Constable Webb. The chief must have been dragged away from a night out; he was still wearing his black tailcoat, starched shirt and bow tie, hair carefully parted, shoes so polished they reflected the light. All three of them looked broken apart by what they'd seen.

Kendall motioned him in. 'How's Reed?' he asked.

'The same, sir.'

'Any leads?'

'It wasn't a robbery, sir. He still had his wallet when they found him. I think it has to do with Alfred. Revenge.'

He saw the chief constable's face darken.

'Revenge against one of my men? Who's Alfred?'

Harper laid it all out once more, sure in his mind that Alfred had been behind the attack.

'As soon as you have anything, put every available uniform on to it. What about these murders in the Leylands? Where are you on that?'

'I'm starting a sweep for the killers in the morning, sir. Now we know who they are, we can track them down.'

'Make it quick,' the chief constable ordered. 'We need them behind bars now. Do you understand?'

'Perfectly, sir. Any more word on those children?'

'Bloody awful accident, lad,' Superintendent Cross said, with the weight of death in his voice. 'The doctors say that more than half of those they brought in won't live.'

There was nothing any of them could say. Just the horror of so many young lives lost.

'Whatever you find, Tom, send word down here to me,' Kendall told him.

'Yes, sir.'

EIGHTEEN

He look the long way back to Millgarth, cutting through the courts and yards that ran between Lands Lane and Briggate. This had been his beat once. He'd been able to name the people in every house, known the men who ran each business. As he glanced down an alley he could pick out the silhouettes of a few figures crouched around a fire, passing a bottle. He breathed out, watching his breath cloud in the air. Good luck to them, he thought. If this cold weather continued, most of them would be dead before the end of the month.

There was little more he could do until dawn. He settled at his desk, taking a blank sheet of paper and dipping a nib in a bottle of ink. At least he could write to Capitaine Muyrère in care of his station in Dijon.

He sealed the envelope. How could he address it? Finally he decided on *Capitaine B. Muyrère, Police, Dijon, France*. It was the best he could do. He left it with the desk sergeant to post, and wandered by the market. Traders were already moving around the open square between the halls, setting up their stalls with fruit and vegetables, and carrying crates around as if they weighed nothing.

He dodged his way through them to the small café that opened every morning at four, its windows steamed over with condensation. The first rush had passed and he had a table to himself; he took his time over bacon and egg and two hot cups of tea. All for just a tanner. A breakfast for a working man.

As soon as the day shift reported for their beats he gave them their instructions. Who to look for, where to start. He picked up the photographs of Hill and Anderson, ready to let the men see.

Jack Anderson. He squinted at the picture. The man had the same heavy jaw and thin lips as the boy he remembered. So his character hadn't changed either, it seemed. It was no great leap from beating up Jewish boys to killing them.

After the constables had left, he stared at the photograph again. Anderson's father had been as bad as his son, he remembered, a man filled with poison. It could be worth finding out if his parents were still alive and where they lived.

Footsteps followed him into the office and as he sat, a constable stood to attention and saluted.

'Constable Dicks, sir. The sergeant said you wanted to see me.'

He had the ruddy face of a drinker, a map of broken blood vessels across his cheeks. The man probably wasn't even thirty yet, but he was already carrying weight around his belly, making the uniform too snug. But the blue jacket and trousers were clean and well-sponged, and he was clean-shaven and presentable.

'You drink at the Anchor,' Harper said.

'Yes, sir. Been my local since I was old enough to have a pint.' He stared straight ahead, not at the inspector.

'You've heard we're looking for four men who drink there.'

'I have. They've been coming in there a while, sir. Thick as thieves, that lot, always off by themselves. They don't mix, if you know what I mean.'

'Have you seen anyone else with them? Someone young, well-off?'

The constable frowned. 'Not as I know, sir. But I don't pay them much mind. I'm usually with my mates, not paying attention. You know how it is, sir.'

He did. Little groups that kept to themselves. It was the same in every public house.

'The Anchor has a reputation,' the inspector continued. 'It's not a friendly place if you're not English.'

'That's right enough, sir.' Dicks kept his eyes square on the wall.

'And you believe in that, do you?'

'Happen I do, sir,' the constable replied after a while. 'But as long as it doesn't affect my work, I think that's my business.'

Harper nodded his acknowledgement. 'We're after these men for murder. If you know where they might be, or if you do anything to stop us finding them, or anything against anyone, I'll have you drummed off the force and in jail. Do you understand me?'

Dicks shifted his gaze to look at the inspector. 'With respect, sir, I don't ask about your views on politics and the like, and I don't believe they'd affect what you do on the job. I know my work and I do it.' He stood straight, wounded pride on his face.

'I don't know anything about those men. If I hear anything I'll tell you immediately.'

'Good. You can go.'

God help him but he believed the man. His answers had the ring of truth. So much for that. He had to move on.

'Sir?' Ash's voice took him away from his thoughts. The man looked refreshed, as if a few hours' sleep had been more than enough. He had to admire the constable's stamina. Outside there was the first hint of early light.

'Let's go out to Woodhouse Moor,' Harper said.

A copper from the Woodhouse sub-station showed them the spot. The earth under their boots was like stone, the wind whipping in cold from the west.

'It was right round here, sir,' the bobby said.

There was nothing to see. The ground was too hard for foot-prints, no trees or branches close by. And it was far enough from any road to be completely black at night. No one around to see anything or spot any faces. Harper wasn't going to learn anything here. He'd never expected that he would, but he still needed to see it, to fix it in his mind.

'What do you think?' he asked Ash. The man twitched his thick moustache and took his time before answering.

'If you ask me, it must have been more than one man who attacked the sergeant, sir. Mr Reed was a soldier, he knows how to defend himself.'

The inspector nodded. Billy would have been able to fight off one. But not two, not in the darkness. Or there could have been three or four. Even five . . .

As they walked back to the station he gave Ash his orders. He wanted him in charge of the sweep, to keep the bobbies on track.

And what about Billy? How could he discover who Alfred was, and who he'd used for the beating? Christ, he felt absolutely useless. But he was going to find them. He'd make certain of that.

He forced himself to concentrate on the murders in the Leylands. Jack Anderson, he thought. How would he find where the family lived? Finally an idea came to him and he walked down to the Leylands, over to Noble Street. He passed the house where he'd grown up and knocked on the door of number twenty-seven.

The Burlands had lived here since before he was born. Only old Len was left now after his wife died two years ago. Harper heard the shuffle of feet, and then he was looking down at the man.

He remembered when Len Burland seemed like a towering man with thick muscles and a ready grin. Now he appeared to have shrunk into himself, not even coming up to the inspector's shoulders, his body withered by age. An ancient, embroidered smoking cap warmed his scalp, wispy wild hair poking out underneath, and a shawl covered his shoulders.

'You're Tommy Harper, aren't you?' he said, peering up. His voice was smoky, hoarse. 'Come in lad, come in.'

The kitchen was hot, a kettle sitting on the side of the range. Burland shuffled across the floor, and moved it on to the hob, standing over it as it began to steam.

'You'll stay for a cup of tea, won't you?'

He needed to be on his way, but he knew that tea and a chat was the price for information. The old man probably saw very few people. Company was a prize to be relished. The street, the area, had changed completely in his lifetime. The familiar had become foreign.

The tea was strong, a dark, rich brown. He sipped and looked up to see Burland staring at him.

'You're a copper now, they say. Made your way up.'

'That's right, Mr Burland.'

'I'd never have guessed you for a rozzer when tha' were little. Always having to give you a clip to keep you in line.'

'It must have worked.' Harper gave him a smile.

'Your mam and dad were that proud to see you in the uniform.' He shook his head. 'Aye, well. Memories are all well and good, but you're not here for them. Your face is too set for that.'

'No,' Harper admitted. 'I'm not. Tell me, do you remember the Andersons, Mr Burland?'

He was the last one left around here who would have known them. The inspector just had to hope that the man's memory was sharp.

'I do,' the old man replied with feeling. 'Nasty buggers they were, the pair of them.'

'They did a flit, didn't they?'

'Aye, long time back. You'd still be a nipper, then.'

'What happened, do you know? Where did they go?'

Burland scratched the white stubble on his chin. 'You're taking me right back now, lad. Behind with their rent, I suppose. That was the usual reason.' He shrugged. 'I don't even remember, it were that many years ago.'

'Did you ever hear where they went?' He knew it was a long shot, but it was the best that he had, the only direct link.

'Like as I recall, they went over round Mabgate somewhere. I seem to recall he had a brother over there or summat. Why the interest now, lad?'

'They had a son named Jack.'

Burland shook his head. 'If you say so. He doesn't ring a bell with me.'

Harper finished the drink and pushed the saucer away. 'I need to find Jack.'

'Good luck to you, then. It were what, twenty year ago?'

'More or less.'

'They could have moved on dozens of times since then. They were allus feckless.'

'It's a place to start.' He stood. 'Thank you for the tea. And the information.'

'It's nowt. I heard you got yourself wed.'

'Last year. She owns the Victoria in Sheepscar.'

Burland grinned, showing a single front tooth. 'You've got your head screwed on, lad. Can't go wrong if you marry a woman wi' a pub.'

Mabgate. It wasn't that far away, less than half a mile. The Anchor public house was in Mabgate. Clem Fields had a room there. The road called Mabgate was long and straight, going through the heart of the area, with the huge Hope Street foundry filling both sides, full of fire and thunder. A little further along, the Mabgate woollen mill pushed its face to the world. Carts moved along, pulled by horses, pushed by hand. An omnibus trundled away in the distance.

Harper walked through to the streets that lay behind the bustle. This was a place where people would know their neighbours. They'd remember names. He needed to speak to the older women; they were the ones who saw and remembered everything.

But before he had the chance to knock on any door, a boy dashed out of a ginnel, straight towards him, stopping just two feet away.

'Can you help me, mister?' he asked breathlessly. His shoes were too big for his feet, flapping as he ran. With thin knicker-bockers, no stockings, nothing more than a shirt and a jacket, he wasn't dressed for the bitter weather. Hair clung to his skull and his skin was almost blue with cold.

'What is it?' the inspector asked.

'Can you give us a farthing? I've not et since last night.'

'Why?' the inspector asked. 'Why haven't you eaten?'

The boy looked to be seven or eight, with clear blue eyes and sores around his mouth, the thinness of starvation in his bones.

'Me da and ma din't come home.'

He'd heard the story far too often. Back when he walked a beat there'd been so many children like this one. He'd go and find the parents and make them come home. But this wasn't his patch. He didn't know anyone here.

'Where do you live?'

'Just round the corner,' the lad answered warily. 'Why?'

'I tell you what I'll do,' Harper offered. 'You help me and I'll give you tuppence.'

The boy's eyes widened at the promise. A fortune. 'What do you want, mister?'

'I'm looking for a family called Anderson who might live somewhere round here. You ask and find out where they are and the money's yours.'

The boy smirked. 'That's easy. Go to Strode Street, back past Globe Works. Everyone knows 'em. Old fella and his missus. Third door along.'

Harper looked at him. 'You show me. If you're right, I'll give you sixpence.'

'A tanner!' The lad's eyes widened. 'I'm not lying, mister.'

'Then show me.' He took off his scarf and handed it to the lad. 'You look like you can use that.'

The boy looked at him, then took it and wrapped it around his neck. 'Come on,' he said.

The boy stood off to the side while the inspector knocked on the door. A thickset man answered, wiry grey hair standing up on his head.

'What do you want?' The words were a challenge. The man folded his arms, blocking the way into the house.

'You're Mr Anderson?'

'What if I am?' he asked.

'I'm Detective Inspector Harper from Leeds Police. Are you related to Jack Anderson?'

'Maybe. Why?' The man kept his hard stare.

'I'm looking for him.' The inspector looked back. 'Do you know him?'

'Jack? He's my brother's lad,' Anderson allowed. 'What do you want with him?'

'Where does your brother live?'

The man's face softened into sadness. 'He's passed away, both him and his missus. Five year ago. Why?'

'When did you last see Jack, Mr Anderson?'

'It was right before New Year. He's married, got nippers. Why, what's he done?' The man's fire and confidence had gone, replaced by worry.

'How long before New Year?'

'The evening before.' The night Rabbi Padewski was murdered, Harper thought.

'What time was he here?' the inspector asked cautiously.

The man scratched his head, thinking. 'Early. Come over to wish us the best before he went out with some lads he knows.'

And his family, wife and children, stuck at home. So many men were the same.

'Did you see him at Christmas?' he asked.

'Aye, he were here all day with his lass and the kiddies. Left about six, after their supper. We're all the kin he has.'

So he could have been out the night before, murdering Abraham Levy.

'Do you know his friends at all?'

Anderson shook his head. 'He has a life of his own, Jack does. Why would he tell us? Allus busy with this and that. I doubt that wife of his sees him much.'

That was what Jack Anderson's wife had told Ash when he questioned her. At home when he had to be, and not a second longer. It was what she knew, what she accepted with her husband.

'What's he done?' Anderson asked again

'I think he's been involved in two murders.' The inspector stared at the man, seeing the colour drain from his face.

'Our Jack? You're wrong there.'

'That's how it looks, sir,' he said. 'That's why I need to know where he might be.'

'Jack? He might have a set-to but he'd never kill anyone,' Anderson protested.

'Then I'd better talk to him and find out the truth,' Harper told him.

'He's not at home?'

'No. His wife says he hasn't been back since New Year's Eve. His friends have gone, too.' He paused to give weight to the question. 'Sir, do you know where I can find him?'

Anderson raised his head. He looked ten years older now. 'I don't, and that's the God's honest truth. But our Jack, he wouldn't do that.'

Harper thought of the boy who bullied the Jewish children at school and his father full of hate.

'Do you have any guesses as to where he might go, sir?'

'No, son, I don't.'

The boy was waiting at the corner. 'You really a copper, mister?'

'I am,' he said with a smile.

'You catch a lot of crooks?' He hurried to keep pace, shuffling in the large shoes.

'A few.'

The lad's eyes grew wide again. Harper felt in his trouser pocket for a sixpence and brought out a shilling instead. He tossed it up in the air. The boy caught it and looked at the coin disbelievingly.

'Get yourself something hot.'

'Are you sure, mister?'

'Positive.' He couldn't save all the waifs and strays on the street, but he could help one or two.

'What about your scarf?'

'Keep it,' he said.

NINETEEN

As soon as Harper entered the station people wanted to talk
to him. Before he could even remove his hat and coat they
were there: two constables with questions and Tollman
hanging back, waiting. He dealt with the men and turned to the
sergeant.

'Well?'

'Ash said to tell you there's nothing from the sweep yet, sir.'

The inspector nodded. 'Has the super been in?'

'Not yet. I heard he's gone over to Wortley. Terrible what
happened there, isn't it, sir?'

'It is.' He thought about the night before and the faces of the
parents he'd seen at the infirmary.

Sitting at the desk, he rubbed his face with his palms. Flames
jumped in the fire but he didn't feel any warmer. Tollman reap-
peared and put a cup of tea in front of him.

'You look like you can use that, sir.'

He was so tired that he couldn't think properly. But he needed
to keep his mind clear. There was so much to do to catch the
Leyland murderers and find whoever had attacked Billy Reed.

Alfred. He had to be the one who'd almost killed Billy Reed.
But he had no idea who the man might be. The man had money,
he was well-spoken and young, and he hated foreigners. It didn't
help much. Harper didn't even have a place to start.

He was draining the dregs from the cup as Kendall arrived. The
superintendent's face was almost grey as he passed through, into
his office. Harper followed. The man was slumped in his chair,
still wearing his heavy overcoat, hat tossed carelessly aside.

'Fourteen of them burnt, Tom.' He barely seemed to have the
strength to speak. 'Eight dead so far and there'll be more.' Kendall
shook his head. 'I've seen a lot in my time, but nothing like this.
They're all so bloody young.'

'I'm sorry.'

'It was an accident, too. That's all it was, nothing more. Just a

single moment . . .' His voice trailed off into emptiness. 'I stopped
in to see Reed before I left. No change yet. That girl of his was
still with him.'

'Elizabeth will stay there as long as they let her.'

'What have you managed to find so far?'

'Nothing yet, sir. I'm going to try all my snouts and see what
they've heard. If they know who Alfred is.'

The superintendent sighed. 'What about these murderers?' He
looked up. 'Tell me something good, Tom. I need it.'

The inspector listed the orders he'd given and his search for
Jack Anderson.

'It's all needles and haystacks,' Kendall said in frustration when
he'd finished. 'Any other ideas?'

'I wish I had,' Harper said helplessly. 'I've been racking my
brains.'

'Keep searching. But I want you to go back to the Leylands
sometime today,' Kendall ordered. 'Let them see you, so they
know we're concerned. Tell them we know who did it and we're
hunting them down.'

'Yes, sir.'

'With luck that'll satisfy them for now.'

'Sir?' Harper said.

'What?'

'You don't look too well. Maybe you should go home.'

Kendall snorted. 'I wouldn't dare. If I tried to sleep now I'd
just keep seeing those kiddies. I'm better off awake. If there's any
change with Reed I'll send someone to find you.'

Through the morning and for most of the afternoon he went to
every place he could think of; public houses, cafés, the men grouped
on street corners, huddled against the freezing weather. He asked
his questions so often that he felt he'd still be asking them in his
sleep. Had they heard anything about the attack on the sergeant?
What did they know about a man called Alfred?

But no one had any answers for him. They were telling the
truth, Harper was certain of that. Even with men on the fringes
of the law, someone trying to kill a policeman would loosen their
tongues. Yet there was nothing. The name Alfred brought nothing
more than shakes of the head.

Not a bloody thing. He was no further on than he'd been that morning. Harper could feel the frustration and the anger growing. Billy was more than another copper, he'd become a friend, someone he trusted with his life. And he couldn't even begin to find out who'd attacked him.

Finally, his voice hoarse and his feet sore from the miles he'd walked, he reached the Leylands in the late afternoon. There were people on the streets, running their final errands before the Sabbath began at dusk. Sewing machines still hummed in the sweatshops before going silent for a day. But the inspector could sense the mood: quiet and filled with sorrow. Men passing on the streets in dark suits, hats and beards glanced at him then away again. Women kept their eyes on the ground ahead. They knew full well who he was. No one would acknowledge him. No smile, no hello.

He found Constable Forsyth walking his beat on Templar Street. The man greeted him with a brisk salute.

'Any news of Sergeant Reed, sir?' he asked.

'Nothing new,' Harper answered. It seemed he'd said it a hundred times today.

'Do you know who did it?'

'Someone called Alfred. Young, well-to-do. Does it mean anything to you?'

The constable shook his head. 'Sorry, sir. What about the ones who murdered Abraham and the rabbi? Have you found them?'

'We're still looking.' He felt impotent, floundering and drowning.

'Some of the locals were out patrolling last night,' Forsyth said. 'Bobby Maitland told me this morning.'

The inspector let out a low breath. It was what he'd feared, people starting to take the law into their own hands. He didn't need this on top of everything else.

'How many, did he say? Who are they?'

'Not that many, sir. That's something, I suppose.' Forsyth frowned. 'Six of them. You know Abraham Levy's brother, young Samuel?' Harper nodded. 'He's one of them.' The man leaned close. 'Truth is, they're all scared, sir. I've been trying to tell them that we'll look after them, but . . .' He shrugged.

Fear and mistrust. It was a dangerous combination, he thought.

'I'll talk to Rabbi Feldman,' the inspector said. 'Maybe he can calm them.'

The doors to the synagogue still smelt of sap. Inside, a charcoal brazier was burning at the far end of the building, giving out a little heat in the frigid air.

Feldman stood, examining the scroll pulled wide in front of him, preparing for *Shabat*, the Sabbath. He was still wearing his overcoat and gloves, a yarmulke pinned to his thin hair. The rabbi pulled off his glasses and peered across the room.

'Inspector,' he said. 'Have you found them?'

'Not yet. But we know who they are now.' He approached the table where the rabbi was working. 'It's just a matter of time until we catch them.'

'Time.' Feldman gave a weak smile. 'That's something none of us really has, isn't it?'

'We'll find them soon enough. They'll hang,' Harper told him firmly.

'I hope that's true.' He frowned. 'What about your sergeant? I heard what happened.'

'He's strong. He'll pull through.' Harper clenched his fists as he spoke.

'May God be listening to you, Inspector. Sometimes I wonder if he's turned a deaf ear to the world.' He moved a wooden pointer across the scroll, over symbols in a language Harper couldn't read. 'Tomorrow at *shul* I'll tell them all to have faith. That they have to believe.' Feldman glanced up, eyes questioning under thick brows. 'But how can I do that when I'm not always sure myself?'

'Have you heard about the patrols, sir?'

'Of course. And before you ask, yes, I know my nephew's involved. I begged him not to do it. I ordered him, but he's not going to listen. None of the young ones will. They call themselves the Golem.'

'The Golem? What's that?' He'd never heard the word before.

'I'll tell you, Inspector, but you'd better sit down.' He waited while Harper perched on the seat, listening intently. 'Long ago, in Prague, all the Jews believed they were all going to be killed or expelled from the city,' Feldman began, the tone of his voice changing as he dredged the story from his memory. 'But they were lucky; they had a very wise rabbi, a man named Judah Lowe ben Bezalel. He'd studied hard, he'd read all the old texts, and he had an idea. He went down to the river, dug out some clay and made the figure of a man. The rabbi knew the right words to say, all the rituals to make the clay come alive, and he knew the *shem* – the name of God – to place in his mouth. And the Golem came alive. There are some who say the Golem did what he was made to do, and protected the Jews of Prague from harm. But others claim the Golem fell in love with a girl who rejected him and he began killing people himself. Whatever really happened, the rabbi took the *shem* from the Golem's mouth and it fell to pieces.' He paused. 'It's a story with a lesson, Inspector. Creation is a thing for God, not man. We don't have the power or the wisdom for it.'

'But they've taken the name.'

'Oh yes,' Feldman said wearily. 'That's the young, they only make out what's directly before them. They see the surface, they don't understand yet that there's far more beneath. Do you want me to tell people that you know who the killers are and that you're looking for them? If you want me to, I will. But it won't make them feel any safer. Do you know what safety is, Inspector?'

'It's what we give them,' he answered. 'The police.'

'No' The rabbi shook his head. 'If you're Jewish, safety's a bubble. Very fragile and easily shattered.'

Raised voices came from the back room of Cohen and Sons as he entered, the bell tinkling as he opened the door. The afternoon had grown so close to Friday evening that Harper was surprised the place was still open. The Yiddish words stopped abruptly and Cohen came through, his face red, trying to compose himself.

'Tom.' He took a deep breath.

'Your son?'

Cohen nodded. 'Israel. The boy's *meshugah*. Have you heard about this patrol?'

'The Golem.'

'Yes. He wants to go out with them. Do you know what my father would have done if I'd said that?'

Harper remember old Mr Cohen as a stooped, timid man, the soul of kindness.

'What?'

'He'd have hit me so hard I'd still be feeling it next week.' He pursed his lips and shook his head. 'All Israel tells me is that he has to do it.'

'Keep him away from them, Moses,' the inspector warned.

'Why? What do you know, Tom?'

'Nothing,' Harper answered. 'Honestly. But stop him for his own good. If they're out on the streets, sooner or later there's going to be blood.'

Cohen took off his spectacles and rubbed his eyes. 'I see.'

'I meant it, Moishe.' The inspector could hear the urgency in his own voice. 'If they carry on, I can guarantee that something will happen. People could die. The Golem is just a tale. This is real.'

'Of course.' He nodded. 'Thank you. I'll talk to him again.'

'Do. Please.'

Harper turned down North Street, heading home to the Victoria. With luck, Moses would stop his boy. Whether he did it by persuasion or force didn't matter, as long as he kept the lad at home. Sooner or later the Golem would find someone. Fear always bred violence; he'd been a copper long enough to learn that lesson. And that would bring even more violence, with the police picking up the pieces and trying to restore order. He'd gone twenty yards when he turned and retraced his steps into town, trudging along the Headrow to the infirmary. He was certain Elizabeth would still be there. He'd take her home with him. She needed rest.

So did he. He hadn't slept since the night before last. And in the morning he had his appointment with the doctor.

The cold drove through to his bones. Even marching, he couldn't feel any warmth. The air was thick and sooty, bitter on his tongue. The hospital came as warm relief, lights glowing softly in the gloom.

Elizabeth was still on her chair by the bed, still holding Reed's hand. She looked as if she hadn't moved since the morning. Billy was still unconscious.

'Come on,' he said gently. 'Let's go home.'

She followed without question, like a woman in a trance. In the hackney, Elizabeth looked around without seeing.

'I'm sure he knows you're there,' Harper told her.

'I can't feel him.' Her voice seemed far adrift.

'He's there. And don't you worry, we'll have him back, large as life and twice as ugly.' He tried to smile. He desperately wanted to believe his own words, to will it to happen. At the Victoria she

climbed the stairs like someone ascending a mountain. He held
the door and followed her through. Annabelle was waiting, rushing
to embrace Elizabeth and raising her eyebrows at her husband
with a question. He shook his head.

'Come and sit down, love,' Annabelle said. 'There's tea in the
pot and something to eat in the oven. You must be hungry.'

'I can't eat,' Elizabeth told her.

'Yes, you can,' Annabelle told her. 'You're not much use if you
get poorly, too.' She fussed and cajoled, putting a plate of oxtail
and potatoes in front of the woman, then placing the knife and
fork in her hand and standing over her like a mother with a child.

Harper ate hungrily, barely tasting the food but happy to have
it fill him. The fire was warm and lulling in the grate. Slowly, he
breathed out, letting the day leave.

'How are things moving along with the shop?' he asked.

'The carpenter's measured. Another week and he should have
the shelves up and he'll make a start on the counter,' Annabelle
said. 'The sign painter's coming on Tuesday.'

'Shop?' Elizabeth asked quietly. 'I didn't know you had a shop.'

Annabelle smiled. 'A couple of bakeries. It's nothing fancy.'

'You're opening another?'

'Just over in Burmantofts. See if it can make a bob or two.'

He'd forgotten that Elizabeth worked in a shop. Soon the women
were talking quietly, comparing ideas and experiences. At least it
brought her out of herself and had her thinking about something
besides Billy. Harper finished the cup of tea and rose.

'I'm off to bed,' he said. 'It's been a long day.'

The sheets were cold and his nightshirt felt awkward and uncomfortable against his skin. His mind wouldn't slow down, spinning
around everything he needed to do in the morning and delving
back, wondering whether he'd missed anything during the day. He
knew he should be out there, still searching, still trying to find
Alfred. But he was dog-tired, so weary that his whole body ached.
He had to rest, to come at it fresh tomorrow. And this time he'd
bloody well get somewhere. At least Elizabeth hadn't asked how
the search was progressing. He couldn't have lied to her.

Harper still hadn't drifted off when Annabelle slid under the
covers and pushed herself against him.

'Thank God you're warm,' she said with a small shiver, putting an icy hand against his face. 'What have they said about Billy at the hospital?'

'There's nothing they can do until he wakes up and they can see how bad it is. And they don't know how long that'll be.'

'Poor lass,' she said quietly. 'I gave her something to help her sleep. She needs it. When we came in on the train from Middleton she was telling me how her first husband died down the pit. If she could make Billy better by herself, he'd be up and running now.' She hesitated. 'Do you think he'll make it, Tom?'

'I hope so.' He stayed quiet for a while. 'At least the talk about shops made her think about something else.'

'I tell you what, she knows her stuff. If she lived in Leeds I'd hire her like a shot. Get a smile on her face and she'd be wonderful with customers.'

'Let's hope she has one soon.'

'Do you know who did it?'

'I think so,' he replied. 'But I don't know how to find him. Not yet.'

'You've not forgotten the appointment tomorrow, have you?' Her voice was taking on a dreamy, sleepy quality. He stroked her hair.

'No,' he told her. 'Don't worry.'

TWENTY

'Tilt your head to the side, Mr Harper,' Dr Kent ordered. 'A little further, please. Good.'

He felt awkward with his head resting against his shoulder. Exposed. His jacket was hanging on the back of the chair, and he could hear the doctor moving around behind him. Annabelle looked at him, bottom lip pinched between her teeth, reticule clutched on her lap, an inch of ankle and button boot showing under her gown.

The inspector had woken a little after four, groped for his clothes and left for Millgarth, the bitter air icy in his lungs. In the office he riffled quickly through the reports. Nothing new in the search for Fields and the others. He tossed them aside in frustration. The word was out on Alfred, rewards offered for any information on the attack on Reed. All the grasses had been told, but there hadn't been a peep yet. And no more word from the hospital. He had Tollman telephone the infirmary for a report. Everything was still the same; Billy hadn't woken.

By eight he'd toured the early cafés, talking to a succession of snouts, offering money for any leads. But it was as if Alfred didn't exist. No one had heard of him. He was sick of seeing people shake their heads.

At quarter to nine he walked across the hard ground of Park Square and into the doctor's office for his appointment. Annabelle was already there, thumbing through a periodical; she smiled as she saw him. She'd dressed in silk, a fashionable bustled gown of purples and lilacs that showed off her shape, corset laced tight, her hair wound up under a black velvet hat.

'We took a hackney and I left Elizabeth at the hospital,' she said.

'Anything more?'

She shook her head. 'I looked in. He's still the same. At least she slept last night.'

'You should take her over to the new shop with you,' he suggested.

'That's not a bad idea,' she agreed thoughtfully. 'I know she wants to be with him, but it would be good to drag her away for a little while. Maybe I'll do that.'

The elegant young clerk came to escort them to the consulting room. Harper's mouth felt dry. He was scared, afraid of what he might hear. As they rose, Annabelle gave his hand a small squeeze.

Kent listened carefully as the inspector recounted the problems with his ear, making notes on a page. He asked questions about the recent hearing losses, his experiences with other doctors, then had him sit on the chair that caught the light through the window.

'I'm going to examine your ear now, Mr Harper,' he explained, easing in the cold metal of an instrument and peering through a lens. 'There's plenty of wax there,' he said after a while. 'I can remove that and it will help, but it's not the cause.' And he asked Harper to tilt his head.

'This will feel warm,' the doctor said. 'It won't hurt. I'll put a little cotton wool in after. Keep it there for an hour.' It was an odd sensation, curiously pleasant. It relaxed him, and then he felt the cotton and his hearing vanished in the ear. 'You can raise your head now, and sit by your wife.'

'What did you put in there?' Annabelle asked.

'Just some olive oil, warmed slightly. Nothing remarkable.' Kent smiled. His appearance was immaculate, expensive and professional. A spotless frock coat and striped trousers, the crisp wing collar and black tie. His hands were scrubbed, nails clipped short, teeth white and even. Every inch a gentleman. 'You can find it at the chemist.'

'I have some at home,' she replied. 'I've always used it for earache.'

'It's good for quite a few things.' He moved his gaze and ran a hand over his chin. 'Mr Harper, I have to confess there's nothing I can see that would account for your problems.' The man's manner was formal and precise.

'What can I do, then?' the inspector asked.

'You have to understand, there's so much we don't know.' Kent steepled his pale fingers in front of his face. 'I can't tell you what causes the temporary loss of hearing you've been experiencing. And I'm afraid I can't guarantee it won't continue or grow worse.'

'So there's nothing,' Harper said flatly. He felt cheated, that he'd wasted his time coming here.

The doctor removed his spectacles and polished them on a snowy handkerchief. 'I wouldn't say nothing. Use the oil every week and keep your ears very clean. That will prevent the wax building up.'

'But?' Annabelle prompted.

'Your hearing will degenerate as you grow older,' Kent continued. 'That happens to everyone, of course. The blow you received affected something inside your ear. You already know that,' he continued before Harper could speak. 'It means the process will probably happen sooner rather than later. I've seen cases like this before. There will be more episodes of hearing loss but it will return, if that's some comfort to you. With luck, the worsening will take some time.'

'I see.' Kent was supposed to be the best in Leeds. He'd expected something more, somehow, some strand of hope for all the money they were paying. Instead, all he'd heard was the same thing he'd been told before. He was under sentence of deafness and no one could tell him when it would begin. He stood up. 'Good day, then.'

They stood on the steps outside the building. A few people were walking around, rich women wrapped in their furs, men strolling at their side. Carriages were parked along the road.

'I'm sorry, Tom. I thought he might have something.' She put her arm through his and they began to stroll up the street.

'So did I.' The years ahead looked bleak.

'Just as long as you know that whatever happens, we'll do it together.' Her fingers squeezed hard against him. 'You understand?'

He smiled, bobbed his head and kissed her. 'I do.'

Annabelle grinned. 'Anyway, you'll look handsome with one of those ear trumpets.'

He felt as if he'd been underwater and was slowly rising to the surface. But the distance seemed like miles and miles, each one a slow struggle. Finally he thought he was breathing air again and forced himself to open his eyes.

Everything was a blur. Colours, green and white that blended together, faint shapes he couldn't make out. He tried to raise his head but he didn't have the strength. He felt something touching his hand and a voice that seemed to come through tears.

'About time you woke up, Billy Reed. You've been sleeping long enough.'

He'd dreamed. He remembered that. Of places he'd been in the army. Barracks in York and Kabul. The warmth and the blue sea of Gibraltar. Travelling across to India in a ship. He'd even been able to smell the stench of the hold vividly, just as if he was there. He'd had conversations with old comrades, many of them long since dead, but with him in his mind.

'Billy?' He turned his head slightly towards Elizabeth's voice. Her face was still blurred, nothing even or clear, no matter how much he blinked. But it was better than it had been an hour before, he thought. 'I've missed you, love.'

He let his mouth ease into a smile and moved his hand to take hers. His whole body ached, it didn't feel like it belonged to him.

He'd dreamed about Elizabeth, too, he remembered suddenly. They'd been somewhere near the sea, somewhere sunny and peaceful. He strained for the details but everything evaporated like mist.

'How did you know I was here? Who told you?' It was still an effort to speak, to form the words and force them out. 'Water, please.'

He felt the cup against his lips, her hand supporting the back of his head and he drank, four gulps, then five, wetting his mouth and tongue and sliding smooth down his throat.

'Mrs Harper came and brought me,' she said.

'What about the children? Where are they?'

'Don't you worry about them,' Elizabeth said. 'Me mam has them. And the Harpers are looking after me. I'm staying at that pub of hers.'

She'd had to explain to him what had happened, how he'd ended up here. He hadn't lied, he simply had no memory of it at all. He'd been on an omnibus, he knew that. It had been stopped a long time. He recalled leaving it, the cold wind so sharp it could cut his face. And that was all until he woke up.

The doctor had examined him, shining a light deep into his eyes, testing his reactions. He hadn't said a word. Reed could hear people in the distance, the cry of someone in pain, feet moving swiftly. He'd been unconscious a long time. But he still felt tired.

'I need to sleep,' he told her.

'You go ahead, love. I'll be here.'

He smiled again and drifted away.

Harper spent an hour sending out squads of constables to search in twos and threes. Superintendent Kendall was back in Wortley. The toll of children who'd died in the fire was up to nine, another five not expected to last the day. The city was in shock; he'd seen the front page of the *Post* that morning, all the sorrow and questions. The assault on Reed had been a story on page two.

The Wortley tragedy was terrible, but he couldn't afford to let it touch him. He had too much to do. He was about to leave and go out searching, when Sergeant Tollman came through.

'There's a lady to see you, sir.'

'Who? Did she give a name?' It couldn't be Annabelle, he'd only left her a few minutes before.

'Mrs Le Prince, sir.'

The inspector sighed. He didn't have time for her. He couldn't do anything about the Le Prince disappearance; he'd banished it from his thoughts. But he needed to be polite. She moved in the right circles; she knew people. He sat her down and offered a cup of tea, then listened attentively as she spoke and produced several sheets of paper from her handbag.

'I've had a communication from a friend in New York, Inspector. Her husband has heard that Mr Edison has plans to file a patent on a single lens moving picture camera.'

'Isn't that what your husband intended to do?'

'Yes!' she said triumphantly, waving the letter. 'Don't you see, this is proof that he could have had my husband murdered!'

He knew she must be frantic, wondering what had happened. If she'd brought him something definite, he'd have helped her however he could. But this . . .

'I'm sorry,' he said gently. 'Is there anything to say this Edison has filed his patent?'

'No,' she answered with a sniff. 'He hasn't done it yet.'

'Then I'm afraid there's no evidence.' He turned as Tollman knocked on the door and slipped in.

'I'm sorry to disturb you, sir, but I thought you'd want to know. They've just telephoned from the infirmary. Sergeant Reed has regained consciousness.'

'Thank you,' Harper said, feeling the relief flood through him as he stood. Please God, Billy would be able to tell him what had happened. 'Make sure the super knows. And would you send word to Mrs Harper, please.' He turned to the woman. 'Mrs Le Prince, I'm afraid I need to go.' He'd never have a better reason for leaving someone.

'We haven't finished yet, Inspector. There's more.'

'I'm sorry,' he told her. 'It'll have to wait. This is urgent.'

Ash was waiting by Tollman's desk.

'Come on,' Harper told him.

The first snowflakes began as they walked up the Headrow.

'Ground as cold as this, it's going to settle,' Ash said, scuffing his sole over the paving stones. 'Going to be nasty later.'

'How do things stand? Any word?'

'Not as you'd notice, sir. There was a sniff of the murderers out towards Armley yesterday but it was nothing. They might have left Leeds.'

He'd considered that the night before, in the hours before sleep arrived. But his gut told him they were still here.

'Two of them are married, they have children. They're not going to run. Would you?'

'No,' Ash admitted. 'I'd want to see my family.'

'We have men on their houses in case they go back.'

'What about the ones who attacked the sergeant, sir? Any leads yet?'

'Maybe Billy remembers,' was the best reply he could give.

By the time they passed the Town Hall, there was already a thin covering of snow on the ground and the flakes flew against their faces. Inside the infirmary they shook themselves, leaving small puddles on the tile floor.

Elizabeth was sitting by the bed, stroking Reed's hand and talking to him in a soft voice. The sergeant's eyes were barely open. His face was thin and worn, the stubble a thick, dark colouring on his cheeks.

'You scared the hell out of us, Billy,' Harper said with a smile. 'I hope you're ready to get up now.'

'I might need a while yet.' His voice was a raw croak.

'You know I'm going to need to ask you some questions very soon.'

'I know, but I don't remember it, Tom. None of it.'

'Nothing at all?'

Reed gave a small shake of his head and the inspector glanced over at Elizabeth. She was frowning, glowering at him. He knew why; she'd just got her man back and he was stealing her precious time with him. But the sergeant was awake, he could speak and make sense, and Harper thanked a God he didn't really believe in. It would take a long time but he was on the mend. He reached out and patted the sergeant on the shoulder, trying not to show the disappointment he felt inside. He'd been relying so much on Billy being able to give him chapter and verse.

'You get some rest. You've got someone here who'll look after you.'

The inspector found the doctor talking to one of the nurses. He was a young man with a heavy beard and an intense, hunted look on his face. The best he could manage was hope.

'He's woken well. But it's going to take a while, Inspector. We still don't know if there's lasting damage.'

With a nod Harper left, jamming the hat on his head as they walked back out on to the street. The snow was coming down thick as fog; he could barely see ten yards ahead. But not pure, not white. In Leeds it was always fell grey and ugly, tainted by all the smoke in the air. Already, horses and carts were beginning to slip on the cobbles. Traffic would soon be at a standstill. He hunched his shoulders inside his coat.

'What do you want to do now, sir?' asked Ash.

He didn't know. He truly didn't know.

TWENTY-ONE

'**S**ir.'

Harper had only taken a pace inside the door at Millgarth before Tollman was calling him. The inspector tried to brush the layer of snow from his shoulders and stamp it off his boots.

'What is it?' he asked as he wiped moisture from his face.

'There's a body. It sounds like it could be Fields.'

The inspector looked at Ash and the constable raised his eyebrows questioningly.

'Where is it?' Harper asked.

'Meanwood Road, sir. Out just past the leather works and the Methodist chapel.'

'How long ago did they find it?'

'A bit over an hour or so, sir.'

'Right, we're on our way.'

'Sir?' Tollman said.

'What?' he turned in exasperation.

'How's Sergeant Reed?'

'He's awake, right enough, and talking. Making sense, too.'

Tollman grinned 'That'll be a first for him. It's good news; I'll pass the word, sir.'

*   *   *

At least the tram was running along Meanwood Road. People were crammed inside, avoiding the cold of the open upper deck, the air heavy with the smells of wet wool and sweat. Harper stood, clinging tight to a leather strap and watched Ash talk to the conductor as if they were old friends.

The constable had all the makings of a good detective, there was no doubt about that. He asked the right questions, had a sharp eye and the kind of easy manner that drew people out without them even realizing. They needed more like him, ones who thought on their feet. His size didn't hurt, either. His eyes might twinkle and he smiled a lot, but he was tall and broad enough to make people think twice before challenging him.

Harper leaned forward, trying to pick out any landmark through the window. Someone had pawed at the glass, trying to wipe away the condensation. But the snow was so heavy it was difficult to be certain of anything. Finally he heard Ash call out and he threaded his way through the people.

'It's right around here somewhere, sir.' They moved slowly up the street. At first, the warmth from the bodies on the tram made the flakes melt on them. Within a minute it was clinging and coating them in white.

'Over there.' Harper pointed into the murky distance beyond an imposing stone building. 'That looks like waste ground.'

Ash sniffed. 'Right by the leather works, too. Can't mistake that smell, can you?'

The copper looked like a white statue. His cap and cape were covered with snow, only the face showing a frozen pink.

'I'm Detective Inspector Harper. You have a body here?'

The man moved, the flakes cascading off him as he brought his arm up for a salute. So bloody young, the inspector thought. He barely looked old enough to grow the moustache intended to make him look mature.

'It's behind there, sir.' The bobby gestured at a small hillock in the middle of the waste land. A sapling with bare, thin branches struggled on the summit. 'Some lads were on their way up to the park and stopped here to play king of the castle. They're the ones who found him.'

Harper led the way, crouching down and rubbing dirty snow off the body. Pale hair, white skin that was icy to the touch. It could be Fields. He lifted one of the man's hands close to his face and the strong stench of fish hit him.

'It's Fields.'

'Makes you wonder who killed him,' Ash said slowly.

The inspector kept brushing until he could see all the man's body. There were marks on the neck. He shifted the head for a clearer look. 'Strangled. Probably happened right here.'

The uniform had turned away, deliberately not looking. It was probably the first murder he'd seen.

'What houses are there in the area?' Harper asked.

The constable gulped in a little air. 'The streets over there are the Serbias and those are the Herberts back behind the chapel, sir.'

'You know the people?'

'Yes sir, this is my beat.'

'Get yourself round the houses and start asking if anyone saw or heard anything last night. If you're lucky, they'll give you a cup of tea. If you find anything, send word to Millgarth.'

'Yes, sir.' He marched away.

'What are we going to do with this one?' Ash wondered.

'One for King's Kingdom, I think.' It was their name for the office of the police surgeon, Dr King, over at the station in Hunslet. 'See what he can tell us. You stay here, I'll have him picked up as soon as possible.'

'Yes, sir.'

No objection, no resentment at standing out in the cold and snow, Harper thought. Ash would make a bloody good detective.

Reed didn't know how long he'd slept, but when he woke his vision was a little clearer. It was still blurred, but he could make out more detail. And Elizabeth was there at the bedside waiting for him.

'Feel better?' she asked. He did, he realized. Stronger. More a part of the world. He frowned, trying to remember.

'Was Tom here before?'

'Yes,' she told him. 'You said you didn't know what happened when you were attacked.'

'I don't.' He shook his head gently. 'I really don't.'

'Don't you worry about that for now, Billy. I've got something for you to eat. You missed dinner, so it's gone cold. But it doesn't look too bad. Come on.'

Tenderly, she eased him up until he was sitting, plumping the pillows against his back. He looked around the bare room, able to discern the shape of a table, the bedstead, her hair pulled back into a bun.

She fed him like a baby, spoonful by spoonful. It was soup of some kind, still faintly warm, thick and nourishing. As he began to eat he realized how hungry he was, chewing the slice of bread and swallowing it eagerly, washing everything down with tea that was barely lukewarm. When he finished Elizabeth mopped around his mouth with a serviette.

She left him with a nurse when he needed the bedpan, and sat with a sigh when she returned.

'It's snowing. Must be two or three inches. Nothing's moving out there.'

He could picture it. Silent, empty, only ghosts around, footprints quickly covered, as if they'd never been there.

'Do you remember what I asked you on Boxing Day?' Elizabeth asked.

He tried to recall. They'd talked about many things.

'No,' he answered honestly.

'I asked what your intentions were.' She hesitated. 'It's just that all this, it's made me think, Billy.'

'What?' he asked slowly, not certain he wanted to hear her reply. His gut lurched at the threat of losing her.

'Seeing you there, not knowing if you'd wake up and wondering what would happen if you . . .'

'I'm here,' he assured her, twining his fingers through hers.

'I know you are. But it made me understand. I always want you here. What if Mrs Harper hadn't come for me? I wouldn't even know what had happened. You could have died and I'd never have found out. I've already lost one man.'

'I'm a copper.' He felt breathless and desperate. 'Things can happen.'

'I know that, love.' Her voice was calm, soothing. 'I'd not stop you from doing that any more than I'd have stopped Martin going down the mine. But I love you. I've fallen for you. And I don't know what you want.'

'I want you,' he told her and he believed it with all his heart.

'Do you?' Elizabeth asked. He could hear the plea in her voice. 'I need you to be honest, love. Don't just tell me what you think I want to hear.'

'I want you,' he repeated, not sure if she was crying or not. He could make out a hand reaching into the pocket of her dress, then swiping at her face. Reed felt like one of those men he'd seen at the circus, walking along a high wire. One slip and he'd be falling and falling, away to the ground.

She sniffled and caught her breath, then moved and quickly kissed him. 'Mrs Harper said something when we were coming down here this morning.'

He could taste her on his lips. 'What?' His voice was a croak.

'She's opening another bakery. She said that if I lived in Leeds she'd ask me to manage it for her.'

'Where is it?'

'Burmantofts.' Elizabeth's tongue stumbled over the unfamiliar word. 'Is that right? That's what she told me, any road. Do you know it?'

He waited a moment, wanting to be sure of what he was about to say. 'We could get married. You and the children could move to Leeds.'

She was silent for a long time. He wondered what she was thinking, hoping it was the same as him.

'We don't have to.' She sounded tentative, trying to find her way around the thoughts in her head. 'We can live over the brush if you want. I don't mind, Billy. Really, I don't.'

'Whatever you want,' he told her, feeling the exhaustion creep over him. 'I need to sleep some more. You go and talk to Mrs Harper, see if that job's still open.'

Harper sent the cart to collect Fields's body. Later he'd walk over to Hunslet and see what Dr King had discovered. He shrugged off his coat, scattering snowflakes across the floor to melt. Kendall gestured from his office.

'Close the door, Tom.'

He turned the knob, cutting out the noise from outside.

'Have you been to see Reed?' the superintendent asked.

'As soon as I knew he was awake. He can talk, but he doesn't remember what happened.'

'That's common enough.' Kendall grimaced. 'Maybe it'll come back to him in time. What about the body?'

'It's Fields. I could smell the fish on him.'

'What do you make of it?'

'I wonder if he's a sacrifice.' He'd had time to consider it on the walk back into town. 'Maybe his friends think if we have his body, we won't bother going after the rest of them.'

'Friends.' The superintendent snorted.

'Something that puzzles me, sir,' Harper said.

'What?'

'Why were they out Meanwood way? None of them live there.'

'Maybe that's why they were there. Staying out of the way.'

'Perhaps,' the inspector agreed. 'I'm going to have Ash go through all the pubs out there, to see if anyone knew them.'

'That's a good plan.' Kendall nodded and let out a slow breath. 'The funerals of the kiddies out at Wortley are going to start on Monday.' He glanced out of the window at the falling snow. 'Even in this.'

'It'll never be the same out there, will it?'

'No,' the superintendent agreed grimly. 'You know, they're already arresting con men in Wortley. They say they're collecting for a memorial. They won't be the last, either. You think you've seen how evil people can be, and something new comes along.'

'We'll never be out of a job, that's for certain.'

'Sometimes I wish that wasn't true. What about the attack on Reed? Any progress?'

'Not yet. I can't even find a single lead on Alfred. No one's even heard of him.'

'Keep pushing,' Kendall told him. 'I need results.'

The quickest way to reach Hunslet was to walk. With Ash at his side, Harper crossed Crown Point Bridge over the River Aire. Snow swirled around them and the bitter wind blew hard.

The police station was down Hunslet Road, a building of soot-blackened brick. The inspector pushed open the door and turned to go down a staircase, then along a corridor that smelt of carbolic.

Harper could hear a wavering voice behind a door singing something he didn't recognize.

'I didn't know Dr King liked opera,' Ash said softly, his voice echoing on the tiles.

'He's an odd man.'

Now somewhere around eighty, the police surgeon had been in his job for years. He was a commanding presence, with a voice that boomed and demanded, but he possessed sharp eyes and a quicksilver mind. He ruled down here. King's Kingdom. It was no place for the faint-hearted. He dissected bodies and carried out his experiments on stray limbs and organs; no one dared to ask where they came from.

The inspector pushed open the door and entered. King had Fields naked on the slab, flesh so pale the blue veins seemed to shine through his skin.

'I was wondering how long before you'd be down here,' the surgeon said without turning. 'I know what you're like. Always impatient.'

'What have you found, sir?'

'You can see for yourself, the marks on his neck. Strangled from behind. He put up a fight, though. There's flesh under his fingernails.'

'When did it happen?'

King frowned as he wiped his hands on a dirty rag. His waistcoat and shirt were spattered with blood and other stains; there was something yellow on his collar.

'Last night,' he said slowly. 'It's difficult to be certain with the weather. I can't be more exact than that.' King glanced at Ash. 'Someone new?'

'Constable Ash. We're trying him out as a detective.'

'Welcome, lad. At least you haven't passed out. Most of them do, the first time here.'

'You'll have to do better than this, then, sir,' Ash said with a grin.

'I could, don't you worry about that. I've spent most of today looking at the bodies of those children who died in the fire. This actually makes a pleasant change.' He paused. 'That sergeant of yours has come round, I hear.'

'Yes. And he's talking.'

King nodded. 'That's a good sign. They'll look after him at the infirmary.'

'I hope so.' He paused. 'What else can you tell me about Fields?'

'Is that the one on the table? Well, if you don't know he worked with fish, you're a worse detective than I imagined. Gutting them or something, I'd guess. There are small scars all over his hands and arms. I thought he might be an albino at first, but he's not. Malnourished, of course, but that's nothing remarkable. I can cut him open and tell you his last meal if you like,' the doctor added wryly.

'No need, sir.'

'For right now, that's all I can manage, then,' King said gruffly. 'Miracles cost more.'

'Pity I'm on a policeman's salary, then,' the inspector said, and the doctor chuckled.

Outside, the wind blew snow hard into their faces as they set out towards the river.

'Is he always like that, sir?' Ash asked.

'No. You caught him on a good day,' Harper replied.

TWENTY-TWO

R eed was sleeping when the inspector arrived. Elizabeth was dozing, too, head down on her chest, hands gathered primly together in her lap. Harper tapped her lightly on the shoulder and she stirred.

'Come on,' he whispered. 'Let's go back to the Victoria.'

'But—' she started to object.

'Billy's going to need plenty of rest. He'll still be here tomorrow.'

For a moment he thought she might refuse, but she gathered up her coat and followed, stopping at the door to glance back. Elizabeth stayed quiet in the hackney, watching the snowy streets. It was already dark, so little traffic around that Leeds could have shut down. The cab moved slowly, the driver preferring caution over speed. Harper directed him to Marsh Lane before going on to the Victoria, to Lewis's shop for three portions of fried fish and chips.

She followed him up the stairs and into the rooms above the public house. He took her coat and hung it on the peg, and picked up a poker to push it into the banked fire.

'I'll do that,' Elizabeth offered. 'Make myself useful.'

'I'll find some plates,' the inspector said. 'I don't know about you, but I'm starving.'

She smiled, the first expression he'd seen on her face that day.

'I could murder a cup of tea.' Elizabeth stopped herself, put a hand over her mouth and reddened. 'I suppose I shouldn't say that to a copper.'

He filled the kettle and settled it on the hob, then took the food out of the newspaper, searching in the drawer for knives and forks. Harper heard the door close and Annabelle's voice. He sensed her behind him, then felt her arms around his waist.

'Fish and chips and making tea?' She kissed the back of his neck. 'You must be looking for a job here. I'm sorry, love, but my servant's position's already filled.'

'You couldn't afford me, anyway.' He handed her a plate.

'I'm sure we could come to an arrangement.' She winked, looked around and asked in a hushed voice, 'How is he? Thank you for sending me the message.'

'He's been awake and speaking, and he seems like Billy. Fingers crossed.'

'That must be a weight off her mind,' Annabelle whispered and went into the parlour, sitting at the table. Fish and chips was a working man's supper, hot, filling and cheap, and just the thing for a bitter, snowy night.

'It's good news, isn't it?' Annabelle said to Elizabeth. She nodded her reply, wiping the start of tears from her eyes.

'He can't see properly yet, not clearly, but it's getting better. And he's sleeping a lot.'

'That's natural, the nurse said,' Harper told her.

'Yes, she said that to me, too.' She looked at Annabelle. 'Thank you. For coming to fetch me. For everything.'

'It's nothing. You and Billy, you're family.'

'We talked a bit when he was awake,' Elizabeth began hesitantly. She took a drink of tea. 'We might get married.'

'Really?' Annabelle asked, eyes widening with pleasure. 'He meant it?'

'I told him we didn't need to be wed.' She blushed a little. 'I just want to be with him.'

'However you do it doesn't matter,' Annabelle agreed. 'Men never understand that, do they? Daft as brushes, the lot of them.'

'You live in Middleton,' Harper pointed out.

'I know.' Elizabeth lowered her head. 'But . . . Mrs Harper said something to me yesterday.'

He looked at his wife and saw she was smiling.

'About the shop?' Annabelle asked.

'Yes. I . . . I didn't know if you really meant it.'

'Oh, I did, love. The job's yours if you want it.'

Harper sat and listened as the women talked. He finished the meal, letting it settle warm in his belly, and drank the tea, reaching to pour himself another cup. Within two minutes they'd moved on to finding a house to rent, where the couple should live with enough room for the children, when Elizabeth could start work.

'It'll be a while before Billy's back at the job.' He spoke into a brief moment of silence.

'Doesn't matter, Tom,' Annabelle told him. 'She'll look after him. And you'll have him good as new again when he's ready.'

The two of them didn't need him here. They were busy making their plans. He slipped out of the room and down the stairs, scraping away the frost on the inside of the landing window to look into the darkness. The snow had stopped but it lay thick on the ground. Roundhay Road was deserted.

The bar downstairs was subdued, dotted with the few regulars who'd appear no matter what. A fire burned in the hearth, a full coal scuttle standing next to it. Two old men playing dominoes, a pair of widows with their small glasses of stout. One or two others scattered around.

'We won't make any money tonight,' Dan said. He was standing behind the bar, reading the evening newspaper. 'Pint, Tom?'

He stood at the bar, sipping and chatting, nodding to those he recognized. A cabbie came in needing a warm, downed a glass of gin in a single gulp and left again.

'I'll be glad when this weather breaks,' Dan sighed. 'I can't remember the last time it was this dead.'

'Give it a few days. It'll pass,' Harper told him.

'Aye, in time. She won't be happy when she sees the takings, though.'

'I think Annabelle has other things on her mind right now.'

Billy married, he thought. That was a turn up for the books. He knew the sergeant liked Elizabeth but he'd never really spoken about her. Not that he ever said much about himself; still, the man had always seemed a confirmed bachelor. He'd visit the infirmary again in the morning. He needed to see if he'd remembered anything about the attack. Or about agreeing to marry. God help him if he'd forgotten that.

But it didn't bring him any closer to finding Alfred. He was going to need Reed for that, for some memory to appear. Either that or more luck than he'd ever known. He was going round in circles and finding absolutely nothing. He was failing and it hurt.

The inspector dawdled in the bar, making occasional conversation and sipping the beer. Half an hour passed, long enough for the women to put everyone's lives in order. Finally he pushed the glass away and climbed the stairs.

The parlour was empty, the door to the extra bedroom closed. Annabelle was in the kitchen.

'Elizabeth gone to bed?' he asked.

'She was flagging, poor thing.' She turned and gave him a peck on the cheek as she washed the plates. 'Married, eh? Who'd have credited it?'

'Not me.' He leaned against the counter. 'But she'll be good for him.'

'How's your ear?'

He shrugged. He'd been too busy to give even think about it since morning. An hour after leaving the doctor's office, he'd removed the cotton wool, seeing it bright orange with wax. But his hearing was just the same; no better, no worse.

Annabelle dried her hands and turned to look at him with hungry eyes. Her lips curled in a sly smile and she began to lift the front of her dress, showing stockings all the way to the knee.

'What colour garters today, Tom? Take a guess.'

'Red,' he answered. His breath felt tight in his chest.

'If you're lucky you'll find out in a minute.'

*   *   *

When Harper woke, everything was silent. He sat up slowly, careful not to disturb Annabelle. It was Sunday. The factories were all still for the Sabbath, the shops closed. He washed, brushed his teeth with Jewsbury and Brown's dentifrice, and dressed quietly, cutting a thick slice of bread and spreading it with jam before putting on his overcoat, muffler and hat. Almost quarter to six by the clock in the parlour. No rest for the wicked. Or for the police.

At least the wind had dropped outside, but a good four inches of snow covered the street and thick grey clouds hung low with the threat of more to come. He set off walking towards Millgarth, chewing as he moved. God only knew when he'd eat again today.

There was no traffic on the roads and hardly any footprints showing on the pavements. For a while, at least, felt as if he had Leeds to himself, the only person alive among all the buildings. With no chimneys belching smoke, the air felt a little cleaner, and the smudged white coating made the place feel fresher, like a coat of paint over something old and tired.

The restful mood evaporated as soon as he walked through the door of the police station. He was surrounded by noise and light and the smell of wet woollen uniforms. In the office he went over the reports. Nothing. All they had was Clem Fields's body from the empty ground in Meanwood. Not a hint of Hill, Briggs or Anderson.

And no Alfred.

A constable brought tea. He read and thought. They needed to flush the men out somehow. He was still pondering it when Ash arrived, freshly shaved, his moustache trimmed, suit carefully brushed clean.

'I want you to go to all the pubs along Meanwood Road,' Harper told him. 'Bang on the doors if you have to. Take those photographs you have. See if any of the landlords recognize them.' It was a long shot. He knew that. But Fields's body had been found out there. It was slender but it was something.

Right now, anything was worth a try.

At eight he walked along the Headrow, Ash at his side, past the empty Town Hall to the infirmary. The gas lamps still glowed; dawn might have broken but Leeds was still sullen with darkness. He stamped the snow off his boots and strode along the corridor.

'Wait out here,' he told the constable.

Reed was sitting up in bed, pillow plumped behind him. The bruises on his face had darkened but he looked more alert, turning his head to the sound of the door opening.

Harper stopped and stared at him. 'For a condemned man you don't look too bad, Billy.'

The sergeant blinked. 'Condemned? What? What are you talking about?'

'I hear you're getting wed.' He sat on the chair. 'Congratulations.'

'True enough.' He gave a raw chuckle, his voice still rough and gravelly. 'I love her, Tom. I want to be with her.'

'Then good for the pair of you,' he said with a grin. 'I'll warn you, though, she and Annabelle were discussing all the details last night. Thick as thieves.'

'Does she . . .' He tried to clear his throat, reaching for a glass of water and taking a long swallow. He moved slowly, as if everything took great effort. 'Does she have the job?'

'Apparently so. Looks like you're going to be moving.'

Reed grinned. Two of his teeth had been knocked out, leaving black gaps in his smile. 'I don't mind.'

'Just as well.' He paused. 'We found one of the killers. Fields, the fish gutter.'

'Where?' He was curious, the first hint of the outside world, his real world, in days.

'Meanwood Road. He was dead. Strangled. My guess is one of the others did it.' He paused. 'The attack. I need to know, Billy. I'm sure it was Alfred.'

'I've tried.' The sergeant shook his head in frustration. 'Really, Tom, I've tried. I just can't remember it at all. The last thing I know I was on a bus that had stopped.'

'There must have been more than one of them.'

'I don't know,' he said emptily. 'I can't remember. None of it.' He tried to bunch his fingers into a fist but the bandages stopped him. 'Bloody nothing.'

Harper began talking urgently. 'It must have been revenge. Had to be.' He listed the reasons on his fingers. 'You weren't robbed. That's strange enough. So someone was after you, and this murder is the only thing you've been working on lately.' The inspector sat back, straightening his jacket. 'You said Alfred looked at you as if he knew you.'

'Maybe,' Reed admitted after a few moments. 'He scared me, I remember that.'

'It wouldn't have been too hard to follow you from the station.'

'Tom,' Reed pleaded, 'if I knew, I'd tell you.'

'Just keep trying, Billy, please.' He was about to say more when the door opened and Elizabeth walked in. She'd borrowed one of Annabelle's dresses, too tight around her waist, the hem damp and trailing on the floor. She hesitated, unsure whether to enter.

'Come in, love,' Reed told her and glanced at the inspector. 'Tom, I'll try.'

Harper nodded and stood.

'It's wonderful news.' He looked at Elizabeth. 'I don't envy you keeping him in line, though.'

She smiled. The sleep had taken the strain out of her face. 'I'll train him well, don't you worry about that. Right, Billy?'

'We'll see,' the sergeant said happily.

'What did he want?' she asked as she settled on the chair. She took off her coat then unpinned her hat from her hair, and rested them on the bed.

'To see how I was. He's a good friend, you know that. And he needs to know if I'd managed to remember anything.'

'Have you?' she asked, her fingertips stroking her arm.

'No.'

His vision still wasn't right. For a few seconds his eyes could pick out every detail of her face, then it would start to wobble a little. A few more days, that was what the doctor had told him on his rounds. He'd given Reed a full examination then declared he'd been lucky; there didn't seem to be any lasting damage. Even so, it would be weeks, maybe a month or two, before he'd be ready to return to work. Time to mend and regain his strength.

Earlier, when he was alone, he'd slowly pushed back the covers and tried to stand. But he simply didn't even have the strength to push himself to his feet. He was an invalid. A baby. Weak.

It gnawed at him. Shamed him. How the hell could he have let someone jump him that way? He'd been a soldier, he knew how to fight. But instead he'd been beaten bloody and broken, and he couldn't even recall it happening. Now he was stuck here, useless to the world, in a place where he spent his days breathing in the bloody carbolic soap they used everywhere.

The only good thing to come from all this was Elizabeth. Married. Six months before, he'd never have believed it. But he had no regrets, no second thoughts about proposing. Becoming a father to her children terrified him, but he'd manage. He'd do his best.

'I love you,' he said.

TWENTY-THREE

The black bulk of the Town Hall brooded behind them, the snow deep and dirty on the pavement. Harper looked longingly across the Headrow to the Victoria Cocoa House. The windows were dark, the place closed. Sunday.

'I could use a drink of that,' he sighed.

Ash smiled. 'Something warm, sir? Come with me.'

He crossed the road and cut down a small alley that led off Park Row to a tiny yard. He brought his fist down three times on a wooden door, paused, then three more times before turning to wink at the inspector. After a short wait, Harper heard a key turning and the door dragged open.

'Mr Ash!'

The man was small, and clothed in layers of rags. His face was grubby with ingrained dirt, his hands mostly hidden in fingerless gloves. He ushered them into a warm kitchen.

'Not seen you in a while, Arthur,' Ash said. 'Looks like you're doing well.'

'Getting by, getting by,' the man said. He scuttled around. His sharp nose and constant movement reminded Harper of a rodent. 'How about you, Mr Ash?'

'Mustn't grumble, Arthur, thank you very much. This is Detective Inspector Harper. We thought you might be willing to make us a cup of that cocoa.'

'Of course, of course.' The man's movements quickened as he worked, surprisingly deft and exact. In a few minutes the inspector was drinking and letting the cocoa warm him inside and out. Arthur stood apart, head lowered, rubbing his hands together.

'That's grand,' Ash said, and Arthur beamed.

'It's very good,' Harper agreed. 'Hits the spot.'

By the time they were back in the alley, the door closing behind them, he felt refreshed, ready to face the rest of the day. He fumbled his watch out of his waistcoat. Almost nine o'clock. Time to do some real work.

'How did you know someone would be there?' he asked.

'Old Arthur lives just off the pantry,' Ash told him. 'Been there donkey's years, since Mr Stephens opened the place. Known him since I was little.'

The constable was full of surprises, Harper thought.

'See what you can find on Meanwood Road.'

They needed to find Alfred. But the inspector had tried everything he could imagine and found nothing at all. Now all he had was the hope that something would break, some thread he could follow. No one would be around so early on a Sunday. He needed to do something, to be somewhere. Anything to get these feelings out of his head.

It didn't take long to reach the Leylands. The grubby snow had been trampled down by people on their way to work. The Jewish Sabbath had ended the night before. This was just another day here. Harper could hear the machines humming and buzzing in the sweatshops, and voices chattering away in Yiddish.

The weather kept most people off the streets, but somewhere in the distance children were shouting, playing a game of some kind. Off to the west the clouds were heavy, pale and pearlescent. At least the wind had dropped.

He found Forsyth on Melbourne Street, standing on the corner outside the Brunswick Brewery. It was a place that brought back too many memories for Harper. He'd reported for work there six days a week, twelve hours of rolling and stacking barrels, then cleaning out the empties before going home, aching and exhausted. After that, becoming a police officer had seemed like sweet relief; all the miles walked on the beat were easy.

'Any trouble last night?' Harper asked. There'd been no word of it on his desk.

'No, sir,' Forsyth said. 'The Golem weren't out. Can't blame them. Not likely to be many creeping around in this snow.'

A night without angry young men was a good thing, even if the weather was the cause. Maybe a break would take the fire out of their blood.

'What's the mood?'

The bobby weighed his words before replying. 'It's changed since the rabbi's funeral, sir. There's been plenty of muttering. A lot of them are scared there'll be more killing. The young ones are angry; most of them idolized Mr Padewski. There's a few round here who think this Golem thing is right, sir, and enough who reckon we're not really trying to find the killers.'

'We found one of them yesterday,' Harper pointed out.

Forsyth said, 'I've been telling them till I'm blue in the face. Do you know what one of them said to me today? "It's easy to call a dead man a killer." And that was Mr Hyman. He's fifty, not one of these young hotheads. Putting them in the dock is the only thing that'll satisfy them, sir. They don't trust us any more.' The admission seemed to pain him.

But he was right, the inspector knew that. People wanted arrests and trials, and a hanging for retribution. They needed to see justice done.

'Just tell them we're doing everything we can, will you?' Harper said.

'I'll try. What about the others you're after, sir?' Forsyth asked hopefully. 'Any closer?'

'Not yet,' he admitted. 'But keep that to yourself.'

'And what about Sergeant Reed? Do we know who did that?'

'I know,' Harper said. 'I just can't find the bastard. If you hear anything about someone called Alfred, young, well-off, I want to know straight away.'

He started on the walk out to Roundhay, tempted to stop at the Victoria as he passed. But he kept going, out along the long, slow hill up to Harehills. On a good summer Sunday this was a gentle stroll. With the snow and ice, each mile seemed twice its normal length as his boots slipped on the ground.

Eventually the houses gave way to woods and the start of Roundhay Park itself. The air was clean, the surface just unbroken acres of white across Soldiers Field. He followed the Wetherby

Road, finally turning up the drive of Oakwood Grange and knocking on the door. His legs ached and he was grateful when the maid showed him through to the parlour where a fire burned in the grate.

He had to wait for a quarter of an hour until Lizzie Le Prince and her son Adolphe arrived, but that was no hardship. It gave a chance to ease the cold from his limbs and dry out his boots a little. She'd taken the time to put on her glad rags, he saw, an expensive silk gown with a fashionable small bustle at the back, her hair up in an elaborate style. Or perhaps she always dressed that way. She took one look at him, turned and called for tea.

'I'm sorry, Inspector. I hadn't expected you to call.'

'I wanted to apologize for leaving so suddenly yesterday,' he said. 'I didn't want you to feel I was ignoring you.'

'Of course.' She gave a tight smile. 'I heard about your colleague. I understand. It's very good of you to come out here.'

It was also wise, Harper knew. Mrs Le Prince's father had the ear of the chief constable and councillors. The woman might have no evidence, but there wasn't any point in making enemies where it wasn't needed. He already had enough of those.

The maid arrived with a tray, placing it on the low table in front of the hearth.

'Sit down, please, Inspector.' She poured for them all.

'You said you'd received a letter,' Harper began.

'Yes. From a friend in New York. Adolphe, would you fetch it, please? It's on the bureau.'

The young man returned in a moment and she picked out a sheet.

'Here we are,' she said. 'She's heard that Mr Edison plans to file a patent on his moving picture camera before spring. He appears to have brought his plans forward. What does that tell you?'

'I don't know,' Harper replied truthfully. 'I'm not privy to the whole situation. The best I can do is try to pass on the information to Capitaine Muyrère so he can investigate. He should be arriving in New York. After that, it's up to him.'

'I'd be very grateful if you would.'

'Of course.' He gave a small bow and finished his tea. 'Was there anything more?'

'Not for now, Mr Harper.' She extended a hand for him to shake.

'I'll be in touch if I learn anything more. Give my best wishes to your wife, please.'

It was easier walking downhill, less tiring. Even so, he was weary by the time he reached the bottom of Roundhay Road, and slipped into the Victoria. Annabelle was behind the bar, chatting with three of the regulars. He pointed upstairs and she nodded, calling Essie to take over.

'Long morning?' she asked as they embraced by the fire. She slapped lightly at his fingers. 'Watch where you put those hands, they're freezing.'

'I'm on my way back to the station. Mrs Le Prince sends her regards.'

'Very nice of her.' She brought bread and jam through from the kitchen and settled at the table. 'That should keep you going. Tea's mashing.'

'I stopped in to see Billy again this morning,' he said as he ate.

'How is he? Any better?' She swept her cap off her head, brushing out her hair with her fingers.

'Much. Except he still doesn't remember what happened.'

'I hope he remembered he's getting wed.'

'He does. Even seems happy about it,' Harper said with a laugh.

'Just as well, for his sake. He's getting a prize there.' She cut herself a slice of the bread and smeared it with raspberry jam.

'Elizabeth arrived just before I left.'

'She's popping back to Middleton this afternoon.'

'To tell the children?'

Annabelle nodded. 'And get some fresh clothes. Those kiddies really love him, from what she says. Her mam will be sad to see them go, but it's not the moon, is it?'

'Just a few minutes on the train.'

'I'm going to take her over to Burmantofts tomorrow. She can see the shop and we can look around for a house. I think George Hardy owns a few places over that way. I'll ask him; they'll be as decent as they come and he won't charge the earth in rent.'

He chuckled. 'You've got it all planned, haven't you?'

'Me?' She batted a hand against his arm. 'I just want to make it easy for them. Seriously, Tom, Elizabeth's a godsend. She knows shops and she's a good head on her shoulders. I'm lucky.'

'Maybe she thinks she is, too.'

'I'll work her hard. I told her that.'

'No harder than you work yourself,' Harper pointed out.

'I can't expect anyone to do more than I would, can I?'

'There's plenty who don't think that way.' He paused. 'Do you think they'll be happy?'

'Yes,' she told him with absolute certainty. 'I do. They just need to get settled before we open.'

'Have you booked the church for them yet?' he asked and she hit him again, harder this time.

The clouds were still threatening as Harper entered Millgarth, but no more snow. He rubbed his hands by the fire in the office and glanced through the papers on his desk. His eyes moved to the clock; Ash wouldn't be back for another hour at least, and no guarantee he'd have found anything.

The inspector sat for a minute, then began to pace around the room. The walls seemed to be pressing in on him, and the minutes dragged by so slowly. Finally he grabbed his coat and walked out into the cold.

Late afternoon and the mercury had fallen once more. The chill in the air seemed to pierce his lungs as he breathed. Harper pulled the scarf over his mouth and nose, put his head down and marched back to Millgarth. He'd gone out to the hospital again; it had been good to talk about the case with Billy. The way things ought to be. They way they'd be again, once the sergeant was on his feet and back at work. Even if it had gone nowhere, he still felt a little better.

Ash was standing with his broad back to the fire, hogging all the heat. But he had a satisfied smile on his face and a cup of tea in his hand.

'Well?' the inspector asked. 'You look like you found something.'

'Do you know a place called the George the Fourth, sir?' the constable said.

The inspector tried to place it and failed. 'No. Is that close to where we found Fields's body?'

'About a quarter of a mile, sir. Turns out a group of men used to come in every Thursday night.'

'Did they now?' he asked with sudden curiosity.

'They'd take over the snug at the back for a couple of hours. Door closed.'

He could feel his heart beating faster 'Did you get a description?'

Ash pursed his lips and frowned. 'That's the problem, sir. The landlord wears spectacles. I've seen bottles that weren't as thick as his lenses. I doubt he could describe me and I was as close to him as I am to you.'

Damn it. Harper slammed a hand on the desk.

'How many of them? Could he at least tell you that?'

'Five. He's certain of that.'

'Five?' They only had the names of four in the band of murderers. And one of them was dead now.

'This is where it gets interesting, sir. The landlord said one of them spoke posh.'

'What?' The inspector shouted the word. Christ. An educated voice. If it belonged to Alfred, that changed everything. He could have used the men to attack Billy. Find Fields's comrades and they'd lead him to Alfred. Harper could feel his blood pumping. He bunched his fingers into fists.

'Did you press him?'

'As much as I could, sir. He just doesn't know.'

'What about anyone else who works there?'

Ash shook his head. 'He only has help during the day. They do most of their trade from the works around there. Nights are quiet. He's not lying, sir, I'm sure of it. He's just old, that's all. And a bit gormless. He's about as much use as a doorpost. It doesn't look as if the place has been cleaned since the Queen took the throne, either.'

'What do you think?' Too many things were suddenly running through his mind.

'It has to be Alfred, doesn't it?' the constable said. 'There can't be two toffs spending time with people like that.'

Harper nodded. For the first time, he began to believe they were getting somewhere. He'd catch the men and pry Alfred's real identity from them. He could almost taste it, and it was sweet in his mouth.

'What now, sir?' Ash asked.

'Did you try the other pubs out there?'

'I went all the way into Meanwood. No one else knew them.'

'Right.' He paced, urgency and excitement rushing through him. 'Go on home. You've covered a few miles today, and you've done some outstanding work. We'll start again in the morning.'

'Yes, sir. The word is that Mr Reed's getting married. Is that right?'

The inspector stared at him. 'How did you hear that?'

'Just talk around the station.'

He hadn't told anyone. No one else had visited Billy. It was as if the gossip had blown in with the breeze.

'It's true, but don't go spreading it yet.'

'Don't you worry, sir. I'll keep it quiet,' he said with a wink. 'Goodnight.'

TWENTY-FOUR

The inspector was back in the office well before seven, early enough to pay the working man's fare on the first tram. A few light snowflakes swirled as he walked through the market, arcs of light from the gas lamps piercing the early gloom. It was Monday and all the factories were back at work. He could already smell the smoke in the air and taste the soot as he breathed.

He hadn't slept much during the night, shifting here and there in the bed until Annabelle complained. He didn't know how to find the killers. But they were still in Leeds; he'd bet his pay packet on that. And Alfred . . . The inspector took a drink from the cup of tea in front of him. He'd see the man in court. He'd make sure of it.

Harper glanced through the reports. The Golem had been out again, but there'd been no trouble. He shook his head. They were fearful and they were bitter. It was only a matter of time before something terrible happened.

Ash arrived right on the hour, looking rested and ready for anything. But there was nothing for him to do. Nowhere to look, no leads to follow. Before Harper could issue any orders,

Superintendent Kendall came through in full dress uniform, shoes bulled to a perfect sheen. The first funerals from the Wortley fire; he'd be attending those today.

'Alfred with the murderers?' Kendall raised his eyebrows as he read the report Harper had prepared. 'Are you sure?'

'As much as I can be. Who else can it be, sir?'

'Any idea who he is yet?'

'No one's heard of him.'

'*Someone* must have. Any more leads on the killers?'

'Not yet.' It hurt him to admit it, to say he'd failed. 'I've had sweeps going through town but they haven't turned up anything.'

'Put more men on it.' He tapped his finger on the paper. 'I want them all and I want them soon.'

'Yes, sir.'

'I had to go to a dinner last night. Councillor May was a speaker. He thinks we could cut a hundred men from the force.' Kendall shook his head in disgust.

'We'd never be able to do our job,' Harper said. 'It'd be anarchy out there.'

'Try telling him that. I wanted to stand up and shout it out.' He sighed helplessly. 'I'm told that patrol was back out in the Leylands last night. What do they call themselves?'

'The Golem, sir.'

The superintendent grimaced in distaste. 'Stupid bloody name. We need this closed before anything else happens there, Tom.'

'I know, sir. I just don't have any idea where to look.'

'Then start over,' he ordered. 'I stopped at the hospital. Reed's improving.'

'Yes, sir. I saw him yesterday. It's still going to take a while, though.'

'He's on the mend, that's what counts.' Kendall's eyes flickered over to the office. 'What about Ash? Is he good?'

'Very. He's been wasted on the beat.'

'Do you want him full-time?'

'We need him, sir. We've been short for a while.'

The superintendent nodded. 'Leave it with me, I'll see what I can do. I'll be gone most of the day, so I'll need you to keeping checking here in case there are any problems.'

'Yes, sir.'

'Those poor families are going to suffer today.' Kendall shook his head sadly. 'Eleven dead in the end. You know the worst part, Tom? We're going to need plenty of coppers there. Penny to a pound the crowd will be full of pickpockets.'

Harper didn't even bother to answer. All the crooks would be drawn to the funerals. They'd see opportunity, not mourning.

Kendall picked up a pen, threw it back down, then stood. 'Right. I'd better present myself at the Town Hall. We're all going out together. Just look after the place today.'

'Yes, sir.'

The next hour flew by with this and that, all the business of running the station. It bought him time to think, but even when the rush had passed he didn't know what to do. He sent Ash out for the morning to supervise the sweeps. Maybe luck would smile on them.

There were papers to read and sign, rosters to check and change. By the time he'd completed all the paperwork it was past eleven and his belly was rumbling. The inspector glanced out of the window. Snow was falling hard again. A bad day for a funeral.

Wrapped in his coat, he made his way through the market. There were few sellers outside today, just the hopeful, eyes searching passers-by for custom. Even Pie Jack hadn't bothered and Pea Ned's booth was empty. If they were gone then business was bad.

The café was quiet, the windows running with condensation, the air heavy with steam. Harper ordered soup and tea. Enough to warm him and keep his belly full during the afternoon. He ate, but the food sat heavily. Too much frustration in his stomach, he thought. There'd be indigestion later.

'Penny for them, Inspector?' Tom Maguire sat across from him and a waitress appeared with his sandwich and cup of tea. 'You don't look like a happy man.'

'Work.' He wiped a slice of bread around the bowl to mop up the last of the soup.

'I heard you found one of the killers.'

'We did. And he was already dead. Not the rest. Not yet.'

'I was going to send you a note this afternoon.' Maguire had shaved his beard, leaving a moustache waxed to points at the ends. It suited him.

'Oh?'

'There are some men in a rooming house up on Arundel Street. Three of them. That's what one of my members told me. Very suspicious, he thought. It might be worth a look. Of course, you didn't hear that from me.' He winked.

'Of course.' Harper smiled eagerly. 'I don't suppose he told you what number?'

'Twenty-six,' he said. 'He dislikes killers more than he dislikes coppers.'

Harper nodded. 'And you?'

'Me?' Maguire gave him an innocent stare. 'I haven't said a word, Inspector.' He took a last, large bite of the sandwich and washed it down with tea before standing. 'I'll bid you good day.'

He'd hoped for luck and it had finally come. He was going to bloody well have them.

Harper hurried back through the snow to Millgarth, and called Sergeant Tollman into the office.

'I need six constables. Big ones.'

The sergeant ran a tongue over his teeth. 'It'll take me about an hour, sir.'

'As soon as you can.' Ash should be back by them. He thought quickly. With this weather, the men probably wouldn't have left their lodgings; it was no day to be walking the streets without purpose. He could feel the excitement rising inside. He was going to arrest them. And he'd make them give up Alfred.

Time passed slowly. He kept checking his pocket watch; barely a minute had passed each time. Ash returned, shaking his head, then brightening once the inspector told him the plan.

'About bloody time, if you ask me, sir.' He smiled. 'I've been looking forward to getting my hands on them.'

'So have I,' Harper said slowly. 'So have I.'

Tollman gave him the nod.

'The beat officer will meet you at the corner of Roseville Road,' he said.

The jail cart was in the yard, a horse in the traces, men in uniform waiting. The snow was still coming down, muffling every sound. Harper shuffled through it. It was up to the top of his boots now, a good two inches more than earlier, and no sign of slowing.

They made a grim procession, but there were few out and about to notice. Most people were at work, or hidden away in their houses. At least they'd be dry, the inspector thought. A few might even be warm.

He tried to picture Arundel Street in his mind. Back-to-back houses, he recalled that. And beyond, plenty of open ground that led to the back of the brick works and the workhouse. He'd need men there to cut off any escape.

They passed the Victoria and made their way up Roundhay Road. He could have sat with the cart driver, but it was quicker and warmer to walk.

The constable was exactly where Tollman had promised, walking in small circles as he waited, saluting the inspector.

'PC Crisp, sir.' He was in his forties, a lean man with some grey in his hair and a serious face.

'What can you tell me?'

'As far as I know, they're still in there, sir. Twenty-six is a lodging house, all right, just the far side of the privies. Run by Mr Grimes. He's a widower, lets out the bedrooms upstairs. Never been too fussed who he takes in.'

'We'll leave the wagon on Bayswater Road. How easy is it to get through to the waste ground at the end?'

'Just over the wall, people do it all the time.'

'How well do you know Grimes?'

'As well as most of them, sir. Enough to pass the time of day.' He gave a quick smile. 'He's not what you'd call friendly. Not with coppers, any road.'

'Right.' He motioned for the others to join him and sent two off to the waste land. Another pair to cover the top end of the street. That left two to go into the house with him and Ash. It should be enough. 'Crisp, when we're ready, I want you to knock on the door. Grimes will open up for you. When he does, I'll come through with the others. If Mr Grimes starts to object, keep him out of the way.'

'Yes, sir.'

Finally, they were ready. Harper glanced at the men in front of him. One looked nervous; it was his first time doing anything like this. Another had his teeth clenched and his truncheon drawn. Ash's face was impassive, giving nothing away. The inspector nodded and they marched down the street, boots silent on the snow.

Crisp knocked and took a pace away from the door. Harper and the others stood on the far side, out of view of anyone peeking through the window. He heard the handle turn and tensed.

'Hello, Mr Grimes, I'm sorry to bother you—' Crisp began, then the inspector was moving, brushing the man aside and pounding up the stairs, the others behind him. Two closed doors. He pushed one open. An empty room. He tried the other.

Two figures sat on the bed, playing cards. They started to rise as he entered, then the inspector moved aside to let Ash and the constables enter. He recognized Briggs from his photograph. The other had sallow skin, lank hair and a face like a rat; that had to be Hill. But there was no Anderson.

'We've been looking for you gentlemen,' he said, satisfaction in his voice. 'I want to talk to you about a few murders. Where's Jack Anderson?'

'He went out to buy baccy,' Hill replied, still astonished.

'Take them away,' the inspector ordered, and ran down the stairs. Crisp was standing in the street, arguing with Grimes.

'Where's the closest shop?' Harper asked.

'Up on Gledhow Road,' the constable told him. 'Why?'

'Come with me.' He began to sprint through the snow, the hobnails on his soles gripping the ground. Crisp struggled to keep pace.

He saw it on the corner, the glow of light through large windows, and he moved faster, tearing open the door. But the only person inside was a small woman behind the counter.

'Has someone been in here to buy tobacco?'

She looked at him with terrified eyes, dumbstruck until Crisp entered.

'Was there someone here buying tobacco?' the inspector repeated.

'Not five minutes since,' she answered warily.

'Big, fair hair?'

She nodded.

'Thank you.'

Outside, he looked around. But with the snow coming down he couldn't see more than twenty yards. Anderson must have spotted them and taken off. He slammed a palm against the brick wall and swore.

'What is it, sir?' Crisp asked.

'We missed one of them.'

'But you still found two,' the constable said. 'That's not bad, is it?'

'No,' Harper agreed wearily. 'A decent day's work.'

They'd dragged Briggs and Hill away without boots or coats, bundling them into the jail cart to go to Millgarth. Now they were in the unheated cells, wet, cold and shivering.

'You take Hill,' the inspector told Ash. 'He looks like he'll cave with a little intimidation.'

'Right you are, sir.'

'And don't be afraid to push him hard.'

The constable smiled. 'I saw what they did to Sergeant Reed. I'll not be holding back.'

Harper was waiting in the interview room when they brought Briggs in, still wearing handcuffs. He was in his thirties, a man with bony arms and a pigeon chest. His cheeks were sunk where he'd lost most of his teeth, and the hair was receding away from his forehead. Old before his time, just like so many. He looked as if he'd barely had a decent meal in his life, and all the food in the world wouldn't be enough for him.

'Sit down.' The man shuffled and settled on the chair. He was shivering. Harper picked up the cup of tea, steam still rising from its surface, and took a slow drink. 'You know why you're here.'

'No,' the man replied, but there was no defiance or force in the word. Good, it shouldn't take long to break him down.

'I'll tell you, then. One, the murder of Abraham Levy on Christmas Eve. Two, trying to set fire to the synagogue on Belgrave Street. Three, the killing of Rabbi Padewski on New Year's Eve. Four, assault with intent to murder on Sergeant Reed. And finally, strangling Clem Fields.' He raised his eyebrows. 'Is that enough for you? Every one of them will get you the gallows.'

'I never,' he objected, but his heart wasn't in the words.

'You went drinking with Fields, Hill and Anderson at the Anchor most nights?'

Briggs nodded.

'Thursdays you'd go the George the Fourth on Meanwood Road.'

Panic crossed the man's face. His mouth twitched.

'You met someone out there every week,' Harper continued.

The man raised his head and jutted out his chin. 'No. We just liked somewhere different.'

Harper threw the cup across the room. It shattered against the wall, liquid dripping down on to the floor. 'Don't bloody lie to me.'

Briggs gulped. 'We didn't meet no one.'

It would wait; he'd come back to that later.

'We found Fields's knife where the rabbi was murdered and fish scales at the scene. We know he didn't do it alone. Someone saw four men.' Briggs wouldn't know it was a lie. 'The description of one of them fits you.'

'Prove it.'

'Where were you New Year's Eve?'

The man looked away. 'Don't remember.'

'You want me to tell you?' He leaned across the table, grabbing the man's shirt and pulling him close enough to see the terror in his eyes. 'You were in the Leylands, killing Rabbi Padewski. And two days later you killed Clem Fields. What did you think, we wouldn't come looking once we had him?'

He waited for Briggs but the man didn't answer, just tried to avert his gaze. The man was shaking with cold, little spasms passing through his body. The inspector let him go, then turned and left the room, nodding for a constable to stand inside the door and watch Briggs.

The office was warm and for a few minutes he kept himself busy, sorting through papers. He stood by the window, staring out. The snow had left a covering that blurred edges and hid shapes. The day had ended, a night fog clamping down to hold Leeds close.

The inspector waited half an hour before going back to the interview room. Briggs looked colder, his body hunched in on itself as he tried to keep warm.

'You know you're going to hang,' Harper began. 'Your friend's singing so loud he should be a choir.'

'He wouldn't.'

'No?' The inspector smiled. 'When someone tries to kill one of ours, we get very nasty. And Constable Ash worked with Sergeant Reed. He took it all personally.' He let the words hang. 'Now, what do you want to tell me?'

'I don't have anything to tell!' Briggs shouted.

'Oh, you do.' Harper smiled and sat. 'And I have all night to listen. There's you, with a wife and children, and we find you in a rooming house. Bit rum, isn't it? Why don't we start there?'

TWENTY-FIVE

E lizabeth had arrived with the end of the afternoon. He'd spent the day shifting between dozing and listening to all the sounds of the hospital – the squeaky wheels of carts, footsteps slow and fast, voices, the clatter of pans – until he wasn't sure what was sleep and what was waking. But none of the old nightmares had visited him since he'd been here.

Time and again he tried to recall the attack. He could see himself on the omnibus, feel the frustration as it sat there, nowhere to go with traffic all around. He could remember climbing off the platform, the hard road under his soles.

And that was all. After that there was still only emptiness. No faces, no voices, no blows.

Reed opened his eyes, throat dry, and started to reach out for the water glass. His shoulder ached as he moved; he still felt weak.

'I'll get that, love,' Elizabeth said. He looked at her, his vision sharp enough now to pick out every feature on her face. Her eyes were wide and she was smiling.

'How long have you been here?' he asked as she held his head and he drank.

'Not too long. You were resting, I didn't want to disturb you.'

'I'm fine. Did you go to Burmantofts?'

She nodded. 'It's a grand little shop, Billy, it'll do well. And we looked at a few houses. Mrs Harper has a friend who owns some property there. He took us to a right nice place. Lovely through terrace. Two bedrooms.'

'You liked it?'

'I did. It even has a garden.'

'Can we afford it?'

'The rent's cheap and—' She stopped herself.

'What?' he asked. 'What's wrong?'

Elizabeth stared at him. He could still see her clearly. His sight had held, it wasn't even beginning to waver.

'I just need to be sure. About us.'

He reached out and placed his hand over hers. 'I'm positive,' Reed assured her. 'Go and take that house tomorrow.'

'I will.'

'What about you?' he asked. 'Moving to Leeds, it's a big wrench.'

She beamed. 'Honestly, I've never been more certain about anything in my life, Billy Reed. My mam's sad, but she's happy for me, too. You'll love the house. I can't believe there's so much room. Two bedrooms! And a woman down the street has a mangle and a big copper for washing clothes.'

He smiled at her. He'd do right by her for the rest of his life.

The door to the room was open. The sergeant moved his head for a moment, glancing at the people who were passing in the corridor. Suddenly his eyes widened and he started struggling to sit up.

'Him,' he croaked. 'That's him.'

Harper marched out of the room, ordering the constable to take Briggs back to his cell. The second session had taken time, grinding through and sweating him until he wore the man down. Five hours had passed until Briggs had finally given up and admitted it all. He'd been there when Levy and Padewski were killed. He'd taken part on the attack on Billy. Helped set the fire at the synagogue. But Briggs refused to plead to the strangling of Clem Fields. That one had been just Jack Anderson. He hadn't even known about it until later, he swore.

The inspector had pushed on, wearing Briggs down. And eventually, there was Alfred. He'd met them the same way he met the other group, talking and drawing them in, offering them money, then arranging to meet them every week out at the George the Fourth.

'How much did he pay you for the fire?'

'A pound each.' Briggs had no resistance left. Harper had pulled down every barrier; all the man had left was the truth. He wasn't going to stop until he'd dug out every scrap. 'But he wasn't happy because it didn't burn the place down.'

'How much to attack Sergeant Reed?'

'A pound. He didn't want him dead.'

'Was Alfred there when it happened?'

'He came along when we were beating him. Told us to leave him, then he bought us all a drink and paid us.'

Whoever Alfred was, he was bloody cold. Harper clenched his fists.

'What about the murders?' he asked. 'How much did they bring you?'

'Two quid apiece.' He looked down at the floor, his voice low.

'Two pounds for a life,' Harper said. He grabbed Briggs's hair and jerked his head up to look into the eyes. 'And you're going to hang. Does that seem like a fair bargain?' He waited a moment, staring at the man. 'The pennies. Why did you leave them on their eyes after you'd killed them?'

The man shrugged. 'He told us to. Didn't say why, just to do it.'

'Who did?'

Briggs lifted his head. 'Alfred.'

'And what's Alfred's real name?'

'I don't know,' Briggs mumbled. 'That's the only name he told us. He never said and we didn't ask, not as long as he was giving us money.'

'You know. What is it?'

'I bloody don't!' He yelled the words.

Harper believed him.

There were more questions to ask, but they could wait for morning. Down in the cells they'd feed Briggs and give him a blanket for the night. He'd have time to think and grow colder. Tomorrow, the inspector would milk the man for the rest.

In the office he'd been standing by the fire for a few minutes, taking off the chill of the interview room, when Ash entered, a grim smile across his face.

'What did you get from Hill?' Harper asked.

'Mr Hill has admitted to killing Levy and Padewski, the fire and the attack on Sergeant Reed,' he announced with satisfaction. 'What about you, sir?'

'The same.'

'I sent him back down.' He hesitated. 'He did slip and hurt himself, sir. Should I write it up in my report?'

'Just mention it like that. Accidents happen.'

The constable nodded. 'Slippery floors and clumsy men. It's a devil of a combination, sir. But he seemed happy enough to talk once I got him started.'

The inspector could see the grazes on Ash's knuckles.

'What about Alfred?' he asked.

'Oh yes.' The constable beamed. 'Gave him up after a little persuading. But they only knew him as Alfred. Never got a real name.'

The inspector nodded. He'd hoped for more, for some clue, but he hadn't expected that Hill would know more than his friend. 'What about Anderson? Does he know where he might be?'

'If he does, he's not telling.'

'Briggs doesn't have a clue, either. He's going to spend the night thinking about his own mortality.' He sighed. 'Write up what he told you, and we'll go at them again tomorrow.'

'Yes, sir. At least we've got them.'

'We have.'

But it wasn't finished yet. There was one more still out there. And there was Alfred. He sat at his desk and rubbed his temples, trying to ease the headache that throbbed between his eyes. He didn't even notice Tollman enter.

'There's been a telephone call from the infirmary, sir,' he began, and Harper's stomach lurched. Bad news. 'Seems Sergeant Reed has something he needs to tell you urgently.'

He dashed through town, cutting through the courts and lanes. Smoke rose from the chimneys, lights burned in the public houses, and he heard the raucous sound of voices.

At the corner on to Great George Street, the infirmary just yards away, he felt it. The hearing went in his ear again, just as surely as if someone had turned a switch. The inspector stopped for a moment, closing his eyes and breathing deeply.

He placed a hand over the right ear, then moved it away. It wouldn't help, he knew that, but he could hope. Not a thing. He remembered what the doctor had said. It would keep happening, it could come – and it would go. And finally it would never return at all.

Harper stood up straight and entered the hospital.

He'd expected to find Elizabeth there, but Reed was alone in his room, sitting up in the bed.

'You've remembered?' he asked breathlessly.

'I saw him,' the sergeant said. 'Alfred. He was here.'

'Here?' He looked around the room. 'Where?'

'He was going down the corridor. It was just the back of his head, but I knew, Tom. It was him.'

'I'll—'

'I sent Elizabeth to ask one of the nurses.' Reed continued, his voice was low and intense. He stared up at the inspector. 'His name's Phillip May. He's Councillor May's son.'

'God.' It fitted. He had money and power. The councillor hated foreigners. Like father, like son. Harper had met him once, briefly. He had the memory of a good-looking young man, fastidiously dressed, with an educated voice.

'Do you remember him there when you were attacked?' he asked desperately.

'No. I keep trying, but there's nothing. It's just blank.'

'We got two more of them,' the inspector told him. 'Arrested them this morning. They've confessed to beating you. They admitted the murders in the Leylands, too, and the fire at the synagogue. There's one still out there.'

The sergeant sighed. 'Who are they?'

Harper kept his head angled to hear properly. 'Tim Hill and Robert Briggs. They didn't know Alfred's real name. He never told them.' But he had it now. In the morning he'd go and arrest Phillip May. 'I need you to try to remember what happened, Billy. If you can put Alfred there, we'll really have him. No jury's going to doubt the word of a policeman.'

'What the hell do you think I've been doing all day?' He was filled with frustration. 'Do you know what they did this afternoon? They helped me out of bed. All I could manage was two steps. Two bloody steps, Tom, then they had to put me back here. I marched across fucking Afghanistan and now I can only manage two paces.'

'You'll get better, Billy,' the inspector told him. 'Just take your time.'

Reed turned his head. Tears were running down his cheeks. 'Two steps. Don't you think I'd remember everything if I could?'

*   *   *

He sat by the fire. The cup of tea on the chair arm had turned cold as he stared into the flames.

'Penny for them,' Annabelle said, and he tried to smile.

'I don't think they're worth that much.'

'The hearing's not back yet?'

He shook his head. 'No. It's not that, though. Work.'

It wasn't over yet. Not by a long chalk. But tomorrow . . . tomorrow he'd see it all through.

'Anything I can do?' she asked.

'Not really.' He changed the subject; anything was better than his thoughts. 'Did you take Elizabeth to Burmantofts?'

'I did.' She grinned, her face lively. 'Tom, she's a find, she really is. She had some suggestions for the shop, putting the counter on the other side so customers can see everything properly. All sorts. Do you know what else?'

'What?'

'She said we ought to hire a man with a sandwich board to walk all round for a week before we open.'

'To advertise the place? That's not a bad idea,' he conceded.

'We found her a house, too. She talked to Billy about it when she saw him. They're going to take it. I can't believe it. She's perfect.'

He'd seen Elizabeth when he returned, talking merrily with Annabelle in the kitchen. One look at his face and she'd hurried off to bed.

'As long as they're happy together, that's what matters,' he said.

'She loves him, you know that. You've just got to look at her.'

'And he loves her. I think it all scares him, but he'll be fine.' He stretched and saw her staring at him. 'He will.'

There'd been no more snow overnight. He'd barely slept during the long hours, lying on his back, staring into the darkness, trying not to move and disturb Annabelle.

His eyes felt gritty, his tongue large in his mouth, as he caught the early tram. And nothing in his right ear. More than twelve hours on and he was still deaf there, the longest it had lasted yet. Maybe this was it. Maybe it would never come back.

He slipped out into the cold morning, feeling it bite against his cheeks. The air was so thick he almost believed he could cut through it with his hand, acrid and foul. On one of the front seats of the tram a man with a deep, liquid cough kept hawking phlegm into a handkerchief. Harper alighted on Vicar Lane and marched through the streets to the *Yorkshire Post* offices. The librarian was already there, cutting old articles to go into marked folders. The inspector explained what he needed. Ten minutes later he was back on the street, a photograph safely in his pocket, and he made his way to Millgarth Station. The constables were just leaving for their beats, a flurry of salutes as they passed him. He drew Forsyth aside.

'I need you to tell the people in the Leylands that we got the men who killed Abraham Levy and the rabbi,' he said. 'They admitted it yesterday.' There was no need to mention Alfred. Not yet.

'I'd heard, sir.' His face was serious. 'But we didn't get all of them, is that right?''

'One's still out there,' he admitted. 'We'll catch him. And find out if those bloody Golem were out last night. I'll be along later.'

'Yes, sir.'

Sergeant Tollman was in his usual position at the desk, checking through the log.

'Constable Ash in yet?' Harper asked.

'Went through to the office not five minutes ago, sir.'

'Right. Bring Hill and Briggs up to the interview rooms.'

'It's still early, sir. They won't have eaten yet.'

'Then they can skip a meal,' the inspector said.

'Yes, sir. It says here that Mr Hill seems to have injured himself.'

'The way I heard it, he fell down.'

Tollman shook his head. 'Clumsy buggers, these criminals, aren't they, sir? I'll see they're brought up directly.'

Ash was hogging the fire, genial and smiling as the inspector entered the office. 'Good morning, sir. Think we'll wrap it up today?'

'With luck.' He gave a big grin. 'Sergeant Reed's identified Alfred.'

'Really? He remembered what happened?'

'It was pure luck. Alfred was visiting someone at the infirmary and Billy saw him.'

'So we know who he is, sir?' Ash asked hopefully.

'Oh, yes.' Harper smiled. 'He's Councillor May's son.'

He was about to say more, but turned at the sound of boots running down the corridor. Then the door swung open and Tollman was there, his face almost grey.

'You'd better come down to the cells, sir,' he said breathlessly.

TWENTY-SIX

Harper ran, Ash on his heels, Tollman close behind, down the stairs and into the chill of the cells. Each one had a solid metal door with a flap to look inside. A constable stood by one, looking so pale he had to lean against the wall. The key was still hanging in the lock.

Harper pushed the door wide and walked in. Hill was there, hanging from the barred window. Under him, a chair had been kicked away on to its side. The blanket from the sleeping shelf had been torn into strips and knotted together to make a noose. The man's feet dangled inches from the floor, a small pool of piss between them. The inspector reached for Hill's neck, feeling for any pulse, and hoping. But there was nothing. The man's skin was cold and waxy under his touch.

'Bloody hell,' he heard Ash mutter.

'Who was on duty down here last night?' Harper shouted. To the constable waiting outside, he said, 'Cut him down and get hold of Dr King. I want him taken over to Hunslet to be examined.' The bobby dashed away in search of a knife.

Tollman was back behind his desk, hands firmly planted on the wood. He looked shaken, as if he couldn't believe what he'd just seen.

'Who was looking after the cells last night?' the inspector demanded.

'Constable Shaw, sir. We were short-handed, the night sergeant's off ill. Shaw's the senior man.'

'Has he gone home?'

'Yes, sir.'

'Send someone to fetch him. Tell him to report to the super-intendent's office as soon as possible.'

'Yes, sir.'

He didn't even give Kendall time to remove his overcoat before he was there, breaking the news. The superintendent stood stock still, hands in his trouser pockets, glowering.

'He's supposed to check the prisoners every hour,' Harper said.

'I know that,' the superintendent snapped. 'How long before he's here?'

'I've no idea, sir.'

'I'll take care of this, Tom. It's my station and I'll get to the bottom of it.' He pulled out a pipe from his jacket pocket and lit it, puffing furiously as he held a match over the bowl. 'Christ, what a mess.' Harper was shocked; in all his years here, he'd never heard the super blaspheme. 'I'll tell you what, Shaw's going to be off the force before the day's done. He'll be lucky if he's not up for negligence.' He paused. 'Have you seen Reed?'

'Yesterday. He's identified Alfred.'

'What?' Kendall started to rise. 'Who is he?'

'Phillip May, sir.'

'The councillor's son?'

'Yes.'

For a long time the superintendent stayed silent, puffing on his pipe, eyes narrowed in thought.

'Did Reed remember the attack?'

'No, sir.' He explained what had happened. 'I got a photograph from the Post this morning. Phillip May's in it. I'm going to show it to Briggs for confirmation.'

'Do that,' Kendall said eventually. 'Don't tell him his friend is dead, though.'

'Yes, sir. And after that?' Harper asked. 'Go and arrest May?'

'No.' The inspector opened his mouth, but Kendall cut him off. 'We can't, not with what we've got. Reed's had a head injury, he can't even remember what happened. Any competent barrister would tear him apart in court, and the councillor will start screaming that we're harassing his family.'

'But if Briggs confirms it?'

The superintendent shook his head firmly. 'The word of someone who's admitted murdering two people and attacking a copper? Who's going to believe him? May's lawyer can twist it so it looks like you pushed him to that.'

'There's the bunch from the Cross Keys. Billy was there.'

'And heard nothing directly from this Alfred, according to his reports.' His face softened. 'Tom, if I really thought we could put him away, don't you think I would? But you don't have enough. If Reed remembers him being there when he was attacked, that would do it. But this? It's not enough. I'm sorry. They'd crucify us and we already look bad enough.'

'Yes, sir.' He stood.

'Get me hard evidence and I'll send you after him with my blessing.'

'I'll try, sir.' What could he get? Billy didn't remember what happened.

'Good.' Kendall kept puffing on the pipe. 'And I don't want anyone in the office when Shaw's here. Make sure that other prisoner's under constant guard, too. I don't care if it means putting a constable in the same cell with him day and night.'

'Yes, sir.'

Harper stood by the door of the interview room, his hand tight around the knob. Briggs was in there, waiting, a constable watching him carefully. He took a breath and entered.

'What's going on?' Briggs started to rise from his chair but the inspector pushed him back down.

'Nothing to worry you.' He took the photograph from his pocket and smoothed it out on the table. It had been taken at a charity ball, a group of men in their tuxedos, with drinks in their hands and smiles on their faces. Phillip May was in there, at the back, his face barely visible. But it was the only picture of him the *Post* had in their archives. 'Do you see Alfred in there?' he asked.

The prisoner stared at him for a moment, then concentrated.

'That could be him,' he said grudgingly.

'Who? Show me.'

A stubby, dirty finger pointed at May's face. 'Can't see enough of him to be sure, though.'

'Right. Take him back to his cell, constable.'

'What's going on down there?' Briggs asked. 'What was all that running and shouting about?'

'I told you, nothing to do with you.'

*   *   *

Harper wrapped himself in his coat and scarf, put his hat on his head and walked out of the station to the Leylands. The clouds hung so low he couldn't tell where they stopped and the fog began. Harper covered his nose and mouth as he crossed the road. Under his boots the snow was solid, packed firm by all the feet that had gone before.

One murderer dead at the hands of his friends. Another killed himself in his cell. The superintendent was right, it was a disaster. He should have *thought*, he should have ordered a watch on the prisoners. Damn it. He kicked at the snow, his face set. And one more still out there somewhere. At this rate he'd be lucky get one of them to court. Even if he did, Phillip May would probably go scot-free.

Forsyth stood inside the shop that had once belonged to Mrs Hamilton. He was talking with three or four women, all with their dark, heavy coats and *babushkas*, shopping bags on their arms. They were jabbering away in Yiddish and he couldn't make out a word. He waited out in the frigid air until the constable emerged.

'What were they all talking about?'

'I was telling them what happened. That lot are the biggest gossips around here, the whole neighbourhood will know before dinner time. Then they were full of questions.' He shrugged. 'I told them I didn't know.'

Best not to reveal Hill's suicide, he decided. Let that wait.

'What about the Golem?' Harper asked. 'Were they out last night?'

'Maitland said he saw them, sir. He told them to go home, that we had the killers in custody.'

'Did they?'

Forsyth ran his tongue around the inside of his mouth before answering. 'No, sir, they didn't.'

'Right, carry on. And keep telling people.'

Harper trudged up the hill to North Street, crossed over to the synagogue and through the unlocked door.

Feldman was there, deep in conversation with a pair of smartly-dressed men Harper didn't recognize. The rabbi glanced up, made a motion to wait, and carried on. He was explaining some point, his voice low but insistent.

The inspector sat, hat in his lap, his eyes searching around the building. It was simple enough, plain white walls and wooden seating. The only decoration was around the Ark of the Covenant in the back wall. That was gilded and brilliant, glittering in the soft gaslight. Behind there, Harper knew, they kept the Torah, their holy book.

He'd attended a bar mitzvah here once, when Moishe Cohen had turned thirteen. He'd turned up, dressed by his mother in his Sunday best, and not understood a word of it. All he'd been able to do was follow the others, standing and sitting when they did, and hoping the borrowed *yarmulke* didn't slip off his head. He'd felt as if he'd walked into another country.

Finally the men left and Feldman came over to sit next to him.

'From the Board of Guardians,' the rabbi explained. 'Important men who don't like to wait. Now, you've come to tell me you have the murderers in the cells. I saw the chief constable last night. He told me.'

'Not quite,' Harper began. 'We only have one of them. We found one dead on Saturday. Another hanged himself in his cell last night.'

Feldman raised his bushy eyebrows. 'If you want me to say that's a terrible waste, I will. But he killed my nephew. Forgiveness isn't easy.'

'He confessed yesterday.'

'So that's all of them, Inspector?' The rabbi placed his hands on his knees. Dark age spots, like large freckles, were strewn across his skin.

'There's still one more,' he admitted with a sigh, saying nothing about Alfred. 'I know who he is. He grew up with me in the Leylands. I'll find him.'

And he'd manage it sooner rather than later. The Jack Anderson he remembered from childhood hadn't been clever. He had no imagination or slyness, just brutality. He doubted the man had changed much over the years.

'Then what do you want from me?' Feldman demanded.

'I need you to tell people we've looked after them. We've done what we promised. I want you to make them believe that.'

The rabbi stroked his beard. 'People have faith or they don't, Inspector.'

'And I need you to keep the Golem off the streets before anything happens,' Harper said, in earnest. 'I don't want any more bodies round here.'

Feldman's mouth twitched with amusement. 'You think I have the power to do that?'

'I hope you do. You're their rabbi.'

'No.' He shook his head. 'Rabbi Padewski was their rabbi. They loved him, Inspector. They believed him.' He paused. 'I can counsel them. I can tell them what I think. But I can't make them do anything. And if you believe I can, you don't understand.'

The inspector squeezed his eyes shut for a moment and opened them again. 'Convince them, sir. Please. Or someone innocent will end up getting hurt.'

Feldman sat in silence for a few minutes. The synagogue was quiet. Only a few small sounds penetrated Harper's good ear.

'I'll talk to them,' the rabbi agreed finally. 'But they want to protect their families, their friends. I can't blame them for that, Inspector.' He stared and his face softened. 'I know you're trying. I'm grateful for all you've done. But there's only one thing that will make them stop, and that's when you have the last man.'

'I will,' he promised. All of them, he thought. Every single bloody one.

Feldman nodded. 'Do that and they'll be gone. Until the next time it happens.'

'There won't be a next time,' Harper told him.

'You're a good man, Inspector, but you can't tell the future.' He stood wearily, pushing himself upright with his hands. 'Go,' he said. 'You're a *mensch*, Inspector. God go with you.'

They'd taken Briggs over to the Town Hall, placing heavy chains on his wrists and ankles before they put him in the prison van. The inspector stood by the window and looked out as it left the yard, drawn by a listless horse.

'Anderson,' Harper said to Ash. 'We need to find him. His wife and kiddies are in Mabgate. What family he has lives there, too.'

'He'll either go there, then, or he'll be careful to avoid it completely,' the constable replied.

'He's on his own, he knows we're after him,' the inspector said thoughtfully. 'He can't have much money left. My guess is that he'll try to slip in there soon. Talk to Tollman, arrange to have extra men around there today and tomorrow. Make sure they know what he looks like.'

'Yes, sir.'

'If they see him, have them follow him. But I want to know. I want him for myself.'

Ash left, and the inspector knocked on Kendall's door.

'Come in, Tom.' He sounded weary, as if he was dragging the words from a deep well.

'Did you see Shaw, sir?'

'I hate having to sack a copper.' He picked up a pocket knife and began to ream out the bowl of his pipe. 'But he didn't leave me any choice. Couldn't even give me an explanation. Just an apology.' He tapped the bowl in an ashtray and filled it from his tobacco pouch. 'Did you show Briggs that photograph?'

'He said it could be Alfred.'

'But he wasn't certain?' The superintendent jumped on the doubt.

'You can only see part of his face. If we had May in court—'

'We won't.' Kendall cut him off. 'I've talked to the chief constable. He agrees with me. We can't risk it, not without something far more solid. Not while the councillor wants to cut the force. His barrister would tear holes a mile wide in everything. If Reed remembers him there at that attack, then you can arrest him.' He shook his head. 'What about this other man? Anderson?'

Harper told him about Mabgate and the superintendent nodded his agreement. 'Seems plausible, especially if he's not too bright. God help us if we ever get a clever one, though. I want this closed today if we can. Have you been to the Leylands?'

'This morning. I talked to Rabbi Feldman. The Golem were out again last night. He's going to have a word with them.' It was shading the truth, making it sound as if the rabbi could order them around, but it would pass for now. 'I popped down to see Billy, too. They're getting him to walk a little more today.'

'Good.' Kendall blew a cloud of smoke towards the ceiling. 'I might go down myself later.'

'His fiancée's there with him.'

'Maybe I'll leave it until tomorrow, then.' He sighed. 'At least we'll put one of the murderers in court in the morning.' He looked at Harper and added, 'Two, when you find Anderson.'

* * *

Alone, the inspector walked the streets around Mabgate. The fog
was coming down again, thick as soup in patches, then suddenly
opening up for fifty or a hundred yards. A few women hurried
along to the corner shops and home again. The noise from Hope
Foundry sounded like the hammers of doom ringing, caught and
clamped by the fog. He stood at the corner of Green Road and
watched the girls leave Mabgate Mills as their shift ended. Heads
covered with scarves, shawls tight around their shoulders, old
dresses sweeping along the snow on the pavement, they burst by
in a swarm of chatter. Then, like a flock of birds, they were gone.
None had even given him a second glance.

The hearing still hadn't returned in his ear. But this time he
wasn't overwhelmed with the panic that had struck him each time
before. Why, he didn't know. It was out of his control; it would
either come back or it wouldn't, there was nothing he could do
about it. He was still here, he was still working.

Harper wasn't foolish enough to believe he'd spot Anderson
himself. He just needed to imprint the streets in his mind. If
he had any sense, the man would wait until night to move
around. And if this fog lingered they'd be hard pressed to catch
him at all.

The inspector saw the constables, out and about, keeping their
eyes open. He moved away, hands deep in his pockets. There was
nothing more he could do here. Before he left Millgarth he'd given
orders to send word if anyone saw Anderson. He believed the man
would come. He must be getting desperate by now; he'd need
money and food and shelter.

But truthfully, all Harper could do was hope.

It wasn't far to the Victoria. Along Mushroom Street and Bristol
Street, cutting through by the Rope Walk and the chemical stench
of Sheepscar Dye Works. Close to the pub the air was so thick
that he couldn't even see five feet ahead.

Inside, the warmth of the bar felt welcoming. Men were enjoying
a drink or two after work before heading home to their families.
He slipped through the noise and up the stairs.

The parlour was empty, the fire banked in the grate. He pushed
a poker into it, releasing the heat and the flames, and added a little
coal before he removed his coat. In the kitchen he filled the kettle
and settled it on the hob, staring out of the window.

The fog looked like a dream. Some moments it cleared long enough for him to see the length of the garden. Then, in the next breath, all he could make out was his own reflection in the glass.

He didn't hear her come in; he didn't even sense she was there until she put her arms around his waist and pressed herself against his back.

'You're away with the fairies.'

'Just thinking.' He turned and embraced her. The feather on her hat tickled her face. The kettle began to steam. 'How did you know I was making tea?'

'Sixth sense.' She grinned then looked at him. 'What's wrong?'

Harper lifted a hand to his ear and saw her frown.

'Still?' she asked and he nodded. Placing her hands on his shoulders, she raised on tiptoe and gently kissed the ear. Then she moved away and busied herself with boiling water and teapot as she winked at him. 'Typical man, leave a woman to do the real work.'

'Busy day?'

She shrugged. 'Burmantofts, then round at the other bakeries. There's always something, you know that.' She poured and handed him a cup. 'Elizabeth's taking that house. It has a garden for the children and everything, it's a proper little palace. I saw Ted Lomax earlier. He has that rag and bone business. He's going down on Middleton on Saturday to bring the furniture and the children. She'll have time to give the place a good clean. I said I'd help her.' Annabelle paused and stared at him. 'The hearing's been gone a while this time, hasn't it?'

'I know.' He spooned sugar into the tea and stirred the liquid. 'The strange thing is, it doesn't seem to matter. I don't know why.'

She took his hand in hers and kissed it.

'Together,' she told him fiercely, and he smiled. 'Whatever happens.'

'Were you collecting the takings?' He nodded at the bag sitting in the middle of the table.

'Someone has to.'

'You need to be careful—' he began, but she silenced him with a look.

'I've told you before, Tom, no one would dare. Not round here.'

'There's always one . . .' That was all it took. Someone who knew, someone willing to take the chance.

'What do you want me to do?' she asked sharply. 'Have a bodyguard? This is where I live. Where *we* live. I'm blowed if I'll change. The day I don't feel safe here is the day I move.'

'I just worry about you.'

She nodded. 'I know. But I was managing for a long time before we met, Tom. I'll be fine, don't worry. Honestly.'

He couldn't help it, though. God alone knew how much she had in that bag. Any woman on her own was a target, every copper knew that. It didn't matter where she was or how many people knew her. Someone could see an opportunity to get rich for a while. Annabelle was his wife; he wanted to look after her.

The evening passed but he couldn't settle. They ate and he sat by the fire, trying to read the newspaper. But he couldn't even finish the front page. He put it aside and paced around the room.

'You're like a cat on hot bricks, Tom Harper.' Annabelle was at the desk, coins in piles beside her, entering figures into a ledger. 'I can't think with you up and down all the time.'

'I'm sorry.'

He sat again, but it wasn't going to work. He was on edge, just waiting and hoping for some word that they'd spotted Anderson. Finally he shrugged on the overcoat.

'I'll be back later. I need to check something.'

'It must be important, whatever it is. I've never seen you like this before.'

He kissed her and went out into the darkness. With his first breath he coughed as the fog filled his lungs. He could see no more than twenty yards ahead, not even to the street corner. It would be easy to get lost. Easier still for a man to slip around undetected. The constables would need every bit of luck to spot Anderson tonight.

Harper made sure they saw him, though. The first, on Cromwell Street, saluted as soon as he recognized him. A second, down on Argyle Road, shivered as he stood, with nothing to report. Not a night to be out, not fit for man nor beast.

Harper spend an hour wandering, his footfall light on the packed snow. He was about to give up and go home when he heard the sound. There was nothing like it; a policeman's whistle. It cut through everything, so piercing it could be heard a full half-mile away. He stood, waiting for a second blast, moving his head quickly, hoping his good ear would be able to pick out the direction.

It came again and he started to run, sprinting along the street and sliding around corners. Twice he fell, sprawling across the pavement then picking himself up and dashing on. By the time he reached Accommodation Place he was breathless. He stopped, hand on his knees, trying to cough out the taste of soot and smoke.

The constable was there. Blood from a broken nose covered his mouth and chin and left a dark stain on his uniform. Harper could hear boots pounding along the road, coming closer.

'What happened?'

'He came running down Farrar Street, sir. I tried to stop him but he just reached out and hit me.' He spat a tooth into the road.

'Which way did he go?'

'Off along Skinner Lane.' He pointed.

'Right. Have the others follow me when they come.'

He took off again, his pace a little slower, breathing through his mouth and trying to listen. After a hundred yards the fog thickened once more, folding around him like a pair of arms. Somewhere, off in the distance, he could hear voices.

Another quarter of a mile, past the harsh burn of the lime works, at the corner of Regent Street, he stopped, holding on to the brick wall and trying to catch his breath. Then it was there, just at the faintest edge of his hearing, the clump of someone up ahead, running. Harper started to move. His lungs were on fire but he wasn't going to give up. He wouldn't let himself.

A hundred yards and he couldn't see four feet ahead. The gas lamps were faint, fuzzy balls that glowed above his head. All he could do was pound on and trust.

The sharp clatter of a metal bin tumbling, somewhere off to his right, spurred him onward. Busfield Street, he thought. Anderson was going into the Leylands. The inspector kept pushing, forcing one foot in front of the other. There was a wall at the top of the road, he remembered that, closing off the school beyond. He reached it and leapt, fingers clawed for a hold to push. Come on, Harper told himself, he'd done this often enough as a boy, up and over like it was nothing. With effort he pulled himself up, panting before jumping off into space and landing on his feet, waiting, listening for something. Anything.

Harper felt the pulse pumping in his neck and his heart pounding hard in his chest. There. The creak of rusted metal. Someone was trying to swing the gate open. He took a breath and set off, following the sound.

The snow was packed solid. He had to tear at the gate, pulling with all his strength to create a gap to slide through. Which way now? There was nothing to hear, the fog too thick for him to see. Back streets, the inspector thought. Anyone wanting to get away would keep to those.

He'd grown up here. So had Anderson. The area was so deep in them both that every turn, every pace was second nature, even after all this time. Duck down the road and through the ginnel, out into Byron Street, then along past Brunswick Brewery, the high malt smell cutting through the stink of the fog. Past the old board school and off into the little maze of streets that had been home when they were children. For a second the fog lifted and he could make out the faint shape of a man, his figure grey against the blackness, no more than a hundred yards ahead. The inspector set his jaw and kept running. He'd win. He had to.

His feet pounded along Noble Street, the hobnails punching into the hard snow before going round the corner, knowing he couldn't last much longer. His lungs were blazing as he made the turn on to Hope Street and started the slow climb past the mill.

The fog parted again, just for a second. But it was long enough to see the man pulling ahead. Anderson had added another twenty yards to his lead. His legs were moving steadily, head down. If he made it out to North Street, he'd be able to vanish in town.

Harper forced himself into one last effort. He had to catch him. He kept his eyes fixed in front of him. The mist cleared slightly and he saw Anderson passing under a street lamp. He'd lost his cap somewhere, and the light glistened on fair hair before he turned to shadow again.

Then he wasn't alone. Faint shapes came out of the fog, too blurred to make out properly. He couldn't be sure how many, but for a second they seemed to come together into one large figure. The inspector heard a cry. He tried to go faster, but each pace seemed slower than the one before, like he was running through treacle. He caught the faint glimmer of light on steel. Another cry. And then nothing more.

He was there in less than four breaths. But the only thing that remained was Anderson, sprawled out on the cobbles, warm blood leaking from his wounds to steam on the snow, the life gone from his face, a pair of bronze pennies over his eyes. No one else, not even the sound of running.

TWENTY-SEVEN

By five o'clock in the morning the inspector was hoarse. He'd gone through it all three times and drunk more cups of tea than he could count. First he'd filled out his own report, then he'd repeated everything for a sergeant from B Division who'd peppered him with questions, and finally the superintendent. And he still couldn't hear a damned thing in his right ear.

Kendall had arrived a little after two. He'd waited in his office until Harper had finished with the sergeant, then waved him in.

'Sit down, Tom. The night sergeant showed me your report.' He lit his pipe and kept puffing as he leafed through the papers again. 'You chased him from Mabgate into the Leylands.'

'Yes, sir.'

'And he was set on before you could reach him.'

'That's right.'

'Whoever stabbed him disappeared before you got there.'

'I was less than a hundred yards away,' Harper said.

'But they'd gone by the time you reached Anderson.'

'Yes, sir.'

'And in a few seconds they'd stabbed him eight times.'

'I didn't count the wounds.'

'How many attacked him?'

'I don't know.' They'd been formless, more ghost than human. The fog was too thick for him to count them. He wasn't about to say that for a moment the attacker seemed like a single large figure. The super would think he'd gone mad. It must have been a trick of the light, but it had shaken him.

'This patrol,' Kendall said. 'The Golem.'

Harper nodded. It was them, it had to be. Yet the story the rabbi had told him, of the figure made to defend the Jews of Prague, kept coming into his mind.

'I didn't see any faces,' he said. 'I couldn't identify anyone.'

'So there's no chance of charging anyone with this murder?' the superintendent asked darkly.

'I honestly don't see how, sir.'

Kendall sat back in his chair, staring at the inspector. 'Right, Tom, now tell me the things you didn't put in the report.'

'Sir?'

'Come on,' the superintendent told him. 'I trained you, remember? I taught you how to think for this job. I *know* you. There are always things a copper doesn't put down on paper. How did you know where he'd go?'

'I didn't,' Harper answered honestly. 'I just followed.'

He tapped the page. 'You wrote here that the fog was too thick to see him.'

'It was. But he made noises, and there were places it all lifted and I could get a glimpse for a moment.'

'Why do you think he went into the Leylands?' Kendall pushed. 'For god's sake, Tom, he'd killed two people there. It's not the sort of place he'd go back to.'

'He grew up there, sir. He knew it, knew his way around, the same as me. We both went to school there.' He shook his head. 'I don't know. Maybe he thought he'd be fine.'

'You know I'm going to have to explain this to the chief.' The superintendent gritted his teeth. 'He wanted to parade the three of them, to show everyone we're really doing something. Instead we've only got one, another dead, a third who killed himself and the fourth murdered by people we can't identify. And nothing to help us take Phillip May. It makes us look stupid.'

'I'm sorry, sir.'

The superintendent puffed at the pipe. 'Too late for recriminations, I suppose. It's happened. I'll tell you something, Tom.'

'What, sir?'

Kendall gave a small smile. 'You did a good job following him.'

'Thank you.'

'And perhaps it's a good job you weren't closer.'

'Sir?'

'They might not have cared who they were stabbing.'

No, Harper thought as he sat at his desk. They wouldn't have attacked him. They got what they wanted. An eye for an eye. The Golem had given the Jews of Leeds their revenge.

He could have gone home, washed, shaved and eaten breakfast before returning to work. Instead he crossed through the open square behind the covered market. The first traders were already setting out their wares, scraps of vegetables and apples left over from the autumn.

The café on the far side was doing a roaring trade in cups of tea and hot food for the early arrivals. Open at four, most of its business was done by eight, and it closed after dinner.

Eggs and bacon filled his belly, with a doorstep of bread to wipe up the last of the yolk and grease from the plate. He took his time with the tea. There was too much to consider.

Harper couldn't have caught Jack Anderson. He hadn't put that in his report and he hadn't told the super. He'd been losing ground all along Hope Street. He was flagging, he couldn't have lasted for another minute. But Anderson still had plenty of stamina. But for the Golem, he'd have escaped.

A boy came around selling copies of the *Post*. He bought one. The headline was still the children in Wortley. Anderson's death, long after dark, made a small *Stop Press* item. By the next edition all that would have changed. Fresh news to fill the front page.

He folded the newspaper and returned to Millgarth. The fog had lightened a little, but still hung low and acrid.

'I heard what happened, sir,' Sergeant Tollman said. 'Good riddance, if you ask me.'

The inspector nodded and walked through to the office. Ash was seated at the desk, reading through the report.

'Morning, sir.'

'Morning.'

'It looks like we're all done with this, then. Sounds like you did well to keep track of him.'

'No, we're not finished yet,' Harper told him and the constable's expression turned quizzical.

'But we got all of them.'

'We don't have Alfred. Not yet.'

As the hands on the clock turned to six, he stood. 'Come on,' he said, putting on his overcoat and hat.

'Where are we going, sir?

'The infirmary.' They woke the patients at six each morning. By the time they arrived Billy would be alert. There'd be time to talk before Elizabeth came.

The hospital was alive with the sound of footsteps, all the coughing and moaning of illness. The sound of someone crying out floated down from upstairs. As they reached Reed's room the inspector said, 'Wait out here.'

'Yes, sir.'

All the noise had woken him. Voices as they passed, the rusty trundle of a trolley in the corridor. A nurse brought tea and helped him sit up. The cup felt awkward as he tried to clasp it in his bandaged hands. Every bruise on his body hurt, tender patches starting to flower from purple into green and yellows. The door opened and Harper entered. He looked exhausted, as if he hadn't slept. The sergeant held up the cup.

'You're too late, Tom, they served it five minutes ago.'

The inspector shook his head and sighed. 'I've been drinking it all night. My back teeth are floating.'

'What happened?'

'Anderson.' He sank wearily into the chair and told the tale. No gloss or varnish, he just recounted what had happened.

'And you didn't see the ones who killed him?'

'I'm not even sure how bloody many there were.' He rubbed his eyes and ran a hand through his hair in frustration. 'You're not going to believe this, Billy, but I swear that for a second there was just one of them, a giant. My mind must have been playing tricks.'

Reed looked at him. There were deep shadows under Harper's eyes. He looked gaunt, weary far beyond sleep, his gaze intense and wild.

'Look at it this way,' the sergeant offered. 'He'd have hanged, anyway. This was faster than a trial.'

'I know.' Harper clenched his fists, looked down at his hands and opened them again. 'But I wanted him for myself.' He glanced at the sergeant. 'Childhood debts.'

'It's done now. You can't change it.'

Harper shook his head. 'It's not over. There's still Alfred.' There was an edge to his voice, somewhere close to manic. His gaze was fierce.

'But I saw him. I found out his name,' Reed objected.

'I know.' He ran a hand across his mouth. 'The chief and the super won't do anything about it.'

'Why not?' The sergeant could hardly believe what he was hearing. 'For God's sake, Tom . . .'

'They said his barrister would take you apart in court.'

'What?' He didn't understand.

'You've had a head injury, you didn't remember what had happened, you just saw the back of his head.'

'But it was him. I know it was.'

'It was. I got a photograph from the *Post* and showed it to Briggs. All he'd say was that it could be Alfred, but I know he recognized him.'

Reed frowned. 'Then what's the problem? Why won't they arrest May?'

'Because his father's head of the bloody Watch Committee and he can afford the best lawyer money can buy. And who's going to take the word of someone who's admitted two murders, arson, and attacking a policeman?'

'But what about the Cross Keys? I saw him there. I talked to him.'

'You didn't hear him give any orders, Billy,' the inspector pointed out. 'He's been very bloody clever.'

'So what do we do?' the sergeant asked bleakly.

'There's one thing . . .' Harper began.

'What?'

'If you remembered what happened that night and he was there. Any jury would take that.'

'I've told you, Tom. There's nothing.'

'Try to remember. Please, Billy. Just try. Please. It's got to be in there.'

Reed closed his eyes. He didn't want to see the pleading in the inspector's gaze. How many times had Harper covered for him when he was drunk and lied for him when the sergeant's temper had flared and he'd become violent? Tom was the closest friend he had in the world. Without him, Reed would have been drummed out of the force long ago.

He stayed silent for a long time, breathing slowly. It hurt. The pain of it was tearing at him. He knew the debt he owed. And now it was being called in. Whatever the truth might be, he had no choice but to pay.

'I remember,' he said finally. 'Alfred was there.' It came out as little more than a whisper. He didn't open his eyes again until the inspector had gone.

Ash was standing in the corridor, waiting patiently. Harper came out of the room and began walking.

'Come on,' he said. 'There's somewhere we need to go.'

There was purpose in his stride, fire in his eyes. All the tiredness had fallen away.

'Where, sir?' the constable asked.

'Meanwood. It's time to finish this.'

The omnibus moved too slowly. He tapped his foot and drummed his fingers on his thigh while Ash sat quietly next to him, staring out at the street. Harper kept pulling out his watch to check the time. Finally he stood, impatient.

'We'll walk,' he said. 'It'll be faster.'

Out here the air was cleaner. The smell still came from the factories that lined Meanwood Road, but it was fainter. Hardly any fog; there was even the merest hint of blue sky behind thin clouds.

Councillor May's house sat back from the road. It was solid, built of heavy Yorkshire stone, weathered by the years. One corner was rounded, climbing into a tower, the slates on the roof rising to a point, crowned with a weathervane, not turning in the still air. The building looked as if it had stood for a century or more. Footprints and the tracks of carriage wheels marked the snow on the long drive.

'If you don't want to come in with me, I'll understand,' he told Ash. 'You can just go back to the station.'

'Are you certain the councillor's son is guilty, sir?'

'Positive.' He didn't hesitate before answering.

'Then I'm with you.'

Harper pressed the bell push. This house was going to come tumbling down.

A maid answered, looking down her nose at their appearance. They were a ragtag pair and he knew it. On foot, no expensive clothes; they could have been tradesmen.

'What do you want?' she asked haughtily.

'I'm looking for Phillip May,' Harper told her.

'He's not up yet.'

'Then you'd better go and wake him,' he told her curtly. 'I'm Detective Inspector Harper with Leeds Police.'

The rank flustered the girl. Before she could say anything he stepped past her, into the large hall, Ash right behind him. Finally she dashed off.

It gave him chance to look around. Portraits lined the stairway, all those grand faces peering out of history. The floorboards were heavily polished. An umbrella stand sat in one corner, and a small, delicate table was pushed against the wall. He turned and saw himself in the mirror. Like death warmed over, he thought. Pale, gaunt, his eyes haunted. Quickly, he turned away. It wasn't something he wanted to see.

The heavy footsteps didn't come from upstairs. A door slammed and the councillor himself appeared. He was dressed for the day, an old-fashioned suit with the jacket almost to his knees, belly bulging against his waistcoat, thin hair parted in the centre, the sideboards white and bushy over his cheeks. May's face was florid, blazing with fury, jowls shaking as he walked.

'What the bloody hell do you think you're doing here?'

Harper stood his ground. 'I'm Detective Inspector—'

'I know who you are,' he barked. 'I asked what you're doing here.'

'I'm here to arrest your son, sir. For conspiracy to murder and assault with intent to commit murder.' He looked May directly in the eye.

'I'm giving you to the count of three to turn around and get out of here.'

'No, sir,' the inspector told him. 'I'm not going anywhere without your son.'

May's face turned a darker colour. 'Do you know who I am? I'm in charge of the Watch Committee. I can telephone to your chief constable and have him give you the order to stop. You'd best use your brain right now.'

'When you talk to him you can say that Sergeant Reed has identified your son as one of his attackers, sir.' He gave it a heart-beat for the words to sink in. 'That's the word of a police officer.' He kept his gaze on the councillor. 'Sir.'

'You really don't know what you're doing, Inspector.'

'But I do, sir,' Harper told him. 'I'm doing my job.'

'Walk away. Now.' He glanced over at Ash and lowered his voice. 'The pair of you. We'll say it never happened.'

'Thank you, but we'll wait for young Mr May, if it's all the same to you, sir,' Ash told him with a friendly smile. 'Since we've come all this way.'

'I'll have him out in an hour,' May said, and Harper knew he'd won. No one was going to be given bail for murder and trying to kill a copper. Not even a councillor's son.

A figure appeared at the top of the stairs. He looked as if he'd dressed in a rush, his tie uneven, hair hardly brushed. But he still had the rich burnish of money about him, the best anyone could buy. And his eyes burned with a dark fire.

'Philip May,' the inspector announced, 'also known as Alfred. I'm arresting you for assault of a police officer with intent to murder.'

TWENTY-EIGHT

The last Monday in January and the snow had finally gone. Only a few dirty patches remained, scattered in deep shade across the parks and waste ground. The cobbles still shone from the early rain. The clouds had skittered away to leave blue skies and a sun that held precious little warmth.

Harper left Millgarth and stopped at the café by the market for his dinner. As he ate, he searched through the *Post* until he found the article he wanted. Ships were still searching for a missing French ship, the *Vincennes*. It had been due to dock more than a week before in Brest, sailing from New York. Hope had almost faded, he read, as no one would be able to survive the January waters of the Atlantic.

Three days earlier, the morning the story broke, he'd received a letter at the station, simply addressed to *Inspector Harper, Leeds Police, Millgarth, Leeds, England*. He didn't know the handwriting and the stamp was unfamiliar. He'd torn it open and pulled out a thin sheet of paper. The words had been scrawled quickly and it took him a little while to decipher them.

Dear Tom,

Today I go home! I feel as if I've been gone for months, and this New York is colder than Leeds. I didn't expect any success here, I was prepared to fail, but I think I've worked out what happened to Msr Le Prince! Hard to believe, no? I'll tell my superiors when I return and let them take care of the rest. Me, I'll be glad to sleep in my own bed, with my wife, and to go back to solving real crime again – did you find your murderer?

Now I must go and buy that dress for my wife. There are so many shops here – how is a man supposed to choose? The *Vincennes* sails this afternoon and for once I'll be glad to put to sea.

Thank you again for your help and hospitality, my friend.

Bertrand Muyrère

He took it from his pocket and read it through again, although he felt as if he knew every word by heart. He'd told Annabelle and held her close as she cried. She'd liked the Frenchman. He had, too. A good copper who deserved a long life, not a grave in the ocean, with his wife and children bereft. It was a reminder that the thread of life was fragile; it could break so easily. And it sounded as though his discovery had vanished with him.

He finished the food and pulled the watch from his waistcoat. Almost noon. He crossed St Peter's Square, passed the gasworks and on to Beckett Street. He had a rhythm in his stride and a smile on his face. His hearing had finally returned the day after he arrested Alfred; touch wood, it hadn't gone again since.

It wasn't far to walk. Out beyond the House of Recovery, before the workhouse and the cemetery, on the corner of St Agnes Grove. He stopped a few yards away to admire the place. The windows gleamed, the green paint stood out bold and fresh, the letters in gold: *Harper, Bakers.* A board outside advertised *Grand Opening. Fresh Bread, Cakes and Fancies.* At least there was some joy today. It was Annabelle's new shop, and he was proud of her.

Inside, a pair of women were working busily, cutting bread and making sandwiches for the workers who wanted them for their dinner. Elizabeth was serving a customer, placing a large loaf next to the pikelets and a pair of small pastries for tea on the counter, while Annabelle wrote out the receipt and took the money, checking the coins before putting them in the drawer. The shelves were mostly empty, so much already sold during the morning. The bell tinkled as the woman left with her purchases and Annabelle turned to him with a grin. She was dressed exactly like the rest of the staff, a simple black dress with a long white apron and small cap. No one would have guessed she was the owner.

He'd suggested she wear her best gown, the silk whose reds and blues shimmered together like liquid. She looked at him and shook her head.

'They don't want to see someone who looks like Lady Muck queening over it all. I want to bring them in, Tom, not scare them off. I'll dress just like the others and work.'

The new black and white tiles on the floor were dirty with footprints, the air filled with the scent of fresh bread.

'Business good?' he asked.

'Better than I'd hoped,' Annabelle told him with a nod. 'And we've hardly started.' She took a handkerchief from her sleeve and wiped her face. 'Come here and give me a kiss.'

He leaned across the counter and put his lips against hers. 'You've done a grand job. It looks wonderful.'

'You'd better tell Elizabeth that, then. She's the one who had most of the ideas.' He turned and the woman lowered her head as she blushed. 'If it carries on like this it's going to be a little gold-mine. Do you know what she suggested this morning? Come three o'clock we start lowering the price on stock so we sell out before closing. That way there won't be anything sitting overnight and we won't waste anything.' She turned to one of the women. 'Abby, why don't you put the kettle on, there's a love. We could all do with a brew. You want one, Tom?'

'I can't stop. I just wanted to be sure it had started well.'

She smiled. 'We've been run off our feet. Can't ask for better than that.'

'Has Billy been in?' the inspector asked Elizabeth.

'First thing. He should be at home.'

'I'll pop by and say hello while I'm up here.' He kissed Annabelle again. 'We can go out tonight and celebrate if you like.'

Her eyes twinkled. 'Where did you have in mind?'

'Powlony's.'

Her mouth made an O. 'Pushing out the boat, aren't you?'

'It's not every day you open a new business.' He leaned close enough to whisper in her ear. 'Just make sure you wear the red garters.'

There was a tiny square of garden in front of the house where the grass grew in tufts, plenty of earth showing through. He knocked on the door and waited, hearing slow footsteps and the tap of a walking stick.

'Tom.' Billy Reed had started to regain some of the weight he'd lost in hospital, but there was still a way to go. All the bruises had vanished, but his face was thin and his hands looked too big for his arms. 'Come on in.'

They sat in the kitchen. The inspector could hear the voices of Elizabeth's two youngest upstairs and raised his eyebrows.

'Edward and Victoria. She has him playing house,' Reed explained. 'Better leaving them to it. I only get in the way.' A few more months and they'd start school; Billy had told him that on his last visit. Emily was already there, and Annabelle had found a job for John, the older lad, over at the terracotta works, learning how to make tiles. 'It was bedlam in the bakery earlier. Couldn't move for women wanting to buy.'

'Been busy all morning, they said. It looks like it'll be a success.'

'I'm glad.'

'Annabelle was singing Elizabeth's praises.'

The sergeant smiled proudly. 'She's a worker, no doubt about that.'

'How about you? Getting better?'

Reed shrugged. 'Slowly.'

A week had passed since Harper had last been here. Billy was still limping, leaning heavily on the stick. He'd stayed long enough for a cup of tea then, the talk brief, polite and distant. The way it had been since that morning in the hospital.

The inspector had been in court when Reed gave his evidence in Phillip May's trial. The sergeant had limped to the stand and sworn on the Bible. May's barrister wasn't a fool, not at the price he charged. He knew better than to call a policeman a liar. And the evidence was damning. On the stand, Billy named May as one of the men who attacked him on Woodhouse Moor. There was a sharp intake of breath at the evidence. Reed kept his eyes on Harper as he spoke, holding his gaze, no expression on his face.

The lawyer did the only thing he could, the only way he could try and plant the smallest seed of doubt.

'Are you absolutely positive, Sergeant Reed?'

Billy's eyes lingered on the inspector's face, then he glanced away. 'Yes. I am.'

'You suffered a head injury in the attack, I believe.'

'I did,' he agreed. 'But I remember what happened.'

The very best Phillip May could hope for was a long sentence. At worst, he'd hang. The word was that Councillor May was using all his influence, calling in favours, everything he could to stop a capital sentence. He'd already resigned from the Watch Committee. There were rumours he'd stand down from the council soon.

Outside the courtroom, the inspector saw Rabbi Feldman. He was sitting on a bench, both hands resting on his stick, his face looking as old as Methuselah.

'Did you come for the trial?' Harper asked, but the rabbi simply shook his head.

'I didn't need to,' Feldman replied. 'It was over long before all this. It ended that night.'

'May was behind it all.'

Feldman pursed his lips. 'Perhaps he was. But he's lost all the power he ever had. His father, too.'

'What about the Golem?' Harper had heard no more about them since Anderson's death. They hadn't been out on the streets.

'Gone, Inspector.' The rabbi raised a gloved hand and waved it in the air. 'Vanished. Crumbled. There's no need for the Golem now, is there?'

'And in the future?'

Feldman managed a weak smile. 'Who can tell that?' Slowly,

grimacing with pain, he pushed himself to his feet. 'If you're Jewish, you learn never to say never. Good day, Inspector.'

'Has the doctor said when you can come back on duty?' Harper asked, setting the empty cup on the kitchen table.

'It'll be a while yet,' Reed answered quietly. 'Once the leg's mended properly.'

'I'll be glad to have you. Ash is good, but he's not you.' He smiled.

'As soon as I can, Tom.' There didn't seem to be any pleasure in his words.

The sergeant had let his beard grow back. It made his face familiar. But the light in his eyes had changed, Harper thought. There was contentment there, but something else, too, something he couldn't quite name. The inspector stood.

'I'd better get back. The super will be wondering where I've gone.'

On the step they exchanged a quick handshake. At the end of the street Harper glanced back. The door was already closed.

She pinned her hair up, showing off her long neck, and wore her best gown. He put on the suit she'd bought him for Christmas, with the new collar that folded over and a silk tie. He felt like a rich man, someone who deserved to be sitting across the table from her in Polowny's.

The meal was perfect, the beef cooked just right, the wine a deep, mysterious red in the gaslight. Annabelle was happy, and she deserved to be. He looked at her, filled with more than he could ever say. Love, pride, joy, everything.

'What?' she asked with a laugh as he stared.

'I love you, Mrs Harper.' He beckoned her close and whispered, 'Did you remember the red garters?'

There was a wicked glint in her smile. 'You'll just have to wait and see, won't you, Tom Harper?'

AFTERWORD

Jews from Eastern Europe really began to arrive in Leeds during the 1880s, settling in the area just north of the centre, known as the Leylands. And they kept coming and coming. Signs reading *No Jews Wanted* did appear in Leeds during 1890, and it's true that none of the big mills would employ them. There was anti-Semitism, but no calculated murders, and no major violence until a big flare-up in 1917 that passed relatively quickly. As the Jewish population Leeds settled and became more prosperous, they started to move out to the northern suburbs, and eventually the houses in the Leylands were demolished.

The disappearance of Louis Le Prince remains a mystery to this day. The idea that Thomas Edison arranged his murder is just one of many theories that have been put forward, but it's never been proven.

The fire in Wortley happened on New Year's Day, 1891, at a bazaar in the schoolroom of the church of St John the Evangelist. It was a tragic, terrible accident. In the end, eleven children died in the disaster.